"We need to work out a way to keep the twins together."

Abby felt a rush of relief. "Of course," she said. "Are you planning to leave Wyatt with me?"

"No," Jack said, dashing her hopes in a word. "I'll sublet my place in the city and find a place to rent around here. You know of any place?"

She thought of the land surrounding the farm. The land that Jack owned. And the farmhouse on it that was now hers.

Her gaze swooped across to the precious baby girl she'd been entrusted to raise, and then to baby Wyatt. She loved these babies. She wanted to be near both of them every single day and night. She'd do anything to achieve that goal.

Anything.

"We could both move in here," she suggested.

Dear Reader,

Our yearlong twentieth-anniversary celebration continues with a spectacular lineup, starting with *Saved by a Texas-Sized Wedding*, beloved author Judy Christenberry's 50th book. Don't miss this delightful addition to the popular series TOTS FOR TEXANS. It's a marriage-of-convenience story that will warm your heart!

Priceless Marriage by Bonnie Gardner is the latest installment in the MILLIONAIRE, MONTANA continuity series, in which a "Main Street Millionaire" claims her "ex" as her own. Jacqueline Diamond pens another charming story in THE BABIES OF DOCTORS CIRCLE series with *Prescription: Marry Her Immediately*. Here a confirmed bachelor doctor enlists the help of his gorgeous best friend in order to win custody of his orphaned niece and nephew. And let us welcome a new author to the Harlequin American Romance family. Kaitlyn Rice makes her sparkling debut with *Ten Acres and Twins*.

It's an exciting year for Harlequin American Romance, and we invite you to join the celebration this month and far into the future!

Melissa Jeglinski
Associate Senior Editor
Harlequin American Romance

TEN ACRES
AND TWINS
Kaitlyn Rice

TORONTO • NEW YORK • LONDON
AMSTERDAM • PARIS • SYDNEY • HAMBURG
STOCKHOLM • ATHENS • TOKYO • MILAN • MADRID
PRAGUE • WARSAW • BUDAPEST • AUCKLAND

To Ben
For enduring the tough times,
and for making the good times more special.
To Mom M.
For the many ways you allow Ben and I
to strive for our dreams.

ISBN 0-373-16972-8

TEN ACRES AND TWINS

Copyright © 2003 by Kathy Hagan.

All rights reserved. Except for use in any review, the reproduction or
utilization of this work in whole or in part in any form by any electronic,
mechanical or other means, now known or hereafter invented, including
xerography, photocopying and recording, or in any information storage
or retrieval system, is forbidden without the written permission of the
publisher, Harlequin Enterprises Limited, 225 Duncan Mill Road,
Don Mills, Ontario, Canada M3B 3K9.

All characters in this book have no existence outside the imagination of
the author and have no relation whatsoever to anyone bearing the same
name or names. They are not even distantly inspired by any individual
known or unknown to the author, and all incidents are pure invention.

This edition published by arrangement with Harlequin Books S.A.

® and TM are trademarks of the publisher. Trademarks indicated with
® are registered in the United States Patent and Trademark Office, the
Canadian Trade Marks Office and in other countries.

Visit us at www.eHarlequin.com

Printed in U.S.A.

ABOUT THE AUTHOR

As a child, Kaitlyn Rice loved to lie on the floor of her bedroom and draw pencil sketches of characters. She remembers assigning each one a name and personality, and imagining what their lives might be like. This study of people and relationships—both real and made up—has always fascinated her. By her midteens she was drawn into the world of romance fiction.

Through the years, Kaitlyn's most enduring pastime has been to curl up with a good romance novel, and her fondest dream has been to create full-fledged versions of those character sketches—in book form. She's thrilled to have finally realized that goal. Kaitlyn lives in Kansas with her husband and two daughters.

Dear Reader,

We've been celebrating a lot at our house lately. The acceptance of *Ten Acres and Twins* into the Harlequin American Romance line has meant that I'm being rewarded for combining a few of my favorite things—a joy in family, a passion for writing and a love for romance.

I share a house with one husband, two preteenage daughters, a cat and two dogs. Clutter and commotion are so typical in our home that I've almost learned to enjoy them. Heavy on the *almost*.

As Abby Briggs and Jack Kimball try to adjust to living in a big old farmhouse with one another and a pair of infant twins, it's inevitable that they'll experience the occasional bit of domestic chaos. But Abby's turmoil is about something more essential than misplaced grocery lists or late-night feedings: she's lost her ability to love and trust a man.

I had fun writing about all the ways a charmer like Jack would grow in Abby's heart. I hope you have fun reading about them. Visit my Web site at ww.kaitlynrice.com, and let me know what you think.

Kaitlyn Rice

Chapter One

Abigail Briggs had outgrown temper tantrums well over twenty years ago, when she still wore bandages on her knees and thought marshmallows were a satisfactory lunch entrée.

Still, if someone didn't answer her questions soon, she was considering lying on the floor, screaming like a forgotten teakettle and thrashing around as wildly as the most precocious of toddlers.

Even in her brand-new business suit.

After she'd announced her arrival to the receptionist, she had sat on the edge of the sofa to begin her wait. She must have glanced at her wristwatch at least a hundred times. The second hand kept whirling around its perpetual circle with easy fluidity, but the minute and hour hands seemed sluggish. Twenty-eight minutes she'd waited. It may as well have been twenty-eight hours.

Abby's mother had always said she was intense, while her father called her spirited. They were apt descriptions, she knew, since she'd spent her adolescence diving blindly and defiantly into a sea of mistakes.

Over the years, however, she had developed patience for most things. Anyone who made her living as a gardener learned to wait.

She could scatter a few handfuls of seeds, and in a season orchestrate the blooms of enough bouquets to please every bride, mother, wife and lover in Topeka, Kansas, and the surrounding county. She could plunk the rooted end of a twig into the ground and nurture it for years, until it became a robust tree capable of bearing bushels of fruit so tender their flesh melted in your mouth.

But some things were too hard to wait for, and this appointment must rate at the top of the charts in importance. Whatever that slick lawyer was doing right now, it could hardly compare to the weighty deliberation about the future of two precious babies.

Abby's indignation had risen with every minute, and now she tapped her foot forcefully on the cushioned carpet, trying to achieve a loud enough sound to catch the notice of the delinquent receptionist. But the woman tapped away at her keyboard, apparently unaware of the hateful thoughts being directed toward her pencil-punctured bun.

The painting on the wall above the receptionist's head caught Abby's eye, if only because it was unimaginative. She wondered if any client had ever been distracted by the watery scene. She wanted to slash it with her pen, paint vivid, deep purple figures across it to express a hurt so deep no lawyer's meeting could ever truly mend it.

Paige and Brian were dead, which was reason enough for her impatience, and for the relentless ache in Abby's gut. The fact that her sister and brother-in-law had died a quick death did little to lessen the agony.

Each of them had been only twenty-two years old, and they had left behind much. A wide network of friends and acquaintances. A couple of broken-hearted families. And a pair of adorable twins, not yet six months old.

The sound of footsteps drew Abby's attention to the

conference room door. It swung open, and a tall man
stepped out. His eyes bore the dazed look of a person in
shock. His jaw was clenched, his face chalky. His appearance was worlds apart from the tanned and relaxed
man Abby had met at her sister's wedding, but she
couldn't fail to recognize him—Jack Kimball was Brian's
older brother.

He hesitated midstep when he saw her, as if he was
once again struggling to place her in their out-of-the-
ordinary surroundings. At the funeral, they'd traded arm-
patting hugs and the expected words of comfort, but it
had hardly been a time for renewing their acquaintance.
Now, Abby sat up straighter and smoothed a long wisp
of hair behind her ear. Then she balled her fist and
dropped it in her lap, perturbed with herself for caring
about her appearance.

She knew the exact instant he recognized her by the
renewed hint of life in his expression. He gave a curt nod
as he walked past her toward the exit, offering only one
word in greeting. ''Abby.''

She had scarcely enough time to question his presence
in the law office before the conference room door opened
again. Sheila Jeffries, upstart attorney and daughter of the
firm's founder, poked her head through. ''Miss Briggs,''
she said. ''I'm ready for you.''

Abby picked up a briefcase containing every pertinent
document she'd been able to find among her sister's
things, and went inside. The attorney smoothed her hands
down the lines of her red linen suit as Abby stepped in,
then motioned toward a chair at a corner of the table.

''Coffee?'' she asked. Without hesitating, she walked
over to a setup on the far end of the room to pour herself
a cup.

Abby swallowed. Her throat had been so dry lately.

She wondered how much bodily fluid a person could actually lose by crying. "I'd love a glass of water."

"Certainly." The attorney pushed a button on the wall, and the hum of an intercom pervaded the room.

"Yes, Ms. Jeffries," said a crackling voice.

"Please bring Miss Briggs some ice water."

The hum faded, and the lawyer took a seat across from Abby and started thumbing through the papers stacked in front of her. The only movement on her face was the occasional blink of her perfectly made-up eyes, beneath a pair of perfectly arched eyebrows.

She looked refined. Disinterested. Detached.

As an attorney, she must deal with this type of situation constantly. People died all the time. But since it was her kid sister who'd been snatched away from this earth in a tragic accident, Abby couldn't be detached. She stared at the other woman, shaken by her composure. How could she sit there so calmly, as if the entire world hadn't tilted on its axis?

One of the strangest aspects of losing Paige was having to exist in a world that, for the most part, didn't recognize its loss.

The door opened and the receptionist walked in, carrying a pitcher and glass. She set them near Abby and left the room, closing the door behind her with a soft click.

Ms. Jeffries waited until Abby had poured a glass of water and taken a drink before saying, "You have a document you wanted me to see?"

Abby released the clips of her briefcase, searching inside for the note. "Yes, I do," she answered. "When Paige was pregnant, she asked me to raise her children if she and Brian ever died. No one ever thinks that'll happen, but..."

Breaking off when the lump in her throat got too big to talk around, she shrugged, finally locating the note and shoving it across the table. The smell of roses reached her nostrils, and she willed back the threat of tears that came all too often now.

Her sister had always written to her on rose-scented stationery, as a sort of gentle ribbing about Abby's middle name. A sisterly prank that had begun when they were kids had developed into a loving habit that seemed poignant now. Who would have thought that Paige could die so young?

Ms. Jeffries studied the note. She read the first side slowly, then turned it over to skim the rest before tossing it back down in front of Abby. "This is not legally binding," she stated bluntly. Almost cruelly.

"It's all I have in writing, but I've been taking care of the babies since the night of the accident and...well, actually, I watched them quite often before."

"If you can prove that, it might help," the attorney said. "But a handwritten and unwitnessed letter won't hold up in court."

"And I could lose the twins?"

In the middle of sipping her coffee, Ms. Jeffries answered with a one-shouldered shrug.

"What can I do to change that?" Abby asked, reaching over to touch the attorney's crisp red sleeve.

She frowned. "You're lucky. A few months ago your sister and her husband drew up a will specifically stating what should happen to their children and their property if they died. Paige didn't tell you?"

"No, she didn't. A legal will?"

"I have a copy here. All you have to do is sign a statement petitioning the court for guardianship rights. If the judge agrees, you'll have every right to make decisions on your ward's behalf.''

Huffing out a bellyful of air, Abby wondered why Ms. Jeffries couldn't have shared that information as soon as they stepped into the conference room. She could have been halfway home by now. ''And I'll get to raise the twins?''

''Not both of them.''

A wave of dizziness swept through Abby's head. ''What do you mean, not both? Paige wouldn't have separated them.''

''It appears that, in a way, she has.''

''Who gets the other twin?''

''I'm not at liberty to say until the hearing tomorrow morning at nine o'clock,'' said Ms. Jeffries. ''Either you or the other party has the right to surrender guardianship at that time. If you both agree to uphold the intentions of the will, the judge will likely do the same. If you don't, we'll have to fight it out in court.''

Abby frowned down at the note her sister had written nearly a year ago. Ignoring its scent now, she studied the curlicue letters of her sister's handwriting, scrawled across pink paper. Paige had been young and suggestible. Brian must have convinced her to change her mind. She shouldn't even have been allowed to sign that will.

Abby drew a ragged breath and pressed a thumb and index finger against her eyelids. ''Is there anything else?''

''There is. Do you prefer legalese or plain English?''

''Plain English would be fine.''

''You've been named as the desired guardian for the baby girl, Rose Allison Kimball. You've also been left the house, its contents and the land and structures within the confines of the fenced yard.''

''The farmhouse?'' Abby asked, looking up.

"Um-hmm."

Abby clenched her eyes shut, once again feeling faint. Her usually capable demeanor had been hammered with one too many traumas lately. But at least this surprise had been welcome news—she could continue developing the farm into the profitable enterprise she and her sister had envisioned.

"Are you all right, Miss Briggs?"

"Fine," she said, opening her eyes. "Is that it, then?"

"Look over this document." The attorney slid a paper in front of Abby. "If you agree, show up in court tomorrow prepared to sign it. If you don't, call me tonight."

"Okay."

"The twins are with a sitter now?"

"Yes—with my mother."

"Bring them tomorrow. All family members have been told about the hearing, and some of them may be at court. If all goes as planned, you can take little Rose back home with you in time for lunch tomorrow."

Abby slid the document into her briefcase alongside her sister's note, and left the building without uttering another word.

At this moment, she didn't know which news had been harder to take—the sheriff's department phone call informing her of the car wreck, or this idiotic notion that she might not get to keep both twins.

She loved those babies. She'd been a doting aunt since their birth. She should be the one to raise them.

She climbed into her truck, stashed the briefcase on the passenger seat and stared out at the office building in front of her.

The adrenaline that had been coursing through her

veins in anticipation of this morning's meeting was dwindling, and in its place was sheer exhaustion.

Last night the babies had each awoken twice, at different times. Abby had sat alone in her dark living room, tending to their needs. Worrying about their future. Ignoring her own pain so she wouldn't upset them more.

The fitful night had made her understand the burdens of single parenthood better than she ever would have imagined. Her short period of full-time caregiving had been an intense and powerful lesson.

She rubbed her temple, trying to remember where she'd put her grocery list. Wasn't it on the seat beside her? She lifted the briefcase, searching, and peered over the edge to the floorboard. The sheet was sticking out from under the seat; it must have fallen when she'd gotten out. After snatching it up, she started her truck. She'd have to buy groceries on the way home.

Forty-five minutes later, she walked through the door of her apartment carrying two bags full of baby supplies. She'd bought one single item for herself—a frozen chicken entrée that she could heat later, after the babies had gone to sleep for the night. "Mom, I'm back!" she called out.

Faye Briggs stepped through the kitchen doorway, wiping her hands on a tea towel. "Hello, dear. How did it go?" she asked, taking a bag and carrying it to the table.

Abby followed her, putting the other bag down before giving her mother a hug and a peck on the cheek. "I'll tell you in a minute. Where are they?"

"On your bedroom floor, asleep."

Abby scurried through the apartment, then slowed to peer quietly around the door to her bedroom. Her queen-size mattress covered most of the floor space. Pillows and blankets were stacked alongside every edge, creating a giant, makeshift crib in the middle of the room.

Drawn by some maternal force she'd had no idea she had until two weeks ago, she walked into the room and knelt beside the mattress, looking down at the twins. Rosie's fist was pulled next to her plump cheek, and ringlets haloed her head—just like Paige's had.

Wyatt was beside his sister, his mouth sucking gently in his sleep. His tiny sock had slipped halfway off his foot, so Abby pulled it off and tucked his blanket over his legs.

Although both babies were sleeping soundly, their faces were turned toward one another, as if each one had fallen asleep in the comfort of the other's presence.

Tears blurred her vision. Rosie and Wyatt had already lost both parents. They shouldn't lose one another, too. And she couldn't lose either one.

She had to find a way to keep them both.

When a shadow fell across the bed, Abby realized her mother was standing beside her. "How long have they been asleep?" she asked, swiping a knuckle under her eyes.

"Just a few minutes."

Abby tugged Rosie's blanket over her shoulder, looking down at the babies for one more minute before she got to her feet. Then she and her mother tiptoed out, and Abby closed the door quietly behind them.

They returned to the kitchen and began to put groceries away. "How did it go?" they both asked, and laughed together, too.

"Tell me about your morning first," Abby said as she put a can of formula into the pantry. "Did they eat breakfast?"

"Rosie drank half her bottle and ate a little rice cereal.

Wyatt drank more, but didn't want the food. They took a sink bath, and we went for a walk. They were fine.''

"Good." Abby smiled. Her mother had been great to help out. Losing your sister was terrible, but burying your youngest child had to be heartbreaking. Having the babies around to keep them busy had been a blessing to them both.

"Tell me about the meeting," her mother prompted again.

"It wasn't good news," Abby said. "Paige and Brian made up a will a few months ago, naming me as Rosie's guardian. But someone else has been asked to take Wyatt."

"Oh, no!" Faye gasped. "Who?"

"I don't know. If it's not you, it must be someone from Brian's side. His mom or brother, I suppose." Abby squinted at her mother. "It's not you and Dad, right?"

"No, it's not. We love the babies, but you're young and able…and you want them so much. We got a notice about the hearing, but that was all."

"That leaves Brian's mom and brother," Abby said.

"Would his mom want custody?" Faye asked as she handed Abby a couple of packs of diapers.

Abby stacked them on the countertop and turned to look at her mother again. "Based on what Paige told me, probably not. Brian's mom has her hands full raising a couple of kids from her second marriage. She's only seen Rosie and Wyatt once, just after they were born."

"What about Jack?"

Abby shook her head. "I don't know," she said. "He's single, and seems to live for work and women. Why would he want custody?"

Faye folded the two grocery sacks and handed them to

Abby before picking up her car keys. "Well then," she said, "maybe we'll get good news tomorrow in court."

Maybe.

But Abby didn't want to take any chances. Whoever had been asked to take custody of Wyatt must know by now. She was betting Jack at least knew who it was, since he'd been in the lawyer's office this morning. In fact, she had a feeling he was her culprit.

Why couldn't she do a little detective work?

She managed to marshal enough brainpower to see her mother to the door, but her thoughts were already rushing ahead, developing a plan. Jack was a businessman; he must carry a cellphone. She was fairly certain she'd find his number in the address book she'd found at the farmhouse.

She was going to play on her hunch.

SITTING ALONE at a linen-topped table, Abby glanced at the door every time a shape passed by the other side of the window. He was either very late or not coming at all.

The waitress had bustled by three times already, filling Abby's water glass and asking if she wanted to go ahead and order. The pretty redhead must think she was a pathetic spinster who was being stood up for a date.

Abby didn't care. Her feet were planted too solidly on this good green earth to worry about what some stranger thought of her.

Practical and outspoken, Abby had learned early in life to meet challenges head-on. Not much intimidated her. But she couldn't afford to lose another loved one. Paige and Brian had been enough.

The only thing Abby feared right now was losing one of the twins, and she'd do almost anything to keep them together, and in her life. If Jack was, in fact, the chosen guardian for Wyatt, she was prepared to argue, lie or even grovel if it would persuade him to relinquish custody.

Nearly an hour after their prescribed meeting time, a single shadow loomed, tall and somehow threatening. Abby felt a tingle of awareness surge through her, knowing without looking closer that Jack had arrived. He removed his ball cap as he stepped through the door, and ran a hand through his hair as he spoke to the hostess. Then he turned and spotted Abby.

She smiled briefly, lifting a hand in greeting. He strode quickly to the table, beginning to make excuses before he was even halfway there. "Abby, I got caught up in a business call that took awhile to wrap up. I'm glad you waited."

"It's okay," she said, and then wondered why she felt compelled to appease his feelings at the expense of her own. Surely he could see that this meeting was just as crucial as a business call that he could have dealt with later.

He sat down across from her and put his hat on an empty chair seat. Right away, he began to study the menu.

Abby sipped from her water glass and watched him. Though he wasn't as ghostlike as he'd been this morning, his eyes sported dark circles uncommon to a man as vital as Jack. Brian's death must have been torture for him.

"Have you ordered?" he asked, without looking up from the menu.

"Nope—wasn't sure you were coming," she said, perturbed with herself for feeling sympathetic toward the man she intended to manipulate over dinner.

He looked up quickly after hearing the note of complaint in her voice. "Since I'm late, I'll treat."

"That's not necessary."

"I insist," he said with a wink and a grin. "What's good here?" And with a simple change of expression, he became the man she knew. The one she'd met at the wedding.

Charming. Devil-may-care. Lethally sexy.

"Depends on what you want," she answered tersely.

He searched her eyes. "Are you mad at me for something?"

"Why would I be mad?" she asked, even more agitated with herself for being attracted to him, after all this time.

"I don't know, you just seem…perturbed."

She slapped the palm of her hand on the tabletop with a satisfying thump. "Let's not start things off by arguing."

"I'm not arguing."

She knew that must be the voice he used with his clients when their feathers were ruffled, and she refused to be mollified. "But you're telling me I'm mad, and I'm not—"

She slammed her jaw shut when she noticed the hand reaching between them to pour water into Jack's glass. The waitress was leaning over them, so intent on her chore she seemed unaware that she'd interrupted a dispute.

After topping off Abby's water, she started to scuttle away, only glancing up when Jack thanked her for the water. That one peek caused a sudden shift in her demeanor. Her brisk pace slowed to a hip-swinging saunter as she headed back toward the kitchen.

Jack frowned into his menu again, seemingly unaware of the flirtation. But Abby had noticed, and she wasn't surprised. There was something about the man that made women fawn all over him.

Her sister had always said he was the Romeo type, but Abby knew better. He might very well be a good-time lover to many, but he was a true love to no one. Jack Kimball was your everyday, garden variety Casanova.

Since she'd decided on her menu choices long ago, she took another opportunity to scrutinize him. There was nothing spectacular about his looks—she'd seen men more handsome who didn't hold her attention for longer than the bat of an eyelash. But Jack had something unique.

He was lean and wiry, and his sun-kissed brown hair waved wildly around his head. His style of dress tended toward the casual. Even at the wedding he'd loosened his tie before the last "I Do." He didn't work too hard on his appearance.

But his sky-blue eyes were nice, and probably responsible for half his appeal.

But it wasn't their hue she noticed, it was their expression. Thick lashes framed eyes that drank you in as if he'd never get his fill of your beauty.

If you were the one lucky enough to have caught his attention, that is. For a brief moment in time.

The waitress returned with her pad and pencil. "I see your date arrived," she said, smiling at Abby now. "No wonder you waited so long."

Abby looked back across the table just in time to catch Jack's wink at the young girl. Abby snorted, and said, "He's not my date."

"Really?" The girl smiled brightly at Jack. "Are you ready to order?"

Abby refused to be ignored. She was the lady; she would order first. "I'll have the roast chicken salad," she said, breaking into their mutual rapport. "Vinegar and oil on the side, and a glass of your house white wine."

The waitress wrote frantically. When she was finished, she grinned at Jack again.

He looked across at Abby with a thoughtful frown, then back down at the menu. After a few seconds of silence, it became obvious that he wasn't ready to order.

Abby expected the waitress to hurry off to the kitchen to accomplish something while her prized patron made a decision, but she did no such thing. She seemed perfectly willing to just stand there, staring at Jack.

Finally, he rubbed his chin and said, "I'll have the steak, medium rare. Loaded potato. Bring a salad with the meal, ranch dressing on that… Oh—and bring me a bottle of your best stout beer."

"Will do. Thank you, sir," said the girl, who was probably still in her teens. He had absolutely no business flirting with her, but he flashed her a smile when she took their menus, and kept watching as she sidled away.

After the waitress was out of earshot, Abby lifted world-weary eyes to Jack's. "Doesn't take you long to do that."

"To do what, Abby?"

"To make a killing with the ladies," she said, shaking her head. "Or do a snow job."

"I was only being polite."

"Uh-huh," she muttered, picking up her water glass for the umpteenth time.

Jack sighed audibly, commanding her attention again. "Is that why you asked me to dinner? To insult me?"

She echoed his sigh as she set her glass back down. "I wanted to ask you about the hearing tomorrow."

"What about it?"

Abby crossed her fingers in her lap. "Have you been asked to take custody of Wyatt?"

Jack picked up his own water glass and took a sip,

peering at her over its frosty rim. "Are we supposed to be discussing that?"

"Come on, Jack," she said. "It has to be you or your mother. Paige always told me your mom was busy with her second family. So that leaves you. It has to be you."

"What if it is?"

"Stop it!"

"Stop what, Abby Rose?"

"Asking questions," she said. "Answer my questions with answers." Fidgeting with the lapel of her jacket, she forced herself to take a calming breath. She forced herself to wait. Again.

Jack set his glass down, contemplating it soberly. When he looked up again, the shadows were back in his eyes. "Yes, Brian named me in the will."

Abby stretched her hand toward him, resting it on the tabletop. "But you're not going to do it, are you?"

He covered her hand with his own, evoking a sudden heat that caused a spasm in the core of her body. She felt suddenly needy and aroused.

She slid her hand away, placing it in her lap. But it still tingled from his touch, and making a fist didn't help.

Uncomfortable with her body's betrayal, she forced her mind to return to the question at hand. She was rather shocked that she could think of sex when something as essential as a baby's future was in question.

Finally, he said, "To be honest, I don't know what I'm going to do."

Abby was grateful for his candor. Truly, she was. But she needed absolute assurances. "I want custody of both twins. They need to be together," she announced.

His troubled stare rested on some spot beyond her shoulder. "I don't want to separate them any more than you do," he finally said. "But I can't just sign them out of my life. Wyatt's my godson."

"Wyatt is five months old," Abby said. "He'd be better off with me."

"He's five and a half months old, and he'd be better off if his parents hadn't just died."

She flinched at his bluntness, but dived right into the fray. "I'm the next best thing, and I want him."

Jack didn't respond. Something past her head had caught his interest again.

The waitress had arrived with their orders, interrupting a second brawl at their table by the window. "Here you go, sir," she said as she placed Jack's meal in front of him. "Let me know if your steak isn't perfection itself."

Then she flopped Abby's plate down and said, "Pepper?"

"Yes, please."

The redhead pulled a pepper mill from her apron pocket and twisted it over the salad. When Abby motioned for her to stop, the waitress looked at Jack and asked, "Do you like things spicy, sir?"

Jack shook his head, so the young woman dropped the mill into her pocket, smiled at him one more time and disappeared toward the back of the restaurant.

He picked up his knife and fork to begin cutting into his steak. Abby thought it was just like him to attack his meat first, leaving his salad for later. Although she'd been around him only a few times, she knew he didn't pay much heed to social niceties. He did what he wanted.

She worked that tidbit of knowledge around in her brain, looking for criticism. Instead, she found nothing but respect for his mettle.

She nibbled at her own salad, letting him eat in peace

for a few minutes. Maybe he'd be more amenable when his appetite had been appeased.

After she'd finished most of her meal, she began to deliberate on her next words. She wanted to frame them carefully, seeking the best way of convincing him.

"Do you realize you haven't even asked about the twins?" She hadn't meant to say it out loud, but having done so, she raised her brows in challenge and waited.

Jack looked up, chewing a mouthful of food and frowning.

After he swallowed, he said, "I knew you'd taken them home, and I was trusting you to care for them until this was all worked out. Are they all right? Where are they?"

"They're with a friend. But you didn't ask about them until just now." Abby rested her fork on the edge of her plate, no longer hungry now that she was ready to hash this thing out.

"It's obvious you love those babies. You would have told me anything important." He stabbed his fork into a piece of steak, stuffed it in his mouth and nodded at her.

"I don't know if I would."

"Yes, Abby. You would," he said around his mouthful.

"How many times have you seen them?" she hissed.

"As often as I could get away from Kansas City. Maybe four or five times."

"Have you ever changed a diaper?" She picked up her fork again and toyed with a chunk of chicken on her plate, cutting it into tiny morsels before lifting one to her lips. As she chewed, she scowled at Jack, waiting for the reply she knew was coming.

"No, but how hard can that be?" He kept eating, but now his eyes were sharp with anger.

"Have you ever calmed a crying baby?"

He shook his head and kept chewing.

"You honestly think you can take a five-month-old boy home and figure him out? He's a human being, not a computer."

Jack put his fork down and planted one fist on each side of his dinner plate. "Wyatt is five and a *half* months old," he reminded her. "And if Brian could figure him out, so can I."

"When? Are you going to quit your job?"

He raised one brow. "I can afford to hire a nanny."

Abby nearly jumped out of her seat, her fury was so intense. "So, Wyatt will be raised by some stranger because you're too mulish to admit I'm the best person for the job!"

Jack pushed his plate away and picked up his beer. He downed the rest of the glass without once pulling his eyes away from hers. Finally, he said, "The truth is, Brian left a letter with the lawyer for me to read on the event of his death."

"A letter?"

"Yes."

She swallowed. "I didn't get one from Paige."

"Sorry."

"What did it say?"

He leaned over to pull his wallet out of his back pocket.

"Here, you can read it yourself," he said.

Abby scooted her salad plate aside before taking the letter. She unfolded it carefully, knowing he must treasure this last communication from his brother, then started to read.

Dear Jack,
    Hey, if you're reading this, it means I croaked.
Funny to think about that, but it means Paige died,

too, and that's not funny at all. Paige and I have had our problems, but lately things have been good. We're learning to compromise when we have a fight. One of the things we've worked out has been what to do if the babies need a home. Paige wants her sister to get them. Abby's great, but she's a single woman. A boy needs a man around. You know that. I want you to raise Wyatt if we die. We're naming you as his guardian, and leaving you the land you financed. Please try it for a year, and then if you want to blow it off, you have my blessing. (Give Abby a chance and sell her the land cheap, you old shark.) But try it. You're not doing anything better.

I love you, bro.

                                                        Brian

Abby refolded the paper with shaking hands. How could she compete with the plea of a dead man?

She couldn't. She knew that. But in time she would find a way. She knew that, too.

Looking into Jack's stricken face, she handed him the letter and shook her head. "Okay. You win this round," she said. "But there's something in there that's confusing. They left you the ten acres of land?"

"Yes," he said, shrugging as he slid the letter back inside his wallet.

"They left me the house."

He stared at her for a moment, his eyes glittering with some internal emotion. She wondered if he was going to throw a fit or start blubbering.

He did neither.

His burst of laughter rang out across the restaurant, turning the heads of several nearby diners. "Those two rascals left me a piece of land with no house to live in,'' he said in a voice rich with amusement. ''They left you an old house with no farm to finance the upkeep. And they left each of us a twin.''

''Uh-huh,'' Abby said, her brow pinched. Why was he laughing?

He shook his head, as if she should have gotten his point. ''They were plotting something.''

Despite the circumstances, she had to grin. ''Paige always did grill me about what I thought of you.''

Jack chuckled. ''And Brian always said you were the perfect woman for me.''

Abby's laugh was every bit as loud as his had been. ''They were so naive,'' she said. ''We've already determined that I'm not enough woman for you, haven't we?''

Chapter Two

Jack took measure of Abby's expression as he walked down the courthouse steps toward her, trying to determine whether she was despondent or furious. She was probably both, and he could hardly blame her. None of this felt right, but it was what Brian and Paige had wanted.

Abby had a parent flanking each side. At first glance, Mike Briggs seemed as easygoing as usual. He stood next to his daughter with a big yellow diaper bag looped over his arm. Today, however, his mouth formed a bleak line across his face.

Faye was the only one of the three adults who offered a smile. She stood to Abby's left, holding the twin in white ruffles—that must be Rosie.

Abby had Wyatt clutched tightly against her chest, and looked quite comfortable for a woman who'd been caring for those babies only a couple of weeks. Her lips were pressed against the boy's forehead, and she was swaying from side to side. The tip of the braid she always wore appeared at one side of her waist, then the other like a pendulum, as if keeping track of how many floggings he deserved for taking the boy from her.

Jack paused on the steps to blow out a puff of pure frustration, before charging on down to the group. When he reached them, Abby handed the child over without a word. Her lips were pinched so tightly that a scattering of dimples embellished her chin.

He smiled at her, appealing silently for understanding, but she didn't seem to notice. Her stormy eyes never abandoned the baby.

Turning his own attention to the boy in his arms, he looked down into the face of his brother's child—and his responsibility for about the next eighteen years. Wyatt's eyes were a muddy blue today—somewhere between the gray-blue of a newborn and whatever shade he'd wind up with eventually. They were wide and trusting. Innocent.

A fit of panic nearly overwhelmed Jack, but he squelched it, and put on a mask of bravado for the benefit of Abby and her parents. "Hi, Wyatt," he crooned. "I'm Daddy Jack. I'm going to take good care of you."

The baby stared back. He had grown considerably in five and a half months, but he was still so very…puny. His balled fist lurched wildly through the air, and his face scrunched into an odd contortion.

Nervously, Jack studied the way Faye was holding Rosie with the baby's back against her chest, wrapped in her arms, and gently bouncing. Rosie seemed content with the situation, so Jack copied their stance. The change in position meant he couldn't see Wyatt's face, but since the boy hadn't started screaming, he figured it was working.

Abby and her parents stood watching, placing the burden of goodbyes on him. Since he couldn't offer a handshake, he offered a nod instead. "Faye and Mike, it's been good to see you again," he said. "Next time, let's hope we meet under easier circumstances."

"Of course, dear," Faye said. "This has been terrible

for all of us. I'm just glad your brother and Paige were so happy in the past year.''

Jack wasn't sure whether he was pleased that his brother had grown into his marriage, or sad that the happiness had been so short-lived, so he didn't respond.

Instead, he noted the way Abby had her arms wrapped against her stomach, and he smiled at her again, hoping to soothe her pain. ''Abby, we need to talk about the farm,'' he said. ''May I call you?''

''I guess you'll have to,'' she answered.

Jack started toward his car, carting Wyatt in front of him like a sack of potatoes. He knew four pairs of eyes were probably boring into his back, but he'd gone a few yards before Abby spoke.

''Jack? Don't you want his things?''

He stopped in his tracks and turned around. Of course. The baby's things. He'd been so intent on looking capable that he'd forgotten Wyatt would need special food, and diapers. He'd need clothes and toys and...baby things.

''I have some of it in my truck,'' Abby said, beginning to walk toward the other end of the parking lot.

As Jack followed her, he added idiocy to his growing pile of bad feelings. At least this one wasn't new—she had a knack for making him feel foolish.

Maybe it was her no-nonsense manner. Maybe it was her sober expression. Whatever it was, it always seemed abundantly clear that she wouldn't surrender to his most valiant efforts to charm.

But at least she was in the minority—most women surrendered plenty.

At fourteen, Jack had taken a wide-angled look at his future. As far as school was concerned, he'd been on a path to success. He was sure to graduate in the upper five percent, along with many of his pals in the computer club.

The only problem was that none of them had been surrounded by girls. He'd recognized the narrow perception most of his peer group had of intelligent males, and refused to accept it.

He could do better. He'd used his brains to figure out the most surefire method to win a lady's attention, if not her heart, and a would-be nerd had turned into a masterful lothario.

Since then, most women had been only too happy to catch his interest. Abby was one of very few who'd been resistant. But she hadn't always been. She'd consented to more than one dance at Brian and Paige's wedding reception. She'd even laughed at a few jokes, until they'd talked their way into a squabble.

Now she didn't seem to mind hurtling across the parking lot in front of him, and she didn't try to make polite conversation. Once she reached a big blue pickup, she opened the passenger door and reached inside for a second diaper bag and a box of supplies. "If you'll meet me at the farmhouse tomorrow morning, say around nine, we can get the rest of his things," she said. "This is just a start."

"Sure thing. Phenomenal. Thanks."

Abby set the box on the pavement and looked pointedly at Wyatt. "Why don't I hold him while you put these in your car? Then I'll get his car seat and you can take it, too."

Handing the baby back to her, he looped the diaper bag over a shoulder, picked up the box and strode to his car to stash both in the trunk.

Returning to Abby, he took Wyatt again, and thought about all the juggling involved in transporting a single infant. How had Abby thought she could handle two of them alone?

He was careful to hold Wyatt in the same face-out position, rocking him gently, and was surprised when the boy started to whimper. When Jack bounced harder, the bawling got louder. He cleared his throat. "Abby? Why is he crying?"

"You have a lot to learn, don't you?" she said. "He may be hungry or wet. Try putting your fingertip in his mouth."

Jack scowled. This was no time to make jokes.

Abby opened her eyes wide, set her hands on her hips and waited. She looked serious.

Frowning still, he stretched one hand across Wyatt's chest so he could press a pinkie finger against the quivering lips. Wyatt immediately stopped sniveling and started sucking.

"Good," Abby said. "Your finger should calm him until you can dig a binky out of the bag."

"A binky?"

She chuckled. "A pacifier."

Abby turned back to her truck, leaning across the back seat to disengage one of the car seats. She had the most delicious little tush, and the skirt she was wearing showcased it perfectly. It wasn't too much of a stretch to imagine what she'd look like without it.

Jack smothered a groan and looked away. The last thing he needed was to foster an attraction for Abby.

Keeping his finger in place, he lifted Wyatt onto his forearm and occupied himself with chuckling at the boy's tiny vest and long brown curls. Abby had dressed him like a little man today, but from the looks of things, a trip to the barber would be in order before Wyatt's first birthday.

Abby clunked the car seat down on the pavement and lifted Wyatt from his arms. "I'll carry him to your car," she said. "Installing a car seat takes both hands."

Make that three to four hands, Jack thought a few minutes later as he fumbled with straps and buckles that seemed to make no sense.

It took one extra baby rotation before the seat was secure, but after Abby's more practiced hands took over the chore, Wyatt was in the seat with a pacifier and she was heading back across the parking lot toward her parents.

Jack frowned as he sat in his car and watched her go. Her purposeful walk belied the reluctance she must have felt, and he knew she had to be upset.

He wished he could think of a better way. He glanced down at Wyatt, whose eyelids were droopy by now, and back out the window at Abby.

Her stride hadn't faltered, but somehow, in a morning of mixed-up feelings, her walk made him smile. It wasn't her speed or the lack of artificial sway, so much as the perfection of well-used legs and a sweet round bottom that couldn't help but wiggle. That no-nonsense walk was as entrancing as any he'd seen.

That walk, and his reaction to seeing it, were the only right things about the morning. He kept grinning as he started his car. Quite unintentionally, Abby had graced him with a moment of pure delight.

"Abby? It's me," Jack said, pleased that she had answered her phone. During the last call she had definitely sounded riled. He'd been afraid she would take the phone off the hook, and he needed her advice.

"Yes, Jack. What do you need?"

"I finally got this formula mixed and heated, and then

the phone rang and I didn't get Wyatt fed for thirty minutes. Do I have to start over completely?''

''Hang on,'' she said with a long sigh. She spoke to someone in the background. The string of babbling that followed must be Rosie, playing. In his five hours with Wyatt, Jack had heard nothing but wailing.

''He's been waiting for his bottle for thirty minutes?'' Abby asked abruptly. She sounded as if she was right there beside him. He could picture her with her hands on her hips and that preachy look on her face. ''What's he doing?''

''Lying on the floor, sucking on a pacifier.''

''For thirty minutes? What did you do with the bottle?''

She made a tsk-ing sound, which was totally unnecessary.

There was no possible way for Jack to feel any more inept than he already did.

''It's on the counter, in the kitchenette.''

''For Pete's sake, feed the kid. Why didn't you do it while you were talking on the phone?''

''Sometimes I need to get on my laptop to figure out how to solve a client's problem. I needed my hands free.''

''Jack, wake up. You're a parent now,'' she said, her tone implying exactly how dim she thought he was.

''You may have to call a client back now and then.''

After hanging up, Jack retrieved the bottle from the kitchen and settled down with Wyatt on the hotel sofa. He popped the pacifier out of the baby's mouth and watched in horror as the tiny back stiffened and the tinier mouth opened wide to shriek.

Frantically, he stuck the bottle in. And relaxed. Once that first taste of formula hit Wyatt's tongue, he quieted quickly. "That's my boy," Jack said, feeling as if he'd conquered a major obstacle.

He was going to get this baby business down and get back to Kansas City. Back to his life. Things would go much better there—he'd have his speakerphone, his main computer and his girlfriends to ask for advice. They might not know as much as Abby, but they'd never make him feel unfit, either.

Under the circumstances, Abby's snappy attitude made sense, but he was certainly not dim. He loved a challenge. He could make this work.

Wasn't he the same guy who'd managed to finish high school a full year early? In spite of having little help from a mother who was busy running through boyfriends.

Jack had to keep Brian occupied and fed on many nights, and he'd still been able to attend college, keep a string of girlfriends happy and start his own business. He could learn to care for a person too young to walk or talk.

Besides, for all practical purposes he'd already raised a boy. Although Brian had been older by the time he had taken over the chore, Jack knew that if he could just persevere until Wyatt was about school age, the job would be old hat.

The most important thing, he thought, was a desire to do the job well. Motivation was half the battle with anything.

He could always deal with the guilt later.

But a few minutes after Wyatt finished the bottle, he started fussing again. Jack changed a diaper that was only slightly wet, but the baby kept screaming. Jack couldn't figure out why. He'd have to call Abby again.

"Hullo?"

"Abby, he's been crying for fifteen minutes straight," he hollered above the noise.

"Did you feed him?"

"Yes," he said in horror, thinking there must have been something terribly wrong with the formula. "He drank the whole bottle."

"Did you burp him?"

"Oh…uh, no. I didn't. Hang on, I'm picking him up. Talk me through it," he implored. "Talk loud."

He held Wyatt out in front of him, hoping against hope the child simply needed burping. The baby howled as if a pin was sticking in his belly, but these diapers had Velcro. That formula must have been spoiled.

Next time, his client would wait.

Abby described the burping position she found most effective, and several others to try if that one didn't work. Within a few minutes, the tiny boy had produced three burps that could vie for a record with Jack's beer guzzling buddies. All of the sudden, Wyatt was gurgling and waving his fists in the air contentedly.

Once again Jack thanked Abby for her help and hung up.

After that, the Kimball men had a fairly decent evening. Jack found a soft blue blanket in the diaper bag and spread it on the floor. He let the baby kick around on that while he ate a room service dinner.

Later, they took in the end of a baseball game together. Wyatt hadn't actually developed a fondness for sports yet, but if Jack sat on the floor beside him and spoke animatedly about the wisdom or folly of each play, the baby seemed happy to respond to the conversation.

When Wyatt started sobbing again after the game, Jack fed him—brilliantly, this time. He had the baby fed and burped within a half hour, without a single snag. Then he changed a dirty diaper, congratulating himself on that, too. It had been his first poopy diaper, and he managed it without needing a bit of advice.

He called Abby only one more time that night.

"Hullo, Jack. What is it?" she asked tiredly, after just one ring.

"How'd you know it was me?"

"Are you kidding? You've called at least once every hour for the past six. I was wondering where you'd gone."

"Oh."

"Well, what is it?"

Abby had worked her magic again: he felt foolish. He considered hanging up, but he still needed to know the answer to his question. "How do I take a shower?"

She giggled. "Now you're kidding, right?"

"No, I'm not," he said. "What do I do with Wyatt?"

"It's eleven o'clock. He's not asleep yet?"

"No."

After another exaggerated sigh, she said, "Is there a separate place in your hotel room for him to sleep?"

"Yes, we're in a suite."

"Go pull a mattress off the bed and put Wyatt in the middle of it on his back. Stack pillows on every side. Then—and this is the most important part—leave the room."

It sounded too easy. "Won't he cry?"

"For a while, but if he's quiet within a few minutes, you've made it," she said in a whisper-soft voice that sounded sweet for the first time today. "Then you can go take a shower."

"Good," he said, grateful for her kindness. He'd been through enough already.

"And Jack?"

"Yes?"

"I'm going to bed. Babies wake up at night. You check their diaper, see if they're hungry. You can do that. Don't call me again unless it's an emergency."

SEVEN HOURS LATER, Jack stirred from a light snooze when Wyatt starting moving around. The arm of the hotel room sofa was rock hard, making deep sleep out of the question. But Wyatt had been quiet and comfortable, belly down against his uncle's chest, with a blanket tucked snugly around him.

Jack had tried Abby's suggestion. He had tried hard. But it had been impossible to listen to Wyatt shriek for longer than a minute or two. For all he knew, the child had fallen off the mattress and rolled across the floor. Or maybe the little guy missed his family. Jack couldn't discount that possibility.

Besides, he had the other hotel guests to consider.

So he'd slept on the sofa with Wyatt nestled on his chest. The arrangement had worked wonders for the baby.

Jack himself hadn't slept more than an hour or two.

All those wakeful hours had afforded him plenty of thinking time, and he'd started to come to some conclusions. For one thing, taking care of an infant was a laborious chore—Wyatt seemed to need constant attention.

Where had Jack gotten the impression that babies slept most of the time? So far, Wyatt had cried more than he'd slept. Or so it seemed.

If he took the baby back to Kansas City, he could try working from home so he could tend to Wyatt. He imagined a day broken into scattered segments of trying to feed, change and pacify a baby, while his clients cooled their heels on the other end of the phone line. And Jack had no idea what he'd do when he had to go on a business trip.

In any case, his company would probably fail.

If he hired round-the-clock care, he could spend time with his nephew whenever he wasn't working. Then he'd have a definite hand in the boy's upbringing.

Of course, Jack would have to slow down his social life to a snail's pace. The ladies would have to visit him at home, or see him a lot less often.

But when it came right down to it, he didn't have many options. His working hours were unpredictable, and he didn't have a kindly old aunt nearby to help when he needed it.

Although there were three women he dated regularly, none seemed as if they would want to take on the chore.

He knew for certain that Paula, the woman he'd known the longest, would revolt at being asked to help with an infant.

She might close her eyes to his playboy ways, but she wouldn't tolerate a child. She often said that having children was what other women did when they didn't have the imagination to create an exciting life for themselves.

There was something else that was bothering him, too, and it was the most important aspect of his dilemma. The twins were all that was left of the family Brian had loved. Jack shouldn't tear them apart, especially not after they'd just lost their parents. They deserved to grow up knowing one another. At the very least, they deserved to spend time together as siblings. He shouldn't take that away from them.

But he couldn't just give the boy up, either. That would be letting himself down, as well as Brian.

Jack needed to talk to Abby.

ONE OF THE BABIES was crying.

Abby woke up, stumbled off the couch and headed for

the bedroom to see which one needed her. By the time she'd crossed the threshold, she remembered. Jack had taken Wyatt.

It had required all the self-control she could muster to help that man through his troubles yesterday, when all she'd wanted was to go over there and bring Wyatt home.

Lifting Rosie off the mattress, she hummed softly. The baby began to quiet immediately, but Abby knew she was probably hungry. It was six o'clock, about the time the babies usually woke up.

Trudging into the kitchen to pull a bottle from the refrigerator, Abby warmed it, then wandered back to her rocker with both baby and bottle. She settled in for a while, watching Rosie drink.

Yesterday's events kept replaying in her head like a nightmare. Jack had really taken Wyatt. And then he had called her all day long, reminding her constantly that his knowledge of babies could fit on the wing of an aphid.

She wondered how Wyatt had slept last night, or whether he had slept at all. A brutal stab of longing pierced through her heart, starting her tears falling again.

She let them flow, reassuring Rosie that crying was healthy and healing. The sweet girl looked at Abby as if she understood the pain, seeming oddly wise—until she reached up with chubby fingers and clenched Abby's nose.

Abby's responding chuckle caused Rosie to smile back and kick her feet in happiness. And for all her innocence, she provided a wealth of comfort.

After Rosie had been fed, burped, bathed and dressed, Abby let her play on the floor with a bowl of plastic fish while she gathered some things in a diaper bag.

Yesterday had proved that she couldn't wait for serendipity to solve her problems. Jack had no business trying to fit a sweet little boy into his self-absorbed lifestyle. Paige wouldn't have wanted that, no matter what the will said, and now it was up to Abby to make sure it didn't happen. Somehow.

She wanted nothing more than to raise both twins together, on the farm in the country. After all, that was a modified version of her lifelong dream.

Ever since she was a young girl, a country life was what she had envisioned for herself. She'd wanted to marry some dark-haired, faceless man, raise a yardful of kids and animals, and grow flowers.

Many of the childhood games of ''let's pretend'' she had played with her sister had revolved around that theme.

After her divorce, Abby realized her fairy tale would never include the dark-haired man. She'd made a foolish choice once, and she didn't trust herself to try again. But she'd never forgotten the rest of the fantasy.

Her sister had been more successful in starting down all the right paths, but she was gone now. It was only fitting that Abby should carry on pursuing their shared hopes.

If only she could convince Jack to give up Wyatt.

A few minutes later, she drove down the long dirt lane to the eighty-year-old-house she'd loved most of her life. Jack's silver two-seater sports car was parked haphazardly in the drive, with his familiar blue cap resting on its hood. He'd beaten her here.

She parked behind him and hopped out to pull Rosie from the back seat. A whistle sounded, and she whirled around to find Jack watching from beside a massive white column of the wraparound wooden porch.

His hair was as unruly as ever, and he looked as if he hadn't shaved today. The dark stubble turned his eyes impossibly blue, and a loden-green sport shirt showed off his wide chest. He looked handsome in a homey sort of way. In fact, his relaxed approach to grooming only sparked her interest more.

He looked as if he'd just rolled out of bed.

"You make that look easy," he said.

"What?"

"Getting her in and out of that seat. It took me a long time to figure out those straps again after I got Wyatt to the hotel yesterday."

"Where is he?" she asked, just now realizing that Jack wasn't carrying him.

He pointed to his car. Whether from overprotectiveness, or a complete lack of trust, Abby was peering through the car window within seconds.

Wyatt was in his car seat, sound asleep. The cracked window provided adequate ventilation, and the morning air was comfortable for early August. The boy was in no danger, but still…

"How long have you left him in there?"

"Less than two minutes," Jack said. "He was asleep when we got here, so I came up to look around on the porch."

Abby squinted at him, wondering if he was being truthful. After yesterday, she wouldn't be surprised if Wyatt had been left much longer. Jack might be some guru computer consultant, but he knew nothing about babies.

"Go ahead, touch the hood of the car," he said with a raised brow. "It's probably still warm."

"That's not necessary." She sniffed and carried Rosie onto the porch. Once there, Abby foraged through her purse with one hand, searching for the door key.

"Let me help," Jack offered, holding his arms out.

Reluctantly, Abby handed the baby over just long

enough to locate her keys. Neither he nor Rosie seemed to mind the exchange. He smiled sweetly into the baby girl's face, provoking a sweeter smile from Rosie, and a string of syllables that sounded something like, "Bibibibi deek?"

Ignoring Jack's chuckled response, Abby opened the door and stepped inside. Subdued light from an overhead window set off the foyer's original wood flooring, and somehow the house smelled fresh, despite the fact that it had been closed up most of the past two weeks.

Maybe it was an illusion—she'd always felt welcome when she walked through this doorway—but now just being here put her at ease. As if she'd come home.

Jack followed her inside, with Rosie prattling happily in his arms. "Why don't I get Wyatt and put him in his crib?" Abby offered. "It's still set up in the nursery."

Without waiting for a response, she jogged back outside and lifted Wyatt from the car seat, cuddling him close as she returned.

Jack had disappeared into the house with Rosie, so she headed upstairs to the nursery. She put Wyatt into his own crib and backed quietly away.

At the doorway, she switched on the baby monitor and took the receiver with her. She found Jack and Rosie in the kitchen, looking out the French doors into the greenhouse Abby and Paige had built last year.

Jack was speaking gently to the child, holding her up so she could see out. As soon as Abby walked into the room, he turned and said, "The flowers are thriving out there. Have you been keeping them up?" He shifted Rosie to his other arm, already seeming adept at holding a baby.

Abby's heart fell; she'd been counting on his complete and continuing discomfort with kids.

She put the receiver on the table and went to claim her little girl. "I have," she admitted. "I had been helping Paige start a commercial cut-flower business, and I couldn't let it all go."

"Didn't your family know the man who owned this place?"

"Mr. Apple Man," she began, and paused to chuckle at herself for the mistake. "That's what Paige and I called him when we were growing up, because of the orchards. Actually, his name is Larry Epelstein. When he got too old to run the place, he offered to sell it to us, cheap. He wanted to be sure someone got in here who would take care of his trees."

"Everyone in your family has a green thumb, don't they?"

"Guess so," Abby answered, gnawing at her lip as she looked out at the colorful melange of flowers.

She'd need to water them today, and some of the varieties would need deadheading. She hadn't found the energy to get the blooms to market lately. If things didn't improve anytime soon, perhaps she never would.

Jack touched her arm. "Since we're both here, why don't we talk now?"

Still staring out into the greenhouse, she considered why it felt as if he held her very life in his hands. He seemed to hold a balance of power here. He had Wyatt, and the land the orchards were situated on. She knew Rosie and the house were every bit as valuable, but there was one difference.

Abby wanted what he had.

Pretending a courage she didn't feel, she wandered over to the antique oak table that dominated the middle of the kitchen. "Guess now's as good a time as any," she said as she slid into a chair with Rosie on her lap.

Jack sat across from her, and actually smiled when Rosie started fussing. "Well!" he said. "It's good to know that you can make yours cry, too."

Abby swallowed a bristling retort and forced herself to smile back. "She probably just wants to play," she said. "There's an activity center in the nursery. I'll sneak up and get it."

She plopped the crying baby back into Jack's arms and grinned at his swift change of expression. Now he looked close to tears.

She ran back up to the nursery, reminding herself all the way of how much more effective she'd be if she kept her cool.

After she lugged the toy back down to the kitchen and put Rosie into the seat, her sobbing stopped. But the knowledge that she and Jack were assured a few minutes of peace did little to calm Abby's nerves.

"Okay," she said, tugging at the neck of her T-shirt as she sat down again. "Where should we start?"

"I did a lot of thinking last night," he said as he frowned at his hands, which were folded on the table. "We need to work out a way to keep the twins together."

Abby felt a rush of relief so profound that she hopped up to kiss him. It was nothing more than a hasty smack on the cheek, but as soon as she did it she realized her mistake.

His beard scraped against her lips, making them feel soft and pouty. And he smelled incredible. Manly, like some bracing man's soap, or like ocean air. She hadn't experienced that sort of smell in a long, long time.

A deep, urgent response walloped her so powerfully that she immediately closed her eyes and collapsed back into her chair. When she opened them again, she realized he was checking out her chest.

Apparently, her kiss had affected him, too. Or perhaps he was always ready for an opportunity to check out a female body. Even Abby's.

She crossed her arms in front of her. "Sorry," she said. "You caught me by surprise."

His crinkle-eyed gaze floated leisurely up to her face.

"Hey, don't ever apologize for kissing me," he said. Then he cleared his throat. "I just don't know how to do it."

"Um, do what, exactly?"

"Keep them together."

"Oh, of course," she said, sweeping her gaze to the precious baby girl she'd managed to forget for an instant.

"I'm not ready to give up my place in Kansas City," he explained. "It's a phenomenal town home, near the heart of the business district. Many of my clients have offices nearby."

"Are you planning to leave Wyatt here?" she asked.

Perhaps her hopes were coming true. If he would sell her the land, too, her dreams would be tied up with a tidy bow.

"No," he said, dashing her hopes abruptly. "I'll stay a year as Brian requested. If you run the orchard, the proceeds can go back into the farm. Next fall, we can talk about a fair price for the land, and a way to keep Wyatt and Rosie in contact. Things might be easier by then."

"Maybe."

Jack ran a hand along his whiskery jaw, staring out at the greenhouse. "I could sublet the town home...."

Abby listened as he thought out loud. Since he was moving things in her direction on his own, she decided to let him ramble on before she butted in. Maybe he'd realize he should just leave Wyatt here with her. Forever.

"…and find a place around here. You know of any-place?"

She thought of the land surrounding the farm. There was a cattle ranch on one side and a wheat farm on the other. She shook her head. "There's nothing to rent out here."

Wyatt's howl exploded into the room, causing Jack to jump out of his seat. "Hot damn—" he began, then glanced at Rosie. "Hot *dang,* what is that racket?"

Abby clicked off the receiver. "Just the baby moni-tor."

He stared at the device. "Why is it so loud?"

Abby was already headed for the stairs. "A bad habit," she hollered back. "This house is so big I'm afraid I won't hear them, so I turn it up full blast."

Wyatt quieted almost immediately when Abby picked him up.

She used one of Rosie's diapers to change him, and then carried him back downstairs, thinking all the way.

She loved this baby. She wanted to be near him every single day and night. She'd do anything to achieve that goal.

Anything.

When she got back to the kitchen, she handed Wyatt to Jack, then lifted Rosie out of the bouncer and laid her belly-down on the floor. "This is when a high chair would come in handy," she said. "Paige was thinking about getting one, but the babies only started eating solid food a few weeks ago."

A frown creased Jack's forehead. "Is Wyatt hungry?"

"No, but one baby could sit in a high chair with a couple of toys while the other took a turn in the activity center." Abby took Wyatt and deposited him in the toy's seat. "It's just another source of amusement for the twins."

Wyatt immediately started bouncing and batting at colorful knobs. "You were just ready to play, weren't you?" she crooned.

Opening a cabinet drawer, she pulled out a couple of toys and tossed them in front of Rosie, who propped herself up on sturdy arms to grab a set of plastic keys.

When she dropped them, they produced a clacking sound that must have pleased her, because she snagged them right back up and began hitting them repeatedly against the terra-cotta tiles.

"If I can find a big enough apartment, I could run my business from there," Jack said as Abby returned to the table. "There's bound to be something suitable in town."

"Or we could both move in here," Abby suggested, wondering even as she said it if she was completely insane. "This house has plenty of room for an office, and we could switch off duties so we'd both have time to work."

"You mean we'd live together as roommates?" Jack asked.

"Of course," she said, trying with all her might to make the suggestion seem like no big deal. Even though it was.

A *big* deal.

"I hadn't thought of that," he murmured, staring at her with a bemused expression. "I could set up my office here easily enough, but don't you work at a flower shop?"

"My parents own a flower shop in town," she corrected. "I work at a garden supply warehouse, but I was thinking of quitting, anyway. I could pay my share of the bills with the profits from the cut-flower business."

"Hmm," he said, pushing out his bottom lip and toying with the whiskers underneath. "I like this idea more and more. The babies would have both of us around for a year and by the end of that time they'd be easier to manage."

"Um-hmm," Abby said, worrying about the idea more and more. Could she and Jack actually live here, together?

He might not know her from a garden of weeds, but she was painfully aware of his vitality. Always.

She also knew he led a pretty active social life. Would he want to bring his women here? She began to imagine a revolving door of various women, coming in and out of the farmhouse and cooing at the babies before they vanished into Jack's room to coo some more.

"Sounds cozy," he said, breaking into her angst.

"Doesn't it, though?" She feigned composure, but her alarm grew exponentially as her idea hurtled from impetuous to barely conceivable to likely. And remained, all the while, quite impossible.

Chapter Three

Abby had hauled seven loads of her belongings past the burned-out front porch light before she finally decided to change it. She had just dragged a kitchen chair outside and perched on top to make the adjustment when her new neighbor, Sharon Hauser, hollered from inside. "Donation box, or new location?"

Sharon's matronly figure filled the doorway. She held a bean-pot lamp on one hip, and Wyatt on the other. Her usual smile was missing as she stared at Abby's precarious pose.

Abby held up the bulb and light cover, and chuckled when her friend's big, gummy smile returned. Though Sharon had at least fifteen years on Abby, she was on the same wavelength. Sometimes words weren't necessary.

Abby finished the job and hopped down. As she carried the chair back in, she said, "I asked you here to help with Rosie and Wyatt. I can finish unpacking."

Sharon jiggled both baby and lamp, prompting a happy squeal from Wyatt. "Shush," she told Abby. "Scrap or keep—that's all I need to know."

Abby knew not to argue. She squinted at the lamp. "Keep," she answered. "Put it on the table beside the sofa."

Sharon swept the lamp and the giggling Wyatt off toward the living room, and Abby headed off in the other direction to cart the chair back to the kitchen.

Her helpful new friend was well on her way to becoming a cherished old friend. She had appeared on that very same porch the morning after the accident, and she'd been just as obstinate then about lending a hand. She'd pushed her way in behind a pierogi casserole, explained that she was the wife of the farmer down the road, and had commandeered the babies and the kitchen duties so Abby could deal with the tragic news.

That morning, Abby had been too stunned to argue. She'd been baby-sitting the twins the night before, and had waited up all night for Paige and Brian's return. She'd thought they must have decided to stay out overnight, and reasoned that they'd been having too much fun to let her know.

She had only learned the grisly truth at dawn, after their overturned car was discovered near a dirt road just two miles from the farmhouse. The white-tailed deer Brian had swerved to avoid was found dead a few yards away, and the furrowed path in the steep embankment told the rest of the story. At first, Abby blamed herself. If only she'd thought to call someone, perhaps they could have been saved. But the coroner had said their death was immediate. He'd called it merciful.

Abby didn't know if a healthy young couple could die a merciful death. She only knew they were gone forever, leaving her behind with a couple of babies who would never be orphans as long as she was around.

That night had created a deep and unhealing chasm in her memory. Everything before had become part of a past that was already lost. Everything since was the future.

Uncertain. Frightening. As important as air.

The delicious sound of baby cackles broke into her thoughts and led her down the hall. She discovered her neighbor and the twins—vital components of her new life—cavorting in one of the rooms she had emptied for Jack.

Sharon now held a baby in each arm, and she was spinning lazy circles in the middle of the room. "Looks funny without Brian's exercise equipment," she said. "You sure about this living arrangement?"

Abby glanced around at the generous space, unwilling to voice her turmoil. "Sure I'm sure," she said.

And she was, in a way. At least she was glad to know that Wyatt would be here, in this house, with her and Rosie. Abby might have snagged a rather large stray in the form of Jack Kimball, but since the baby boy she'd tried to lasso was included, it should be well worth it.

"Since I volunteered to baby-sit the twins during the funeral, I've never met Jack," Sharon said. She stopped turning, and caught Abby's eye. "I assume you know what you're getting into."

"I think so," Abby said with a shrug. "Besides, this was the only way to keep Wyatt for the time being."

"Didn't you say Jack was granted permanent custody?"

"I did." She pulled Wyatt away from Sharon. "He's a bachelor, though. He has no idea what he's getting into. I'm predicting that he'll want out within three months."

Sharon frowned. "You know they can learn, right? Most men start off clueless when it comes to their first baby."

"But Jack isn't like most men," Abby said with growing confidence. "He's like Tim, my ex-husband."

"How's that?"

Abby counted off the similarities on her fingers. "He

likes women, he spends too much time in bars and he buys expensive, big-boy toys.''

''Sounds like a typical single man, if you ask me,'' Sharon said. ''My Earl rode a Harley before we got married. He only traded it for the tractor after our third son was born.''

Abby swung Wyatt to her opposite arm and used her other hand to continue her tally. ''Well, now I'm just guessing on these,'' she said. ''But I'll bet that Jack bores easily, avoids commitment and hates self-sacrifice. He's a Tim, not an Earl.''

''What does he look like?''

Abby scowled. ''That's irrelevant.''

''Is he tall?'' Sharon asked with a chuckle.

Abby nodded. No need to deny that particular quality, since Sharon would find out for herself soon enough.

''Brian had nice eyes. Does Jack?''

She thought about a pair of devilishly handsome eyes and shrugged. ''Doesn't matter.''

Sharon's mop of graying blond hair floated triumphantly out of the room. ''Sounds to me as if you've got more than the twins to worry about.''

''Jack Kimball is completely resistible,'' Abby said as she followed her friend into the living room.

''What if you aren't?''

Abby stopped near Paige's plum curtains and pulled them closed. ''Are you kidding?''

Her neighbor turned around and shook her head. ''You said he likes women. You are one, Abby.''

She laughed at the thought. ''I'm not his type.''

Sharon sat on the sofa with Rosie on her lap and tickled the little girl under her chin. ''And that's a problem?'' she said. ''Opposites attract.''

''Stop it,'' Abby said. She jiggled Wyatt. ''This is the

only irresistible bachelor in my life. And besides, even if Jack doesn't know better, I do.''

"You won't have a problem with being chased around this fine, faux leather sofa?''

"That won't happen,'' Abby said with confidence.

Her friend patted the cushion beside her. "Sit down and spill it,'' she said. "What are you up to?''

Abby laughed. She walked across the room and flicked on the lamp. "What do you mean?''

"I recognize that look in your eye,'' Sharon said. "We're finished moving for tonight. Sit and talk.''

Abby set Wyatt on the carpet amid a cheerful clutter of toys, then took Rosie from her friend's arms to put her down there, too. After that she plopped down on the sofa, shrugged and admitted, "I do have a teensy little plan.''

JACK KNEW HE'D NEVER succeed at running his own business if he didn't devote himself to it passionately. He spent most of his weekday hours developing and marketing software, training clients or troubleshooting problems.

Most days, he had lunch delivered to wherever he was working, and often ate dinners there, too. The only personal things he rammed into his grueling schedule were an hour's exercise at whichever end of the day he could fit it in, and a shower and shave after that.

No one could work harder, and he had achieved a degree of success that allowed JK Business Software Systems to enjoy a nice little profit.

He also knew that play restored him, and he worked hard at that, too. He couldn't do well at one thing without focusing ample attention on the other.

Therefore, most of his off hours were reserved for fun—any kind of fun. Wild or civilized, carefully charted or slapdash. His only requirement was that it, and the woman he chose to share it with, held his attention.

By the time Friday night rolled around, he was usually the first in line for entertainment. This weekend was no exception. Although he'd returned to Kansas City to pack for his temporary stint in the country, there was no reason he couldn't squeeze in a few dates with his lady friends.

A year spent in the sticks taking care of two babies, with Abby's solemn eyes judging his every move, sounded exhausting. And long. Possibly joyless. He wanted to cram as much of his usual rakish lifestyle into this weekend as possible.

It had taken him only a few hours this morning to pack his things and dismantle his computer. He'd boxed everything and stacked it by the front door. The movers would pick up a few big items tomorrow and deliver them to the farmhouse on Sunday. It wouldn't make sense to get out there before his furniture did, which meant most of the weekend was open.

It only proved that he led a charmed life—he had plenty of time, and three beautiful girlfriends who should fill it rather nicely. Maybe if he could smooth things over with each of them, an occasional weekend visit might be arranged, making the year a little less arid.

Since Diane happened to be a real estate agent, he called her first. Maybe she could help him find a temporary tenant for his condo. Even if that didn't work out, she was well worth his time. His latest paramour had a cap of sexy black hair and mile-long legs. But his favorite feature by far was the seductive laugh she only used in the bedroom.

He dialed her cellphone number, knowing her Friday morning would have been spent showing houses or scouting out opportunities.

"Diane Westmoreland," she barked.

"Hey, Diane. I'm back in town."

"Ooh, Jacky!" she said, in a tone fairly dripping with carnality. "How good to hear your voice."

"You must be alone," he said, chuckling at the change. She'd gone from frigid to fiery in a second.

"Way, way too alone, big boy."

Good. He would enjoy seeing her, but more than that, he needed her help. "You busy in an hour?"

"There's not a thing happening here that can't be rearranged for you."

"How about meeting me for lunch? We can go to your favorite Italian place in the city."

"Sounds wonderful," she purred. "I'll be waiting."

Wonderful it wasn't. It was closer to woeful. Or wintry.

Once Jack told Diane that he was moving to rural Topeka, her temperature went right back down to 98.6 degrees. And when he explained about moving into the farmhouse with Abby, it plummeted well below freezing.

The mood had been so frosty at lunch, he'd worried that they'd both develop hypothermia. Or at least indigestion.

He spent nearly an hour trying to convince her that he was not involved with Abigail Briggs. He told her that Abby was too countrified, often sharp-tongued and genuinely not his type. For some reason, Diane didn't believe him.

She had finished her meal and gathered her purse to leave before he remembered that he was going to ask her to sublet the apartment for him. He opened his mouth to speak, but after looking at her dour expression one more time, he thought better of it. He'd just have to call her later, after she had warmed back up to room temperature.

There was no point in hiring a stranger just because the wiliest Realtor in town was a little miffed.

Besides, there was no need to be alone tonight—Paula was next on his list. He owed her the choice Friday night slot because she'd been the most enduring girlfriend of his adult life.

Ultrasophisticated Paula put up with his other lady friends and always greeted him with a smile. He was hoping she'd be willing to let him crash at her place whenever he had to come into the city on business.

She surprised him. Their understanding about dating other people seemed to fly out the window as soon as he said the word *roommates.*

"What do you mean, you're going to live with her?"

Jack held Paula's wineglass out to her. She'd always understood his need to date around. This was only a slight deviation from normal, and it shouldn't truly upset her.

"She'll be living in the same place, but that's all," he explained. "We're not romantic. Think of her as a house-mother, if you wish. Or the girl next door."

Paula didn't take the glass, and she didn't look amused. "And you're actually going to help take care of two brats?"

Jack frowned as he sat the glass back down. That had sounded ugly. He knew she wasn't the nurturing type, but now she was slandering his own flesh and blood. "They're only five months old," he said. "Infants can't be classified as brats."

"Future brats, then," she sniffed, standing up to leave before they'd even ordered dinner.

"Paula, you surprise me," he said, as he stood up, too.

"Darling, I'm afraid it's you who has surprised me," she said over her shoulder.

Jack threw a couple of bills on the table and followed

her out, wondering why two out of three of the women who were supposedly crazy about him were giving up so easily.

He wasn't doing anything shady. This was all just geographical. He was moving from a condo in the city to a house in the country, and it was an easy forty-five minute drive between the two. What was the problem?

As they stood near the front of the restaurant, he held out her jacket so she could slip it on. In a desperate attempt to bring their conversation back to its usual witty banter, he said, "If I can ditch the rugrats one weekend and get to the city, may I give you a call?"

"You can try," she said. "I do have a life, you know. I'll tell you what you can do—you can call me when you're finished playing family man. Perhaps then we can move in together." She gave him a peck on the cheek before she slid into her car, which the valet had just parked in front. And then she drove away without a single backward glance.

As Jack watched her go, he didn't wonder at his lack of disappointment. He knew his weekend's diversion wasn't lost just yet. He'd simply call in his third option tonight, instead of waiting for morning.

Zuzu was slightly offbeat, but her unpredictable way of looking at things was amusing. And he'd never once seen her mad. Despite a colorful head of hair whose base tone, he suspected, was red, she was peaceable, often prophetic. He called to invite her out for coffee. Luckily, she was free.

An hour later, he sat in a trendy diner handing Zuzu fresh napkins. "I knew you were going to run off to the country and fall in love," she sobbed.

The sequins on her pink-and-orange blouse glimmered

with each shuddering breath, making it hard for Jack to take her seriously.

"Zuzu, I'm not in love," he said. "Abby and I are just moving in together for convenience. We have never even kissed—"

He clamped his jaw shut when he remembered how much he'd wanted to do just that in the farm kitchen a few days ago, and he tried not to let the thought echo in his brain.

There was no need to bring something like that up now.

"W-well, if you haven't yet, you w-will. I just know it."

"I doubt that," he soothed, moving his chair closer to hers so he could rub her back. Maybe there was still hope for snatching a little romance out of an otherwise wasted evening.

In a singsong voice, Zuzu asked, "Is she pretty?"

He removed his hand. She'd sounded far too childlike to be touching her seductively right now. Sighing deeply, he said, "In a way, I suppose. She seems to have the basic material, but she doesn't try very hard to enhance it."

"But that's worse!"

"Why?"

"Because that means she's a natural beauty."

"I suppose you'd say she's all right in the looks department," Jack said, wondering if Abby would be considered attractive by another woman.

Her eyes were gorgeous—no one else had eyes that bright and clear. But her hair was usually just parted in the middle and tied back. Even at Paige and Brian's wedding, she'd simply wound a braid around each side of her head. He'd never seen her hair loose around her shoulders, and her clothes were usually unassuming.

A woman would think she was plain, he supposed. Only a male would home in on that sexy little body.

"Is she sexy?" Zuzu asked.

He shrugged. He prided himself on being truthful with his dates, but with Zuzu he tried to be extra careful.

In case she *knew*.

Sounding confident now, she said, "See what I mean? You'll be married in less than a year."

"Zuzu, we've talked about this before. I'm never going to get married. There are too many women out there."

"Every man says that," she said. "Every woman knows it only takes the right one."

Jack frowned. He always spent time at the beginning of each relationship establishing a single rule: he'd date whom he wanted, when he wanted.

No commitments, and no cat fights.

"And what makes you think Abby's my Miss Right?"

"Intuition," Zuzu said with a knowing smile.

"Baloney," he responded, with a confidence of his own.

And with that, the otherworldly Zuzu drifted out of the diner, and the astounded Jack returned to his town home alone for the first time in a number of weekends.

Always before, a barren weekend had been his choice—not theirs. He'd had no idea how spoiled he'd been. He walked around among his boxed possessions, wishing he hadn't packed. Wishing the movers would come so he could get to the farmhouse and begin to put the next year behind him.

At least there the baby-care duties should keep him from being bored. It had been nice of Abby to offer to take care of the twins all weekend. He wondered if Wyatt had gone to sleep without a struggle tonight, and if Rosie had babbled nonstop all day.

After an hour of quiet, he called Abby to find out.

"Hullo?"

Her voice was low and throaty. She sounded tired. He checked the time and realized it was eleven o'clock. She'd probably been asleep. He could picture her lounging in bed with a pristine white sheet slipping down the front of her— *Whoa!*

An evening's assorted discussions about the caliber of her assets must have gotten to him.

"Hullo? Is anyone there?"

"Abby, it's Jack. How's it going?"

"Fine. The babies have been asleep for two hours," she said. "They wake up early, so I came on up to bed."

Bed. There it was again.

No matter how hard he fought it, that image of her naked body kept popping into his brain. The only explanation he could think of was that his woman-filled weekend had been a complete washout.

"I'm sorry if I woke you. I just wanted to check on things there," he said with his eyes closed, as if he could block the unwanted mental pictures.

"You mean you're alone? Jack, are you slowing down at the ripe old age of…what, thirty-one?" As she grew more alert, she seemed to extend her talons again.

"There's no need to start a fight now," he said, opening his eyes again.

He should thank her, really. As soon as her tone changed from soft to sarcastic, her image transformed, and he saw her standing with her hands on her hips and her lips pinched together. Wearing *plenty* of clothes.

"I wasn't starting a fight. I was expressing surprise that you didn't have company."

"It wasn't by choice."

That got her for a moment. Then she said, "Poor baby, did your girlfriend get upset by your news?"

"Yes. And I wouldn't scoff too much, since it's your fault," he sniped back.

"My fault? How is that?"

"Obviously, they're upset that I'm shacking up with you."

He heard her sharp intake of breath. "They? As in more than one? But you've only been gone *one day.*"

"Um…yes. I managed to squeeze in a few—just to let them know I was moving, of course."

"Holy cow," she breathed. "Well, did you tell them we can hardly tolerate one another?"

"Not in so many words."

"Well, you should. It would probably help."

"What's the point?" he asked. "I'm coming to live there in the boonies for a year, remember?"

"How could I forget? But if you want to keep them as girlfriends, tell them I'm not feminine enough for you. Maybe you could persuade them to come for an occasional therapeutic visit. One at a time, of course."

"You would put up with that?"

"I'm not so naive that I don't realize you have… needs," she said, whispering that last word in a way that had him closing his eyes again in defense.

"You know, for a country girl, you sound enlightened."

"I'm not backward, Jack."

Brian had always said that Abby didn't get out much. "And why are you alone on a Friday night?" he asked.

"I have two infants here. I don't have time for dating."

"Before the babies, did you date much?"

"I was married before, remember?" she said. "I'd just gotten divorced when Paige and Brian got married."

Of course he remembered.

He'd been the best man to Abby's maid of honor. They'd had plenty of time to talk at the reception. Biting his cheek to keep from chuckling, he said, "We danced a few slow dances, and I almost kissed you."

The silence stretched out until it became uncomfortable. She was probably remembering how well they had fit together before things had broken them apart.

Jack figured that every cell of his brain must have withered away from lack of sex. They were moving in together at the end of this weekend, and he had just reminded her that he'd once been somewhat smitten.

"Abby Rose," he said, borrowing her lecturing tone. "I'm trying to say that you're reasonably appealing. Why haven't you gotten involved again by now?"

"Well, for one thing," she said, "most men don't seem to be attracted to me."

Jack had no idea how to reply. He'd just spent an entire evening explaining to several other women that Abby wasn't his type. However, when you combined that sexy little body with bright eyes and a keen intelligence, she was pretty compelling.

In truth, he couldn't say that he wasn't attracted. He was, and he always had been. It was hard to believe other men weren't just as interested.

"Where would you get that idea?" he finally asked.

She made a sweet, low-pitched sound that must have been a sigh. "My ex-husband told me I was too unyielding to make sacrifices for another person. He said I wasn't womanly."

"He sounds like an idiot, Abby. You are an attractive woman, and you sacrifice plenty for Wyatt and Rosie."

She was quiet again, this time for long enough that he

glanced at the battery light on his cellphone. But finally, she sighed again and murmured a thank-you.

And Jack knew he'd discovered still another tender spot in Abby.

ABBY SPENT ALL DAY SUNDAY hauling her unwanted belongings to a donation center and cleaning her old apartment. By the time she finished, she was tired and grungy and wanted nothing more than a long, hot bath and an evening of peace.

She knew that was probably out of the question, because Jack was returning today. She'd felt it in her gut all day long, and as she drove through the gates to the farmhouse and passed a moving van on its way out, she knew he had arrived. It was time for her performance to begin.

She pulled down her visor and checked her image in the mirror. A day's work had put a bloom on her cheeks, but her hair was acceptably messy and she'd worn a tattered white T-shirt and jeans that were two sizes too big. A streak of crusty brown grease from cleaning out the apartment oven was smudged across one side of her chest, adding that perfect last touch. She was ready.

But she did wish she'd brought the babies home with her.

They would have provided an extra protection, of sorts. They might be too young to serve as chaperons, but they could keep her too busy to think unthinkable thoughts.

Jack's car wasn't in the drive, but when she opened the garage door, she found it parked inside. He'd already made himself at home. She squeezed her full-size truck in next to his sleek little car and came in through the back.

When she walked into the kitchen, she stopped just

inside the doorway and stared. Smack-dab in the middle of the room sat two high chairs, with a lopsided bow tied around each.

She went over to examine them. They were beautiful, state-of-the-art high chairs. Exactly what she would have chosen, if she could have afforded them.

Jack came in from the hallway with a huge smile on his face. "I thought I heard your truck," he said. "What do you think?"

"They're incredible! Where did they come from?"

"Believe it or not, I had free time this weekend," he said. "I went shopping. If they won't work, we can return them and you can choose something else."

His thoughtful surprise had foiled the impression she was hoping to give. Now she just felt gratitude. She shook her head, straightening the blue satin bow on one of the chairs. "They're great," she said. "And there are two."

"Guess that's one benefit to these monstrous old houses. This kitchen is huge. I figured we had room."

"Yes, we do," Abby said, swallowing hard to moisten the dryness in her throat. "Um. Well. Thank you."

Repressing the inclination to give him a peck on the cheek, she stood stiffly in front of him. Awkward and embarrassed, she pushed a loose strand of hair behind her ear and started fiddling with the pink bow, adjusting it so it was round and even.

And cursed herself for wondering what he was thinking as his eyes focused on her. She couldn't meet his gaze, and she couldn't hug him. She'd learned that the hard way.

"No problem," he insisted. "And they're for me, too. I can't imagine how I would handle it if I was feeding Wyatt, and Rosie was hungry, too. We needed two."

"Thanks again," she said, finally allowing her eyes to meet his.

Big mistake.

He stretched an arm out on either side of her, pulling her into a hug as he whispered against her hair, "Just trying to make things work."

She kept both arms crossed in front of her, as if she could ward off her own feelings. But he held on, and his gesture had been so unselfish that she couldn't resist sliding her arms around his shoulders for just a second.

Make that a minute. Maybe longer. Just long enough to warm her insides and set her toes to tingling.

Eventually, he backed off. After frowning at her grease stain for a couple of seconds, he said, "Something's missing."

"What?"

"The twins?"

"Oh! They're down at the neighbors'," she explained. "I needed to clean today, and when I went by to get them they were napping. Sharon said she'd bring them over after they woke up."

"Phenomenal," he said with a smile. "It's our first night of sharing baby duties, and we have free time."

Abby inched backward, toward the door.

She definitely needed time to regroup, and she knew she could find plenty to do outside. "Not really," she said. "I need to head out to the orchards now."

"Really? I'll come with you."

She wanted to refuse. Taking a Sunday evening walk with Jack sounded foolish. No, more than foolish. It was out-and-out dangerous. He'd managed to throw her completely off balance with the high chairs and the hug. Who knew what he'd do next?

Who knew what *she'd* do?

But she couldn't think of a single rational excuse for denying him, so she said, "Of course, it's your land."

"Maybe, but you know I'll let you buy it in a year at a fair price."

There, in a sentence, was most of the reason why she should never allow herself to take walks with Jack Kimball.

Even if he proved to be the perfect roommate. Even if he was polite, gentlemanly and generous. He was leaving. In one year. And he intended to take Wyatt with him.

Which made him the enemy.

She did everything she could to ignore him as they started across the farmyard together. She tried to conjure up the plain and waspish country woman that should be a powerful bachelor repellant, but the image eluded her in the moist August heat.

As they walked along the narrow, wooded path that led into the orchard, the shadows seemed too enchanted, the air too heavy.

Many of the fruit trees had been harvested over the past few months, but a few late peaches and early apples were ripe, making the air smell divine.

The perfection of the moment and the charm of the man worked together to cause her guard to fall. She even allowed her heart to open up, just a little. Just enough.

"How did your family meet Mr. Epelstein?" Jack asked as they made their way through the first grove of trees.

Abby pulled a leaf sample from a young peach tree and leaned down to inspect its trunk. "Through Mom and Dad's flower shop, I guess," she said. "He came around on Saturdays when Paige and I were helping out. Often, he'd bring a basket of fruit to exchange for a bouquet for his wife."

"That must be why you and your sister became gardeners—you spent your childhood in a flower shop," Jack said from over her shoulder.

Reaching up to pull a peach from a branch, she began to examine it carefully. She started walking again as she put the fruit to her nose to sniff. "I'm sure that was it," she said. "When I started college, I flirted with the idea of studying business. It didn't last long, though. I wound up with a degree in horticulture."

Jack put his hand on her shoulder, stopping her momentarily. Confusion showed clearly on his face. "But you were already divorced when we met four years ago. When did you have time to finish college?"

Abby started to walk again, ignoring the pang of regret when his hand fell away. "I was twenty-two when Paige got married, and I'd been out of college a year. Tim and I met, married and divorced during my senior year."

"A whirlwind marriage, huh?" Jack said with a chuckle.

"Guess you could call it that," Abby said, thankful for his flippancy. She really didn't want to go into the details of her single tottery attempt at a lasting relationship.

"If you have a degree in horticulture, why did you insist that Paige and Brian buy the farm?" he asked. "Wouldn't you have been the better choice?"

The complete change of subject made her sense of relief even stronger. "They needed something," she answered, remembering how glad she had been to see her sister get this farm. "I saw signs of trouble in their marriage, and I wanted to help."

"Why? They married too young, just as you did. You were divorced, and you survived. Why not just let it go?"

"My marriage is another story," Abby said. "I don't think Tim ever loved me. Brian and Paige just didn't know how to work out the kinks. Their situation was worlds apart from mine.''

''If he didn't love you, why did he marry you?'' Jack asked, putting his hand on her shoulder to stop her again.

''I refused to move in with him,'' she said, and then wished she hadn't. But Jack was a sophisticated man—he would understand the difference between moving in with a lover and moving in with an acquaintance for practical purposes. Surely he would.

One corner of his mouth lifted in a wry, acknowledging smile, but he stayed on the subject. ''Still, marriage is a huge commitment.''

''And one Tim took very lightly,'' she replied, scowling down at the peach. The pain of her divorce was long gone, but the hurt about her ex-husband's infidelities would remain in her heart forever.

It wasn't about missing Tim, either. She'd realized that a long time ago. Her deepest wound festered because of her complete failure to choose a husband who could even be considered decent. She felt so inadequate in that regard that she didn't think she'd ever regain her confidence.

So she stayed away from men.

She felt Jack's hand slide along her neck and stop just under her chin. He lifted her face with his index finger, until her gaze met his again. ''He played around?''

''He played around.''

She couldn't keep the humiliation out of her voice, or off her face. And she felt silly. These days, how many people let a five-year-old mistake affect them so acutely?

Jack didn't say a word, but he took a step closer.

Amazing, she thought, how powerful that man-woman magnetism could be—especially when you hadn't been around it for a while. Just having Jack's blue eyes skim across her face often felt as seductive as a caress. It made her want to relax and enjoy it, for just a moment.

And now, when his thumb rubbed along the hollow in her neck, she couldn't find the will to pull away.

Those charmer's eyes were gazing straight into hers, and were offering much more than a simple glance. They looked so very, very attentive.

She bit her bottom lip, scarcely daring to breathe.

As much as she wanted to avoid getting closer to him, right now she just wanted to kiss him. And she wanted him to kiss her back.

Wasn't that what he was offering with those eyes? She *ached* for a real, on-the-lips kiss.

The bachelor-repelling plan could start later, when they were out of this enchanted orchard. When this moment had passed. She sighed, wishing she could allow herself just one, single respite. Then she could get back to her lonely resolve.

He took another step closer, bent his head down.

And granted her wish.

Chapter Four

Except he missed.

The short, soft peck on the side of her mouth was too short, too soft and ever so disappointing. Afterward, he moved his face back and kept his eyes closed. He licked his bottom lip, as if he was assessing the taste. Then he popped his eyes open and backed up a few steps. "You shouldn't take it personally," he said. "Men aren't built for long-term relationships."

She felt cheated of her kiss, and suspected that he'd just stifled his own desire. Scowling up at him, she asked, "You don't think so?"

"Hey, I've been a man for a long time. I know so."

He started to walk again, but was still headed out toward the edge of the acreage. Abby was ready to go back to the house, so she stood her ground and hollered, "They can be if they love the woman."

He turned around and yelled, "Old men, not young and virile ones."

Abby's mouth dropped open. "How old is that? Seventy? Human populations would die out."

"Maybe not that old, and maybe not every man," he said as he headed back in her direction. "But a woman shouldn't expect a commitment from a man until he's past the reckless stage.''

When he reached her, she started walking alongside him. "My parents were about twenty when they married," she pointed out.

"So were mine," he said. "My feeble excuse for a dad left when Brian was three. My mother was crushed. She spent the next ten years falling for every man who looked at her."

"That's too bad, but it isn't always that way," she said. "Brian and Paige were married at eighteen."

Abby stopped to put her hands on her hips and glare at Jack. She couldn't fathom a reason for this argument. *She* certainly had no desire to marry again. She just hated his jaded views, regardless of the fact that hers were worse.

"But you said yourself that they had problems, and they were only twenty-two when they died," he argued.

A wave of grief flowed over Abby, and she felt tears looming. Losing her sister had been the hardest thing she'd ever experienced, making her divorce pale in comparison.

She wondered how much time would have to pass before the sorrow didn't hit her like a sledgehammer.

Brushing her palm across her eyes, she said, "This argument is pointless, and we've had it before."

The corners of his mouth twitched. "At the wedding."

Abby grinned back, remembering the preposterous end to Paige's wedding. Abby had been divorced only a few months at the time, and had been reluctant to attend a gathering where she would be expected to mingle and laugh. She had sat most of the evening alone, watching everyone else have fun.

Eventually, Jack had forced her onto the dance floor.

He had used his legendary charm to put her at ease, and had flirted with her mercilessly.

She'd been swept off her feet, until one of them had mentioned the bride and groom. Their opinions about the future of that union were so opposite that they had declared immediate warfare. In fact, their argument had gotten so heated that the entire crowd had stopped to watch.

"We pretty much ended their reception," she said with a chuckle.

He laughed and shook his head. "That we did."

The absurdity of the whole situation struck Abby, who stopped walking and laughed in turn, letting the tension flow from her body.

After a while, she put a hand to her belly and looked across at Jack again. He had stopped, too, in front of a young pear tree. His face was shadowed by its branches as he stood watching her, but she could see his teeth.

He was smiling, seeming to enjoy the laughter he had provoked. He was a charmer, all right.

She arranged her face in a serious expression and began to walk toward the house again. When she felt his arm drop softly across her shoulders, she nearly missed a step.

She needed to shrug it off.

She hadn't counted on liking him, but he seemed to be coming into a difficult situation with a cooperative spirit, and she'd have to be callous to refuse his offer of friendship.

She let the arm stay, but forced herself to remain quiet, until his next comment. "Who'd ever have believed that the two people whose shouting match was the talk of the town that spring would be moving in together four years later?"

Abby's runaway laughter lasted all the way to the house.

Luckily, Sharon arrived with the twins a few minutes later. Abby found it hard enough to keep her mind on her goal when she and Jack were sparring, but the shared laughter made him that much more attractive. It brought him too close, which was something she couldn't afford.

As she introduced Jack to Sharon in the farmhouse kitchen, Abby tried to ignore the easy chatter that flowed between the two of them, about barbershops and computer games.

She tried harder to ignore the sly wink her friend directed her way as she left. Sharon might be perceptive, but she didn't know everything.

As soon as they were alone again, Jack carried Wyatt down the hallway and returned moments later with a paper bag. He buckled Wyatt into a high chair, removed a shiny purple train engine from the bag and put it on the tray.

Wyatt squealed and kicked his feet, seemingly pleased to be sitting up so high. Next, Jack produced a similar toy for Rosie, except hers was a red caboose.

Smiling, Abby fitted her into the seat. "You're just full of surprises," she told Jack. "What else do you have in that bag? Anything for me?"

His grin got bigger, and he plunged his hand back inside. Abby gasped. She'd only been teasing, but apparently he wasn't. He handed her a small beige box.

Biting her lip, she pulled out a heavy, tissue-wrapped item and removed its protective cocoon. It was a porcelain rosebud. Beautifully crafted, its shape was an exact replica of a Gemini rose. Someone had hand painted the apricot-and-pink tints, and it looked as if it had been plucked from the group of rosebushes near the front door.

"To commemorate a new beginning," he said.

Abby was silent as she studied the flower. "It's exquisite," she finally said. "But I can't accept it. You shouldn't be buying me things."

"It was nothing. And I won't take it back to the store."

"You keep it, then."

His jaw tensed stubbornly. "It's yours," he insisted. "Give it to Rosie someday, if you don't want it."

Abby sighed in surrender and reached up to kiss him on the cheek, wondering as she drew close if he would still smell good. But he turned his head at the last minute, and their lips collided.

And held.

Even then it could have been a chaste kiss, but she'd also opened her mouth to whisper her thanks. So instead of a smack, it was an openmouthed stunner of a kiss.

His firm flesh slid against hers, nestling in with a sensuality that felt as hot and smooth as mulled apple cider on a brisk fall day.

She opened her eyes in shock.

And then closed them in pleasure.

And somewhere between her whisper and that first heady taste, she lost herself. The babbling babies faded into the background, and she was aware only of Jack's pliant mouth and the long fingers he rested against her rib cage.

A few seconds later, he stopped. She knew he'd do so eventually, but she wasn't ready yet. She needed more.

She put the rosebud on the table and stepped forward, grabbing his arms to pull them around her waist. Then she tried to grab his lips again, too, with hers.

He backed up about an inch to take a huge, gulping breath, and then plunged forward. Without warning, his mouth opened and his hot tongue dipped inside to tease hers with erotic circles.

A squeal punctured her bubble of euphoria.

Abby opened an eye to look at the twins. Wyatt was smiling at her as if he knew what he had interrupted, and he held his toy out by way of apology.

Absently, she pulled away and took the train, pushing it along on the tray and whispering, "Chuga chuga choo choo."

When she found the courage to look at Jack again, he seemed just as addled.

"Man, I'm sorry," he said as he shoved a hand through his hair. "Guess I was just curious."

"We can't do that again." She wondered if her trembling voice was at all convincing.

"Of course not," he said, a little too fast and much too agreeably.

She managed to make it through the rest of the afternoon without throwing herself in his arms again, but her disgusting lack of willpower had been aided by the fact that he'd taken Wyatt into his office and shut the door.

Living platonically with Jack should be easy. Taking care of the twins was work enough, and she had the greenhouse and orchards to keep up, too. She should have no time for anything else.

She needed to pin a copy of her plan to her brain, because so far she'd been too off-kilter to launch it.

Life in the country wouldn't be boring, even to a big city boy, if she kept offering gratitude and sizzling kisses. No matter how homely and argumentative she made herself out to be.

And there was the little matter of the twins, and making Jack realize all of the sacrifices they required. It would be hard to make him feel incapable as long as he kept provoking delighted squeals from the babies with new toys.

When it was time to feed the twins their dinner, she knocked on his door, holding Rosie on her hip. The door swung open to reveal Jack sitting at his desk, attempting to assemble his computer with one hand. The other was wrapped around Wyatt, who was grabbing at wires with a gleeful expression.

She put a hand over her mouth to cover her chuckle with a cough, and then volunteered to feed both babies so he could work awhile longer.

His appreciation of the offer was apparent in his expression, but in actuality she wasn't trying to be overly thoughtful. She just knew it'd be smart to avoid him.

The twins loved their new high chairs, and Abby celebrated a new milestone by serving them a treat of real mashed bananas. Always before, she'd had to feed them on her lap, one at a time. Having two high chairs made her job easier, and that alone was cause for celebration.

She wasn't celebrating a darn thing else.

After the bananas were devoured, Abby put a teething biscuit on each tray, pointed the high chairs toward each other and made herself a turkey club sandwich. As she ate it leaning over the sink, Jack walked into the room.

She tried to ignore him as he opened the refrigerator and stood looking inside. The soft whoosh of the closing door was followed by approaching footsteps. When they stopped, she glanced to where he was standing. Covetous blue eyes were locked on her half-eaten sandwich.

"I haven't bought groceries yet," he said.

She took a bite. "Umm."

He watched her chew. "That sandwich looks delicious."

She swallowed and smiled. "It is."

"I'd love to eat a sandwich like that about now."

She took another bite. "Um-hmm."

He frowned. "I can see you're not going to offer, but maybe we could negotiate a deal."

"What's that?"

"You make me a sandwich like that and I'll watch the babies for an hour while you do anything you want."

"An hour?"

"Two hours," he said. "One big sandwich for two hours."

Abby kept the sandwich cradled in both hands, but she turned around to lean against the counter and look at Wyatt and Rosie.

They were covered in banana goop and biscuit sludge.

She remembered the making-him-feel-incapable clause of her plan, and nodded. "Deal," she said. "But you have to give them a bath down here in your bathroom. The one upstairs will be in use."

He immediately agreed and pulled a chair next to the twins to wait. Abby threw a man-size sandwich together on a paper plate and set it in front of him. She returned to the counter to put things away, but he stopped her.

"No, go on up," he said. "I can clean up."

Abby turned around again and frowned. He was offering to clean up, too?

"Hit the tub," he said, pointing his finger skyward.

All of the cooperation was very nice. They were the perfect roommates...except for the way his eyes had marauded her body when he'd said the word *tub*.

Or the way she had thrilled at that heavy-lidded glance.

She'd even had the thought that she might be able to wait till later for her bath, so he could join her.

Then, shocked at herself once again, she suppressed the idea and practically sprinted out of the kitchen.

Good plan, she remembered, to get away from him. And as she started upstairs, she scarcely noticed the sound of his voice as he spoke softly to the babies about the wonders of a big, hearty sandwich. Her only thought was about luxuriating in a long, hot bath for the first time in a few days.

And she absolutely did not think about Jack downstairs, twenty feet away, as she stripped and stepped naked into the tub. Well, maybe just a *smidgen.*

By the time she came back down to get the babies and put them to bed, she'd already decided she would hole up in her room with a novel. There was no need to interact with him at all when the babies were asleep. Maybe she could buy herself a small television to set up in her room. She'd stay busy during the day and stay away during the night.

Avoiding his charm should be easy, if she was clever.

IT WAS AN EXCELLENT IDEA, and it worked for a while.

Long days of constant work and skillful baby-care maneuvering passed by without any blatant displays of lust.

She tended to her plants; Jack tended to his computer. She shared her meals with him; he cleaned the kitchen for her. A couple of times she took the twins with her to run errands, allowing him a few hours of peace.

He returned the favor one afternoon by taking them with him to the barbershop. They all arrived home a few hours later with tamer curls and a new set of wooden blocks.

She couldn't help noticing that Jack was more considerate than she'd expected, or that his gentle play with the twins was endearing. But at least she didn't offer up her lips in gratitude.

She made sure of that, no matter how often she thought about it.

The idea probably would have worked much longer, except for one slight flaw.

The one about babies waking up at night. And crying.

Usually, Abby could quiet a baby's cry within moments, and usually, the twins woke one at a time. But not always.

Early Friday morning, Rosie woke and began a long, angry wail that sounded hungry. Abby ran to the nursery to pick her up, hoping to avoid waking Wyatt.

She sat in a rocker and cuddled Rosie, reaching over to plunk a bottle in the warmer at the same time. Rosie quieted, and was contentedly playing with Abby's braid and enjoying her bottle when Wyatt woke up.

He began with a whimper that rose to a cry within seconds. Abby carried Rosie and the bottle to Wyatt's crib, hoping to soothe him.

It wasn't often that she had to feed both babies at once, but she'd done it before. She kept talking to Wyatt, but dashed over to put another bottle in the warmer.

"Need some help in here?"

Her eyes flew to the doorway, where Jack was standing in a pair of well-worn gray sweatpants and not much else.

"No, I can handle it," she answered. She doubted that Jack had heard her, though, since Wyatt's cry had grown to a full-scale bellow.

Jack said something she couldn't hear, and came into the room. She stared at his chest as she sank back down in the rocker. He stopped right beside her, providing a scrumptious view of a lean, flat torso. He pointed toward the bottle warmer.

She pulled her eyes away from places they didn't belong and grabbed the second bottle. "I'm calling this ready," she hollered. "Will you feed Wyatt?"

He nodded, swooped the boy out of his crib and over to the second chair, and whistled in relief when Wyatt quieted. "This must be why there are two rockers in here," Jack said.

He was far too civil for someone who'd been awakened at five o'clock in the morning.

She didn't even answer. She didn't know which was more embarrassing, her shortsightedness for not putting on a robe, or her reaction to seeing him without one.

Good thing Wyatt was there, on his lap, to make Jack think she was looking at the baby. Good thing Rosie was on her lap, too. If she propped the baby up just right, her chest was covered. Maybe he wouldn't notice her embarrassing state of...well, titillation.

He wasn't talking much, either.

She wondered what Mr. Man-About-Town thought about the past week of domestic bliss. Maybe he found it boring, which should be a good thing.

There was the plan and all.

Rosie finished first, so Abby patted her back to let out the bubbles, and went to lay her back in her crib. As soon as she did, she wished she had something to hold, because now she was wandering around the nursery with nothing on but a pair of bikini panties and a long cotton T-shirt.

She felt silly.

She felt naked.

She felt *turned on.*

But Jack seemed to be concentrating on Wyatt, and completely unaware of her discomfort. Except for the couple of times when his focus seemed to move past the baby to her chest and down her legs. Then he looked a little disturbed.

She hoped he was. Plan or no plan.

DON'T THINK ABOUT ABBY that way—she's your roommate. Her breasts are not luscious. All right, even if they are, she's not reacting to you. She's probably cold. Of course her legs would look like that—she makes her living working outside. They are not sexier than any you've ever seen. Diane's legs are longer. Abby's are just better toned.

Don't think about her that way…

Jack wished he could stop sneaking peeks at Abby. He was glad she couldn't read his mind, because she'd probably think he was depraved, noticing her body when they were both in here feeding the babies.

It had been a long time since his hormones had raged on ahead of his brain, no matter how many sexy female parts were paraded around in front of him.

With Abby, the entire package was alluring. The thought of those clever brown eyes glittering into his from up close seemed just as enticing as her parts.

Maybe his problem was that he hadn't had to deny himself for so long. This living arrangement was not a great idea.

He needed to get out and find a date.

"Abby, I can finish with Wyatt," he whispered. "Go on back to bed."

"Are you sure?" she asked.

Her arms were wrapped around her waist. Did she know her T-shirt pulled across her chest when she did that? She must, because she abruptly dropped her hands to her sides and formed them into fists. Maybe she was just as uncomfortable as he was.

A pain tore at his chest, and Jack looked down to find Wyatt's fingers full of hair and his tiny mouth grinning.

Which meant he wasn't drinking, and Jack had been too busy noticing Abby's parts to realize he was done.

Abby still wasn't leaving—hadn't he suggested that?

"You can go on back to bed, Abby," he said more loudly as he unwrapped Wyatt's fist from his chest hair. "I can do this."

"I asked if you were sure," she reminded him with a smile.

She turned around and fiddled with Rosie's blankets, giving him a provocative view of her backside.

He'd never seen her with so few clothes on, but he'd always been fascinated by that bottom. Now he could see the absolute lusciousness of those legs, almost up to a place that was even more luscious. "I'm completely sure," he said through gritted teeth. "Go back to bed."

"If he won't go down, just tap on my door," she said on her way out.

Oh, sure, I'll just tap on your door and join you in bed, he thought, and groaned out loud.

She popped her head around the door. "What happened?"

"Nothing," he grumbled. "Wyatt's fingers got tangled up in my chest hair in a tender spot."

She flew back into the room. "Did you get the hair off his fingers?"

"Yesss! It's off," he bellowed. "Go to bed."

They both looked at Rosie, who nestled her cheek into the crib mattress and made a soft little sigh. Abby put a finger to her lips and tiptoed out.

Finally.

Jack resisted the urge to breathe a sigh of relief.

Instead, he whispered to Wyatt, "Women become

complicated when you're my age, little man. Enjoy them now when things are simple.''

Wyatt yawned and stretched both arms in the air, and Jack spent a few minutes exploring various burping methods before he found the one that worked.

Then he followed Abby's example. He took Wyatt over to the crib and laid him down. After pulling a downy yellow blanket over the boy's body, he backed away.

Wyatt's face crunched into a frown. He drew in a gulping breath. And Jack flew back to the crib and scooped him up.

There was no way he could handle seeing Abby again. If the babies cried, she'd be back here in a flash—flaunting those flirty parts and asking how she could help. There was only so much temptation a man could take, and Jack couldn't navigate around Abby for another second.

He sank down in the rocker again, thankful for its massive size. Brian must have helped choose these chairs, because they were big enough for a long-legged man to sleep in, if necessary.

Pushing the lever to tilt the chair into a reclining position, Jack settled Wyatt against his chest and closed his eyes. He would just rest here until the baby was deeply asleep.

Then he could put him in his crib and head downstairs. Just a few minutes. That's all it should take.

''JACK, WHAT ARE YOU DOING up here?''

He opened his eyes to find Abby's most indignant expression furrowing her face.

Fully dressed now, she stood in front of him in her favorite hands-on-hips pose.

As uncomfortable as last night had been, it had at least

been fair. Now he was the only half-naked adult in the house.

"Guess I must've dozed off," he said, leaning forward to release the chair's lever. As he stood, he realized his arms were empty.

Horrid visions filled his head of Wyatt slipping off his lap and scooting his way to the top of the stairs. Tumbling down. Disappearing into the darkness of the countryside.

"Where's Wyatt?" he asked, noting the baby gate now blocking the doorway. "Is he all right?"

Abby pointed.

Wyatt was on the floor of the nursery, pushing around a jingling ball with one hand, and propping himself up on the other. "He's going to be crawling in no time," Abby said.

Rosie was near her brother, batting at a plush orange giraffe.

"Why'd you sleep up here?" Abby asked again, more quietly.

He looked at her sheepishly. If he admitted that he didn't know how to put a baby down to sleep, she'd never let him try again. But if he didn't, she wouldn't teach him.

"Wyatt started bawling when I put him in his crib, and I didn't want him to wake Rosie," he explained. "I only meant to stay till he fell asleep."

Abby's chuckle floated through the nursery, filling the air and meshing with the sounds of the babies' babbling play. It sounded very right.

He grinned, too, enjoying her laughter.

"I can't tell you how surprised I was to see such a cosmopolitan man sleeping with a baby on his chest," she said. "You looked pretty comfy."

"Sometimes we men have to stick together," he said, thankful that she wasn't angry.

"You'll spoil that baby boy." Her lecturing tone was contradicted by the glowing light in her eyes.

He was tempted to kiss her to see if it would ignite.

"You have to put him down and let him fuss a bit," she said. "Or he'll forget how to go to sleep on his own."

"Maybe next time you can show me," Jack said, unable to look away.

"Sure." She turned to pick up Wyatt.

And just like that, Jack was dismissed. Which was just as well; he needed a shower, a shave and coffee. A few clothes might be a good idea, too.

Heading downstairs, he hurried through his routine, deciding to approach the subject of daily schedules over breakfast. So far this week, Abby had handled the bulk of the baby-care duties. She seemed to view him as a part-time baby-sitter, but he wanted to do more. He still had a lot to learn, and she made a good teacher.

Before he left his bedroom, though, he dug his robe out of a box of unpacked clothes and hooked it over his doorknob. Next time he was needed at night, he'd go upstairs fully covered. Perhaps Abby could give him a lesson in how to put a baby to sleep, instead of how to snuff out a wildfire of sensual imagery.

Unless she came to the nursery in that T-shirt again, or some other scrap of a nightie. The only good his robe would do in that case was cover up the evidence of his desire.

Because one thing was certain—his gentlemanly behavior would never last a year with both of them running around naked.

And if he slipped once, he might slip again. And that

could start an avalanche into a giant heap of complications.

He'd managed to avoid such a thing over the course of his entire adult life. He only got as involved as necessary to gain companionship. But he couldn't do that with Abby. She wasn't the type to play around, and besides, she'd been hurt enough already.

Something about her brought out his latent protective instincts, and he'd brandish a shotgun around his own backside before he added to her pain.

So he had to get out, very soon, and play off some energy. And she had to wear more clothes at night, even if he had to buy them for her himself.

Chapter Five

"Slow down, Abby! Pull in up here to the right."

Abby started to nudge her foot on the brake, but she groaned and lifted it as soon as she saw the car dealership Jack was pointing to.

"We ventured into town to restock the refrigerator," she said dryly. "Not your giant playboy toy box."

"Stop here," he insisted. "You said ten minutes ago that my car was…let's see, how did it go? 'Insanely useless for a man with a child.' That was it."

"It has only two seats and the trunk space is laughable," she pointed out. Then gasped when Jack's hulking torso slammed against her side and a powerful leg crossed hers to stomp on the brake pedal.

"Jack! The twins," she shrieked, chomping on her lip as he grabbed the steering wheel and forced it to the right.

Helplessly, she watched as her own truck hurtled into the car lot, with her in the driver's seat and Jack steering.

As soon as they were safely parked, she swiveled around to look in the back seat. Both Rosie and Wyatt seemed oblivious to any danger. Their pacifiers were waggling furiously in their mouths, and they were slumped in their car seats, staring out the window.

She whirled back around to glare at Jack, but now that

they were no longer moving, she realized how very close he was. His leg was still plastered on top of hers, and his shoulder pressed against her chest.

His solid heat felt welcome against her softness, and he didn't seem to be in a hurry to leave. He turned his head toward hers and opened his mouth, but no words came out. He just let his eyes wander over her face.

As she did with his.

That mouth was sexy, and when he held it open, it was hard not to imagine it slanting across hers. It was harder still to think about moving, but there was something—a seed of a thought somewhere deep in her brain—that she needed to nurture. There was something she needed to remember....

Oh, yeah. The plan.

Today they were taking the twins to the grocery store so he could experience the joys of cranky babies and endlessly long and boring rows of shelved food. This side trip to the car lot was definitely not going to work.

Neither would the kiss she was craving about now.

"Jack, get off," she whispered.

He didn't seem to have heard her, because he didn't move.

"Jack!" she roared. "What are you doing?"

Well, that did it. Wyatt let out a piercing shriek, which was followed by Rosie's deafening howl.

Now the twins were frightened.

Jack scowled as he handed her the keys. Then he untangled himself and scooted over to get out on his side of the truck. By the time Abby stumbled out, he was leaning in the back to remove Wyatt from his car seat. The truck's cab blocked her complaints, so she opened Rosie's door to call across the back seat, "I asked what you were doing."

He lifted Wyatt out and said, "Looking at cars."

Her hands flew to her hips. "I don't have all day to mess around. We came out to get groceries, and that's all."

"This won't take long," he said, winking and smiling before he slammed the door between them and walked away.

By the time Abby caught up, toting Rosie, Jack was staring into the tinted windows of a sleek white four door. "Jack, we need to get back," she repeated as she followed him around the classy vehicle.

He scrutinized the trunk lid. "I just want to look."

"Why?"

He stopped studying the car and frowned at her. "As you put it so candidly, just awhile ago, I need a more practical car now."

Rosie was starting to fidget. "But we don't have to drag the babies around," she said, following him as he strode across the lot. "Just go alone sometime."

He ignored her. He was circling a sunshine-yellow wagon and bouncing the boy to keep him from fussing. Abby followed, but stopped talking.

Car shopping wasn't a lot of fun for babies, was it? After a while, their fidgeting should turn to whining. Especially if some salesman arrived on the scene to talk a mile a minute. Most adults could hardly take such a thing, let alone a baby. Maybe she had a little spare time, Abby decided.

She caught up and made sure she had his attention before she said, "Okay, but I have a lot to do today. Plants and babies don't take days off. You have half an hour."

"This wagon's pretty sporty, and it's as practical as hel—" He stopped and looked at Rosie, who by now was threatening to cry. ''As a helmet. As practical as a helmet.''

Abby looked at the car. It was pretty sporty all right. Way, way too sporty and fun. She had to find something wrong with it.

Frowning in concentration, she peered through the side window and laughed triumphantly. ''Not that practical,'' she said. ''The snow-white interior would show every puddle of baby drool. Come on.''

Abby led him down the row, stopping at a big, battered wagon. She rested a hand on the faded tan fender and said, ''Here's a good family vehicle. There's room enough for kids, groceries and spare computers, and you wouldn't worry about spit-up spots or grocery cart dings.''

There. Maybe now he'd understand about the sacrifices involved in raising a baby.

Jack looked down his nose at the car as he stalked past. ''There's no need to surrender my pride just because I need a bigger car,'' he said.

He squinted across the lot and practically jogged to a sedan in a rich charcoal-gray. Wyatt's vibrating giggle at the bumpy ride grated on Abby's nerves.

When she approached with Rosie, Jack touched his index finger to the little girl's nose and said, ''This is fun, isn't it? And you're not going to bawl at all.''

The traitorous Rosie kicked her legs, pointed at the car and said, ''Deek.''

Jack took off his baseball cap, threw back his head and laughed. ''That's right, sleek,'' he said, and winked at Abby. ''And it has a back seat, a big trunk and a dark interior.''

Abby leaned down to look in the window, and Jack

bent down beside her to whisper in her ear. "And it's as hot as you-know-what."

She glared at the car, looking for faults. She walked around it and stopped when she reached the price sticker. Then she laughed and tapped a fingernail against the glass. "And at this price, you would bawl if anything happened to it."

He shook his head. "I don't know."

She practically skipped across the row and stopped at a boxy green minivan. "The sticker on this one says it was rated safest in last year's crash tests," she hollered. "And you'd have room for babies, groceries, computer junk...and up to four girlfriends."

"Very funny," he yelled back. He opened the door of the sedan and sat in the driver's seat with Wyatt on his lap.

Abby stared across the row at him in that car.

Its trim lines seemed to suit him, and the front end looked astonishingly like a woman's face. A pair of slanted headlights waited for his hands to make them glow, and the grill seemed to smile brilliantly.

The darn thing seemed to be mocking her.

She strolled over to wait while he puttered with the controls, but when he didn't come out within a few minutes, she pulled open the passenger door and sank into the seat.

"I want to drive this," he said immediately.

Wyatt seemed just as excited as he patted his chubby hands on the steering column.

"No more playing today, big boy," she said as she shook her head at Jack. "We have the twins to consider."

"So we'll take them for a ride," Jack said. "You two want a ride, don't you?"

Rosie was too fascinated with the glove compartment

latch to respond, but Wyatt bounced and smacked his hand against the horn. When the car's jazzy beep sounded, he squealed.

"See? He wants to go."

"That's silly. We'd have to move their car seats."

"So we'll move them," Jack said with a shrug. "We can drive around, maybe even take this car to get groceries. Then we can swing back by here and transfer everything to the truck before we head home."

"That's really silly," she said.

"No, it's really fun."

She blew her bangs away from her face. He had a way of thwarting her little lessons in boredom and self-sacrifice.

"For you it's fun. For me it's extra work and wasted time."

He reached down to her seat and started tugging at something under her thigh. When he got his flattened baseball cap out from under her, he grinned and punched his fist inside to pop it back into shape.

Then he put it on *her* head. "Oh, but I'll let you drive first," he said, with a wink and his best "gotcha" grin.

JACK REREAD THE NOTE he'd left on his office desk a few days ago, wondering if he could find a local shop that would pack up a robe and send it over this afternoon. He'd had no idea that a female roommate would cause this much bother to his libido, and frankly, he was surprised.

Although he'd always been attracted to Abby, her sharp edges had held him in check. Somehow, since he'd gotten to know her better, her scrappiness seemed cuter.

He could never resist a little teasing, just to see her eyes flash. He'd had an incredibly good time this morning, convincing her to drive that car. And then he'd wallowed in sheer delight as she gave in to the excitement and sat behind the wheel.

He'd never realized that watching a fully dressed woman drive to the grocery store could be sexy. He needed to keep her fully dressed, at all times, or he might be tempted to help her get fully *un*dressed.

He picked up the private phone he'd set up in his office, and decided to try his only connection to the fashion world. His old friend Paula was a buyer for an exclusive ladies' apparel store in Kansas City—she should know of something appropriate. If she would speak to him.

As luck would have it, she answered on the first ring. And he was relieved by her diplomatic greeting. This was the Paula he recognized. Without hesitation, he asked if her store carried women's robes.

"Of course," she said. "Are you in the market for a ladies' robe?"

"Yes, my mother's birthday is coming up," he said through clenched teeth. The statement was misleading, but it wasn't exactly a lie. His mother's birthday was next month. Only the robe wasn't for her.

"We have just the thing," Paula said more warmly. "Your mother is remarried, with a passel of kids to worry about, right?"

"Right," he said, surprised that she remembered that much. He and Paula hadn't talked about families.

"We have a line of flattering nightwear for the woman who wants to put the romance back into her marriage," she began, sounding like a lingerie copywriter. "There's a silk robe with a lacy peekaboo skirt that's been selling well. We have it in smoke, orchid and midnight."

Visions of Abby's thighs displayed all the way up to her chin danced through Jack's brain. "No. Ab— I mean

Mom wouldn't like that at all,'' he said. ''She likes to be covered at night, in case the kids are up and about.''

Remembering the firm curves underneath that old T-shirt, he wondered at the possibility of finding a thick bunting robe in sludge-green.

Perhaps decorated with shackles. Or wedding rings.

''Doesn't she live somewhere that stays hot year-round?'' Paula asked. ''California or somewhere out West?''

''Arizona.''

''It's still August, darling. No one in Arizona would want to be covered up.''

Paula wasn't as helpful as he had hoped. He ran a hand through his hair. ''Mom does,'' he insisted. ''Do you have anything?''

''Our winter arrivals are due in late this week. I suppose I could pull something from our holiday stock.''

''Perfect. I want something at least down to her knees, and thick. Mom's always cold.''

''What size does she wear?''

Holding his hand out in front of him, he imagined Abby standing there. When he'd kissed her, he'd only had to lean down a few inches. ''She's about up to my nose, I guess. And built nice, for a mom. Slim, but not skinny.''

''We'll say she's about average in height and build. Should I wrap it up pretty and send it straight to her?''

''No,'' Jack said, thinking fast. He needed that robe here as soon as possible. ''I want to put a note in the package. Could it be personally delivered?''

''Personally delivered?'' Paula asked. ''You mean, by me? Darling, you've missed me, haven't you? I'd love to visit!''

Jack slid down into his chair, thinking.

He hadn't missed Paula all that much, but since they'd dated off and on for three years, he knew why she would make that assumption.

And Abby had mentioned him inviting a lady friend, now and again, hadn't she? Maybe a visit from Paula would take his mind off Abby's parts, solving several problems at once.

"Perfect," he said. "Topeka isn't as big as Kansas City, but I think we could find a decent restaurant. I'll take you out to dinner. How soon can you make it?"

"You mean, this week?"

"Absolutely."

"Darling, you must be so anxious to see me. I'll come Friday after work, and I'll bring your mother's gift."

"I NEED TO TALK TO YOU about our nights."

Abby looked up from the double stroller, where she'd just buckled in both of the babies, and squinted toward the porch at Jack. "So talk, but make it quick," she said. "Remember I lost two hours this morning to your little whim."

He stepped off the porch and grabbed hold of the stroller's handle. "Where are you headed?" he asked. "I can talk on the way."

She scowled, wondering why he wasn't tapping away at his computer keyboard. "I need to take pond samples," she said.

"We have a pond?"

She sighed. "Beside the house, at the southern edge of the fenced lot. I need to get that done before it gets dark, and then I have the plants to water and the—"

Jack started across the farmyard in long strides, pushing the stroller ahead of him across the grass. She had to jog to catch up, and as soon as she did she waited for him to speak. But he didn't. He simply barreled along beside her with the brim of his cap slanted against the afternoon sun.

She couldn't see his expression, but she'd bet he had that same distracted grimace he got when he sat in front of the computer. Something had him perplexed.

He didn't say a word until they reached the pond, and then he only asked about the new wooden structure that sat on a tiny island in the middle.

"It's a duck shelter," Abby explained. "Paige built it earlier this summer."

"Where are the ducks?" he asked, looking around.

"She…well, she didn't have time to get ducks."

That was enough to shut both of them up for a while.

Abby dug her pond kit out of the bottom of the stroller and walked down around the shoreline to take water samples.

When she'd finished, she capped the test tubes and stuck them in her jeans pocket.

As she turned to climb the knoll to where she'd left Jack and the twins, she realized he was watching her. But when she got closer, he turned his attention to the water. And he still seemed bothered by something.

Against her better judgment, she decided to put him at ease. He'd said he wanted to talk about their nights. Maybe he was still feeling guilty about the division of labor.

It had taken some swift responses to baby cries, but she'd handled all nighttime duties for a while now. That had been a tough call. Getting up at night was one of the realities of life with a baby, and keeping him bleary eyed would have been a nice addition to her plan.

But she knew she'd just wake up, too, and feel as if she had to check on things. And after that hot and embarrassing night in the nursery, it was obvious they should avoid middle of the night encounters.

She grabbed the stroller's handle and started pushing it back toward the house. "Hey, if you hear Rosie or Wyatt fussing, go back to sleep," she said. "I'll be glad to keep handling the night feedings."

"Oh, but I want to help with the twins," he said immediately. "I'll come up when I hear them both cry." He walked along beside her, and cleared his throat. "We haven't talked about how we're going to handle this, but people like us would probably want to get out of the house occasionally."

"People like us?" she asked, wondering what category he thought they'd both fit into, besides human being.

"Yeah. We're both single," he said. "It's fine if you want to go out on dates. I could watch the twins and...uh, maybe we could work out a schedule."

She thought back to her last date. Sometime last winter, her mother and sister had tricked her into going out with the son of one of her mother's friends who was visiting from out of town. Abby hadn't been fooled again.

"A dating schedule," she said feebly. "What a great idea." There was no need for him to know about the sorry state of her romantic life. She'd just make one up, and he'd never be the wiser.

"In fact, I have a friend coming into town Friday night," he said. "Do you mind if I go out for a while?"

He already had a date?

Swish went the revolving door, bumping her right on the derriere. Abby's heart skipped a beat and she tripped over a clump of grass.

To cover herself, she leaned down to fiddle with a wheel of the stroller. "Of course I don't mind," she said. "Why would I mind?"

He stopped, too, and stood looking at the twins, who were pink cheeked and drooling as they waited for their ride to continue. "I'll make a point to be home by the time the babies are ready to go to bed. About ten," he promised.

She stood back up. "That's not necessary. Take your time with your girlfriend."

"Thanks," he said softly. "But if you'll teach me how to put them down to sleep, you can go out, too. I know you don't think men are attracted, but they would be if you gave them a chance."

Abby started pushing the stroller again. She didn't know how to react. He was probably trying to be kind, but he was making her feel like a pariah. "Oh, I know," she said breezily. "A banker in town has been watching me for ages, probably wanting to ask me out. I think I'll take him up on it."

"Phenomenal," Jack said, following her quietly.

"Isn't it though?" she said, pushing the stroller faster.

LATE FRIDAY AFTERNOON, Abby sequestered herself in the nursery with a novel and a glass of mint tea. The twins had fallen asleep an hour earlier, and she'd told Jack she wanted to wait upstairs until they woke up.

That was partially true. She was waiting—but only until the revolving door quit spinning around. As silly as it was, she had no desire to greet his girlfriend.

Abby read the first twenty pages of her novel without comprehending a word, and tried not to listen to the silent-house sounds that must mean Jack was dressing.

When Rosie chirped a greeting from the crib, Abby rushed over to pick her up, thankful for the distraction. Wyatt woke awhile later, and she handed each baby a toy and promised a round of zwieback cookies, when they had the house to themselves again.

Soon after, the doorbell rang and a female voice floated upstairs. Judging from the careful modulation of that voice, Abby could hazard a guess about the woman's looks.

Perfectly composed in dress and manner, Jack's date would be wearing a chic outfit with shoes and handbag to match. Abby knew the type.

She resisted the urge to spy, and waited until they left before she ventured outside the nursery door. But as she went about her evening routine with the babies she was overcome with curiosity. Would they actually make it to dinner, or just rent a motel room?

That thought should make Abby happy. If Jack was otherwise occupied, she wouldn't have to combat the terrible attraction growing between them. But in truth she was only irritated, so she forced herself to think about something else. Some other man. Now that she'd made her boastful noise about male interest, maybe she could drum some up.

She'd go into town this week. The curious-eyed loan officer at her bank seemed harmless enough—she'd work on him. She was way out of practice with flirting, but maybe it was similar to riding a bike. Maybe she hadn't forgotten how.

She had just buckled the twins into the high chairs for a late dinner of oatmeal and applesauce when the front door opened. Jack was returning, and it was only—Abby glanced at the kitchen clock—eight-thirty!

He spoke softly upon entering, and she realized he must be bringing his date inside. Abby began shoveling mounds of baby food into the twins' mouths, trying to rush them through their dinner.

She refused to be downstairs when he and this woman were shut up in his bedroom. If she heard them in there making noises she would barely recognize after so long, she'd be nauseated.

But Jack came strolling into the kitchen before she'd had a chance to stuff a third spoonful into either baby's mouth. "Abby, I want you to meet Paula," he said. "She's an old friend of mine."

The blonde's navy halter dress showcased a set of evenly tanned and toned shoulders, which were made even more flawless by the pearls at her neck and earlobes. *Bingo*.

"Paula, this is Abby," he continued, seeming pleased with himself.

The woman extended a hand. "How lovely that we should meet," she said in that same cool voice. But the expression was all wrong, because this lady was simmering.

Abby stood and wiped her hand on the hip of her jeans before offering it. "Hullo," she said with a quick smile. "And this is Rosie and Wyatt."

"I'm not usually interested in babies," Paula said as she eyed the twins. "But I suppose these two are... cute?"

"They're absolutely precious," Abby said as she sat back down between them. While she'd been distracted, Wyatt had stuck his hand in the bowl of cereal and slicked it across his hair, making the ends of his curls clump together and spike up adorably.

Abby took the bowl and spoon away from him and began to feed both twins again. Grinning, she said, "Look at that! Now Wyatt's hair is as wild as Jack's when he gets up in the middle of the night."

She tugged her bottom lip in between her teeth as she looked up at Jack's hair.

Paula was looking up there, too.

Jack put a hand to his head and frowned.

Paula folded her arms across her dress and said, "Getting up in the middle of the night, are you, darling?"

"Only if both babies cry," he said.

"Uh-huh," Paula said, in a way that made clear she didn't believe him.

"It's none of your concern, anyway," he said. "And I need to help Abby bathe these babies. You'd better go."

"Hmm. Well. I suppose I should be heading back to the city," Paula said, as if it had been her idea to leave in the first place. But she stood in the middle of the kitchen and looked at Jack expectantly.

"Thanks for bringing the package," he said.

"Walk me out, darling," Paula said, folding her arm around the crook of his elbow and pulling.

Jack shrugged and followed obediently.

As they left, Abby heard Paula whisper, "I see what you mean about your roommate's appearance."

Abby frowned. That whisper had been just loud enough for her to hear, and it had met its mark. She spent the next few minutes wondering what Jack had said, and why this Paula person found it necessary to mention it.

Jack returned a few seconds after the front door had closed. "I'm sorry she was rude," he said. "She was just jealous, you know. I've never lived with anyone, although she has hinted for several years."

"Uh-huh," Abby said, copying Paula's disbelieving tone.

"I didn't tell her much about your looks, Abby. Although I do think I said you were the girl-next-door type.''

Abby carried the bowl and spoons to the sink. She ran water over them and returned to get the babies down from their chairs. ''You don't have to explain,'' she said. ''I guess I can understand why she might be catty.''

''She was that, wasn't she?'' Jack said, taking Rosie from the high chair and holding her while Abby wiped the excess goo from Wyatt's hands and hair.

''She's eye-catching, though,'' Abby said. ''She reminds me of an apple taken from the tree a few weeks early. Her looks are so perfect you get all worked up about how great she'll be, but after one bite you want to spit her right back out.''

Jack's laughter was vigorous and sustained. He laughed so heartily that soon both babies joined in, and the four of them spent a few minutes in fits of giggles.

When everyone started to calm down, Rosie's chuckles had developed into a case of hiccups. Abby filled a bottle with water. ''I'm surprised, Jack. I thought you two must be pretty attached, since she came to visit so soon.''

He shrugged. ''I've been seeing her for a while, but I wouldn't say I'm attached. She's always been an available companion for social events. Anyway, she only came here to do me a favor.''

Abby pictured Paula lying across some hotel room bed purring, ''Would you like me to move my hips a bit more, darling?''

Before Abby could stop herself, she asked, ''A favor?''

''She brought me something from the store where she works. Incidentally, it's something for you.''

She handed him the bottle. ''Tell me that's not true.''

"It's nothing, really—just something that might help us with our nighttime duties."

He walked off with both Rosie and the bottle, and soon returned with a dainty mauve shopping bag. "After the other night in the nursery, I thought you might find this useful."

Abby accepted the bag, grazing Jack's hand in the process. A burst of energy surged through her. Her startled eyes met his intense ones, and she looked away, into the bag. "You got me a piece of lingerie?" she squeaked, staring at the slinky black fabric inside.

He peered over her shoulder, wincing when he saw the garment. "It was supposed to be a robe, to pull on when we both have to help with the babies at night."

Her heart returned to its normal rhythm. He wasn't trying to flaunt her body, he was trying to cover it up.

She pulled the contents out of the bag, and it did turn out to be a robe. Satiny smooth and ethereal, but a robe, nevertheless. "A robe," she said tonelessly. "Thanks."

"Since we'll both be getting up, I thought we'd be smart if we wore something."

She turned around, embarrassed by her own naiveté, and stuffed the robe back into the bag. Whisking Wyatt from the chair, she headed for the stairs. "I agree," she said on the way. "Thanks again."

When would she get it through her thick skull that she wasn't the type to attract men? Tim had told her she wasn't feminine enough…that her very strength was boring.

But Tim had never looked at her with that teasing light in his eyes. And he'd never made her laugh as much as

Jack did. She was beginning to think Tim had been the boring one.

Upstairs, she gathered the twins' bath supplies and went straight into the bathroom. They were sitting up well enough now to be bathed one at a time, with the help of a bathing ring.

Abby ran water in the tub, allowing Wyatt to splash around in it as it filled.

"I brought Rosie up," Jack hollered from the nursery. "I'll entertain her in here. Let me know when you're ready to trade."

"Mr. Cordiality yourself, aren't you?" she muttered to herself. "Without even thinking, you insult me."

"Are you talking to me?" he asked, sticking his head through the doorway.

"Of course not. I'm talking to Wyatt."

Glancing back, she noticed Jack staring at her bottom before he left again. She patted a hand back there to make sure she didn't have a cracker stuck to her pants, and then turned her attention to a more manageable male.

Smiling at Wyatt's cackling enjoyment of the water, she reminded herself that this little boy was worth a tiny nick in her self-esteem. Before Jack had moved in, she hadn't felt great about her relationships with men, anyway. He merely confirmed what she already knew.

She managed to contain her emotions as they switched babies, and even acted normal as they worked together to ready the babies for bed.

But Jack didn't leave after the babies were in their pajamas, and her feelings were too close to the surface for Abby to face him.

"All right," he said. "Now will you show me your magic for laying them down?"

"Of course."

Jack watched over her shoulder as she laid Rosie in her crib. When she tucked the blanket around the baby's body, he moved closer. His breath hit Abby's neck in warm waves, making her very aware of his nearness.

"Rosie goes without a struggle," she said softly as she squeezed between him and the crib. "She always seems happy to snuggle down to sleep."

Taking Wyatt from his arms, she crooned to the boy as she walked the four steps to the other crib. Barely breathing, she nestled him onto his mattress and folded a blanket around him. "Wyatt is trickier," she whispered. "You have to tuck him in securely and let him get settled. He may complain for a few minutes, but he's usually too tired to resist long."

Wyatt's bottom lip trembled as he stared through the cagelike bars of his crib. Until he found his thumb. Once that was in place, his eyelids drooped quickly into sleep.

Abby backed up and bumped solidly into Jack's chest. His hands sprang up around her middle—she supposed to help her catch her balance. But when she was steady on her feet, his hands remained. He brought his chest tight against her back and rubbed his face against her hair.

She closed her eyes and tried not to react. As much as she hungered for his touch, she knew encouraging it would be a mistake. But she couldn't find the will to stop him.

She did resist the urge to turn around and taste his hot, male lips again. But when they touched the nape of her neck in a barrage of nibbles, her contrary spine bent like a willow, until his solid body was supporting her flimsy one.

His hands roamed up from her belly, and he gently cupped a breast in each hand. She felt a moan escape, and when his breath hit the side of her neck, she stole a glance at his face. He was looking over her shoulder, watching his thumbs trifle with nipples that stood out brazenly through her shirt, inviting contact. She forgot to breathe, until Rosie cried out in her sleep, and his hands dropped away.

Abby glanced over to the crib, satisfying herself that Rosie was okay. Then she walked on rubbery legs to the door of the nursery, with Jack following.

When they got outside the door, Abby closed it softly and turned to look at him. He looked back, but offered nothing more than a gulping swallow. She supposed he didn't know what to say. She sure didn't. She also didn't know whether to step into his arms or run away from them.

She puffed out a shaky breath and watched in horror as he reached for her again. Was he going to gather her in his arms and whisk her off to bed? What should she do?

She shouldn't have worried about it, even for a second, because he only yanked at the bottom of her shirt to pull it down smoothly over her belly.

"Good night," he whispered, and walked quickly down the steps, leaving her alone to deal with her unruly desires.

She went to her room and sat on her bed, thinking. She must have let weeds take over in her head and crowd out every sane judgment.

Here she was, spending her days wearing dirt-encrusted clothes and pointing out the hardships of parenting so Jack would get restless and leave. Like Tim.

Yet at the same time, she was battling a persistent fantasy that this doggedly confirmed bachelor, and Wyatt's legal guardian, would fall head over heels in love with her and stay. As no one had. Ever.

It was all complete lunacy.

Chapter Six

Jack opened bleary eyes to the luminous red numbers of his alarm clock. He noted the time and closed his eyes again. Ten-thirty. Good, he had plenty more time to sleep. Last night had been hellaciously long. He'd spent most of it wrestling with knotted sheets and...

Wait, had that said *ten*-thirty?

He looked again and rolled off the bed with a groan. Abby probably thought he was a lazy bum, sleeping the day away.

After stumbling over last night's clothes on the way to the door, he grabbed his robe from the doorknob and tossed it around his shoulders. He needed a shower and shave, and then he'd be out there to help.

Sweet mercy, he was tired. He'd spent hours in front of his computer, at some point even nodding off there. At five in the morning, he'd peeled his forehead off the keyboard and stared at the onslaught of equal signs and brackets that had taken over his computer screen.

He'd made himself wake up enough to repair the damage, and must have gone back to sleep on the way to his bedroom. He had no recollection of removing his clothes or hitting the bed. If Rosie or Wyatt had cried last night, he hadn't heard them.

Fifteen rushed minutes later, he ventured into the main part of the house, prepared to apologize and offer to baby-sit for the rest of the morning. But the house was suspiciously quiet, and a glance out the back door to note the absence of Abby's truck saved him a trip upstairs.

There was half a pot of cold coffee sitting near the sink, and a note on the refrigerator from Abby. She'd written that she had taken the babies with her to deliver a load of flowers to market. She would be home by noon.

He warmed up a cup of the coffee and headed for his office, deciding to use his free time to get some work done. He clicked on his mouse and maneuvered through the steps of his program, but he couldn't make his mind start to work.

For days now he'd only been able to think about Abby. He'd nearly made a catastrophic mistake. Again.

He'd managed to stop himself in the nick of time, so he shouldn't be feeling so out of sorts. He'd done the right thing. It was just that the thing he'd *wanted* to do kept barging into his thoughts, making him miss sleep and sabotaging his attempts to work.

Paula's visit hadn't done any good at all. In a couple of weeks, she'd gone from being an interesting companion to being someone he had no interest in ever seeing again.

He needed to plan another date, with someone else. This time he would return to Kansas City. If Diane and Zuzu were still upset with him, there were usually plenty of willing women in the bars. An evening with one of them should solve his problem.

He took a gulp of coffee, winced at its bitterness and reread what he'd saved last night. Scowling, he read it again. He seemed to have missed a few crucial elements. He'd obviously been tired out when he'd written it. The whole thing was pure garbage. Fingering the cursor to the middle of the screen, he deleted most of last night's work.

The phone's ring jangled his nerves and interrupted what little concentration he could muster. It was a repeat client needing help with a glitch that she'd been trying to straighten out for weeks. Jack spent a half hour talking the young woman through the problem, and hung up.

Picking up his mug, he walked back out to the kitchen and flung its contents down the sink.

It didn't make sense.

He'd been single forever, and had lived alone since Brian got married four years ago. Jack had been here with Abby and the twins for less than a month. But somehow, being alone in the silent old house made him lonely. He missed the babies.

He missed Abby.

He wandered over to the French doors to look out at her flowers. As usual, life was thriving out there. Abby had a knack for taking care of things.

Plants. Babies. Probably men, if she let herself.

He admired her energy, and her honesty, and it bugged him that he'd confused her last night. He'd seen it in her eyes when they were on the landing. It had taken everything he had to walk away from her, but she wasn't the kind of woman he could dally with. She needed more than he could offer.

Besides, she hadn't given him reason to believe she'd be interested in more than a platonic roommate. He knew all the signs of a woman inclined toward romance—he'd been studying them for years.

Women on the prowl behaved differently from Abby. They dropped hints, fiddled with their hair and looked at him from under fluttering lashes.

With Abby, those signs were missing.

Except for a couple of returned kisses and a misplaced moan here and there, she dealt with him in the same brisk manner that she dealt with everything else. She didn't flirt, fiddle or fuss. Even a dim man could figure out that she wasn't asking for more.

He plodded back to his office and sat in front of his computer, doubting that he'd get much done on his program.

His mind wasn't clicking along at its normal pace. The only thing he could see right now was Abby's somber gaze, cast upon him as if he'd done something terrible.

Maybe he just needed a break. Back home in Kansas City, he'd call a buddy and go play handball, or maybe take a lady friend out for a lunch date. But what did a man do to work off a foggy-brained morning when he was in the middle of nowhere?

Ignoring the pile of paperwork next to his computer, he changed into shorts and running shoes, crammed his cap on his head and headed out the front door. The crisp warm clash of sun and north wind sharpened his senses, at once cooling his face and toasting his limbs.

Fully awake now, he raced away from the farmhouse, only slowing when he neared the edge of the property and realized he could hear the vibrating songs of a pond-ful of frogs.

He veered off toward the sound, and circled once around the pond's perimeter. Slanted light glinted across the choppy waves, catching his attention. It soothed his thoughts and brightened his mood.

He'd never had a dad around to take him fishing, but it sounded like fun. He made a mental note to stock the pond with fish and buy a couple of fishing poles. He and Wyatt could learn to fish together.

The idea of sharing a lifetime of discoveries with the

boy pleased him. Jack wanted to be the dad he himself had never had.

When he remembered that his year at the farm would be nearly finished by spring, the morning's gloom settled back around him. He couldn't fish with Wyatt here because the farm essentially belonged to Abby.

And rightfully so. She loved the place—even that creaky old house. She would take care of it. But surely she would allow him to visit with Wyatt. A boy would learn a lot from spending time in a place where there was plenty of dirt to dig around in.

Jack traveled a stretch at a steady jog before he saw Abby's truck emerge through the gates. As soon as he saw it, he gave a robust wave and made an immediate turn toward the house. Although he'd already jogged at least a mile, he sprinted home, glad beyond reason that she and the babies were returning.

He reached the garage just as she was getting out of her truck. "Hey," he hollered. "Let me help with the twins."

She gave a quick nod as she reached in the back seat for Rosie. Jack jogged around to the other side and discovered that Wyatt had been lulled to sleep by the ride. Releasing the straps, Jack pulled the warm baby against his chest.

Wyatt gave a soft little sigh, snuggling down. Jack ran his hand gently along the back of the baby's silky brown curls, feeling an emotion so strong it could only be described as love.

It hadn't taken long for that attachment to grow, and he looked across at Abby, understanding her need to keep the boy with her.

But she wasn't looking at the babies. She was looking

at him and biting her lip. "I assume you found my note," she said as they carried the babies inside the house.

"Yes, I did. You must have gotten up pretty early."

She shrugged. "Rosie and Wyatt slept through until six, so we all just got up then."

He walked up the stairs alongside her, allowing her to place Rosie in her crib and then take Wyatt to put him down, too. Following her back downstairs, he stood in the middle of the kitchen, which managed to be cheerful despite its size, and waited as she trotted back out to the truck and returned with a plastic grocery sack.

Abby's emotions were usually so evident that he knew at a glance when she was happy or sad. Now she was so carefully composed he couldn't read her, but the tooth marks on her bottom lip implied a worry she wasn't expressing.

He knew it had to do with him.

"I do intend to help in the mornings," he assured her. "Guess it's just taking me awhile to adjust to the changes."

Abby began to remove items from her bag. "I'm completely willing to do it all alone, remember?"

He frowned, watching her fill her arms with garden supplies and retreat toward a separate pantry that stood near the door to the greenhouse.

He picked up a box of bone meal and followed her. "Of course I remember," he said as he handed her the box. "I'm sorry about the other night in the nursery, too. That was a mistake."

"I didn't stop you, did I?" she said immediately, looking up from under her lashes with reproachful eyes.

The sun filtered in through the greenhouse windows, hitting her face with full force. He nearly gasped in surprise. Her honey-brown eyes were gorgeous in the light, and she had the lightest spattering of freckles all over her face. Her skin was beautifully flushed and seemed to glow with good health.

He wondered if she was as freckled and glowing all over, and decided just as quickly not to pursue that thought. "No, you didn't," he murmured. "But you barely had time to react, Abby. I overstepped my bounds."

She turned back to the cupboard, moving boxes and bottles around to fit in the new supplies. "Despite what you must think, I'm a normal woman. I can get turned on, just like you. It didn't mean a thing."

She snapped the cupboard door closed and stalked away.

But as she left the kitchen, she said, "You're right about us getting out, though. I have a date Saturday night."

So, THE RECLUSIVE ABBY had a date. Maybe he was a good influence on her, after all. He should be happy for her.

But the news plucked at Jack's nerves all week long.

He spent a lot of time in his room working. Most days, he ate a stack of buttered toast in his room. For breakfast, lunch and dinner. A few times, he drove four miles into town to eat his evening meal at a local diner, leaving Abby and the twins to manage without his company.

He even took an afternoon off to go buy that new car, but as he drove it back to the farmhouse, he knew most of the thrill had been coaxing a bit of spontaneous fun from Abby.

She seemed to be avoiding him, too.

She spent more time upstairs, and would leave terse notes that requested he watch the twins for an hour or two, while she took flowers to market or tended to the trees or greenhouse.

At night, when one of the babies cried, he waited downstairs. He stared at the ceiling and worked through his current program. And forced himself to stay away.

Usually, she had the baby calmed within minutes. His help simply wasn't required.

By Thursday, he knew it was time to head for the city. A client had called, needing on-site instruction, and he'd jumped at the chance to escape. He'd arranged a help session for that very weekend, and told Abby that he had to go on an important business trip that would require several days away from the farm.

When he'd offered to pay for a sitter to help her manage alone, she had only shrugged, eyes snapping, and said that her mother and Sharon would each be glad to baby-sit anytime at all, absolutely free.

He supposed this new distance was more normal in a roommate situation. The fact that he didn't enjoy it as much was just something more to deal with. So what if he was attracted to the wrong woman? He knew how to cope with something like that. He just needed to find someone more appropriate to engage his attention.

This weekend should provide the perfect opportunity.

He and Abby managed to remain civil until Friday morning—but just barely. By that time they were shooting covert missiles at one another with a regularity that had him wondering why he'd ever found her intriguing at all.

Her shrewish behavior was the perfect complement to his brattiness, except her usual sarcasm had taken on a sharper edge that no longer seemed cute. Since he no longer felt like teasing her out of it, the tension was mounting.

As he packed for the weekend, he felt relieved to be leaving. He needed to get to the city and let off steam.

He thought he might have put a permanent dent in his forehead from frowning in the past few days, and his nerves were wound so tight he thought he might explode.

Before he left, he cornered Abby in the greenhouse. She was watering the plants, looking as serene as he'd ever seen her. "Abby, I'm leaving," he announced from the doorway. "I'll be back late Saturday night or early Sunday morning."

She looked up from her plants and smiled indulgently, as if he were an obedient child. "I hope things go well with your client," she said before turning her attention back to her flowers. With the twins off visiting her parents, Abby must be anticipating a few hours of complete freedom.

Whatever the case, that polite coolness was worse than her most cutting comment. "Oh, but I won't just be helping my clients," he sniped. "My nights are free to do as I please."

She glanced up again. The only way he knew his dart had hit the target was from the tiny wrinkle in her brow. "Okay, have a *fruitful* trip," she said, a little more sharply.

He wasn't satisfied with the knowledge that he'd won, and he still didn't leave. He lingered inside the doorway, watching her. Wondering why he wasn't diving for the door as fast as the class troublemaker on the last day of school.

"And you have fun on your date with, uh—what was your banker's name?"

Now Abby seemed truly startled. Her face colored prettily and she stammered, "Duke—er, Delbert. Um, Duke

Delbertson. Kind of an unusual name—I think he's Swedish."

Duke Delbertson—that was a weighty name. It conjured up images of some blond John Wayne type. This banker must be a big guy. Maybe Abby was blushing because she had a crush on this lumbering mass of a man.

Jack's eyelid twitched. "Oh," he said coolly. "I hope you have a good time. We can compare notes when I get back."

"Wouldn't that be a hoot?" she said, looking completely horrified. Then she swished past him on her way out of the greenhouse, leaving him standing alone among her plants.

He strode out in turn and went straight to his brand-new car, which was packed and waiting in the garage. After all, he was a busy man with a full weekend planned; he might as well get under way.

He began the hour-long drive to Kansas City, intending to check into his hotel room first, then spend the remainder of the day tutoring his clients on the use of a new business package.

After hours, however, his options were wide open, and he had the weekend all mapped out. He intended to return to the craziest days of his bachelorhood, partying to an extreme he hadn't indulged in in several years.

He'd call every woman in his book, and the first one who said yes would be wined and dined by a crazed man. Maybe he could play a freckle-faced vixen right out of his mind.

ABBY FIDDLED WITH her bowl of cold blueberry buckle, wondering idly if the twins were asleep by now. She had resisted the urge to call home for the entire hour that she'd been gone, but she hadn't been able to keep her mind on her date at all.

In truth, she hadn't spent every minute thinking about the twins, although they were in her thoughts often. She knew they were fine with her mother. More often, Abby was thinking about Jack. Imagining that his weekend of romance was more successful than hers.

Every once in a while she looked across the table at her companion to make a cursory check on the conversation. He'd spent at least five minutes discussing the government's economic shortsightedness, and he didn't seem ready to break off his speech anytime soon.

If she'd known the banker had been regarding her with an interest in business rather than romance, she wouldn't have gone into the bank last Tuesday with the sole intention of scaring up a date. Right now, in fact, her blatant pursuit of this man's attention compared in stupidity only to moving in with Jack last month.

Things weren't going well in either case.

"Abigail, did you hear what I asked?" said her companion, whose name she had forgotten sometime between him asking her out and her agreeing to come.

She just knew it started with *D*. For dull.

She looked up with a start, and recognized that frowning expression, even if she hardly knew the face. He'd asked her something. Finally.

"What was the question?"

His eyes rolled upward, as if he found her to be outrageously slow. "I asked if you've developed a five-year business plan for your farm."

"Oh, I have goals, but I haven't put a pen to paper yet. It hasn't been all that long."

"Would you mind sharing your thoughts?" he asked, with curiosity honing his already sharp features.

"Actually, I do mind," she answered. "I didn't know we were coming out to dinner to talk business. I'd rather not."

His interest deflated as fast as a balloon in a cactus garden. Sitting back in his chair, he asked, "What do you want to talk about, Abigail?"

Why a rational woman would spend her first date in months thinking about her impossibly off-limits roommate instead of her completely harmless companion.

"Well, what do you do for fun?" she asked.

The banker's eyes seemed to vibrate in their sockets. "Fun?"

She sighed and looked at her watch, trying to decide whether it was too soon to go home. "Do you have a hobby?"

He stared at her, straightening up in his chair after a moment and announcing, "I trade commodities."

She stared back. "For fun?"

He took a deep breath, seeming ready to launch into another Duke-Delbert-Don-or-Dwayne lecture series. "Yes, and other than a few ups and downs, it's been lucrative."

"I see," she said through her teeth.

When he began an exhaustive chronicle of his portfolio, she knew an escape was in order. She didn't waste time trying to figure out a good excuse. She was ready to start digging her way out of this date immediately.

"Um...D-Drake?" she interrupted. "I must have forgotten to tell you, but I need to get home to feed the babies."

"Feed the babies? Can't your mother do that?"

"Well, not the way I feed them," she said, tugging at the lapel of her jacket.

His brows formed a perfect V over his eyes, and he shook his head.

She bit her lip at the lie she was about to tell. Then she said in a hushed tone, "You know...the natural way."

The banker jumped halfway out of his chair and then plopped back down. Cupping a hand beside his mustache, he stared at her chest and whispered, "You're breast feeding? But the babies aren't yours."

She shrugged, and offered a tiny wink. "Anything's possible if you want it bad enough."

"Amazing," he said, already retreating from the lady who'd brazenly flirted with him in the lobby of the biggest commercial lending bank in Topeka.

He picked up the bill, pulling a calculator out of his jacket pocket to double-check the amounts. Then he called the waitress over, suddenly quite receptive to the idea of taking his wacky date home.

Abby didn't bother trying to make conversation as he drove her back out to the farm, and she was fairly certain he'd never ask her out again.

Her fib had ensured that fact. She considered that a good thing, since she had no intention of ever going out with him again. Even if she never had another date, she wouldn't suffer through the D-man's speeches.

She'd known for a long time that she wasn't cut out for romance, and at least in the case of her date tonight, she wouldn't notice the loss. It had been silly to try again.

As she hopped out of the car in front of the farmhouse, she said, "Thanks, Doug. See you around."

He sped off before she'd taken a single step toward the door. She had to dodge the sand that came flying out from under his tires, but she chuckled anyway. Either he was in a big hurry to leave or the staid banker was a stunt driver in his spare time.

She went to the door, eager to get inside and see what the twins were up to. "Mom, I'm back," she hollered as she walked through the living room.

Her mother appeared at the top of the stairs wearing a cow puppet on her hand. "We're up here—and you're early! Did you bring Dwight with you?"

"Oh! *Dwight!*" Abby said as she started up the stairs. "I kept thinking his name was Duke. Or Don. Or Duffy."

Her mother waited for Abby to reach the landing, then patted her arm with the puppet. "You must not have had too good a time if you didn't even catch his name," she said.

Abby snorted, but not from amusement. Her few experiences with men seemed doomed to failure. She simply wasn't good at man-woman stuff. "A girl could learn a lot from Dreary Dwight, the banker. I can say that much."

"You always did prefer smart boys."

Stepping over the baby gate to see the twins, Abby said, "This guy's brains only worked with numbers. Maybe I was just interested in listening to a speech on another topic."

Her mother followed and sat cross-legged on the nursery floor in front of the babies. Bobbing the puppet around in front of her, she imitated the slow lowing of a cow as she said, "Oh, dear, I was hoping Abby's date would take her to the harvest party next month."

Still in her new suit, Abby sat beside her mother and grabbed a lamb puppet from a pile of toys on the floor. To the delight of the twins, she held the lamb up and bleated, "The harvest par-r-r-ty, is it time for that aga-a-ain?"

The cow turned toward the lamb. "Absolutely, it's the same time every year."

"And I won't go, the same as every year," Abby said, forgetting the voice and the hand movements.

Her mother removed the cow puppet and pushed Abby's bangs away from her eyes. "You should go," she said. "Even if you're not concerned with the social aspect, you're an owner now. The party's a great place to make business contacts."

Abby held up her puppet again and moved the lamb's mouth in time to her voice. "But Abby doesn't wa-a-ant to go alone."

Her mother didn't join the act. "Your dad and I will be there, dear," she said. "And you need to get out."

Again Abby used the puppet to say words that were too painful to say in a normal voice. "And here's a news flash—Abigail Briggs, twenty-six-year-old divorcée slash guardian to adorable twins, attends big community bash with parents. Will she ever get a li-i-ife?"

Her mother smiled as the twins chuckled in glee at the puppet's antics. "What about taking Jack, just for fun?"

Abby didn't miss a beat. She swept the lamb around immediately, announcing to all in the room. "Abigail Briggs, twenty-six-year-old divorcée slash guardian, is the talk of the *t-o-w-n* as she engages in a loud quarrel with her male roommate at the annual harvest party."

"That's not going well, either?"

"You could say that."

"Oh, dear."

FOR THE PAST HOUR, Jack had listened as a young couple across the bar exchanged verbal insults. He wondered if the pair of sweethearts knew they had an audience, and why they didn't take their argument to a more secluded place. Even more than that, he wondered why he didn't just get up and leave himself. He'd long since scouted the room for romantic possibilities, and no one here seemed intriguing enough to make the slightest effort.

"Excuse me, handsome," said a voice from behind him. A doe-eyed brunette was standing at his shoulder. She slid a slow hand across his back, flexing her fingertips around his biceps. "May I sit here?"

Shrugging, he turned back to his drink while the woman slithered onto the bar stool beside him. After a few moments, a man with spikes in his hair and a hoop through his nose appeared between Jack and the lady. The other man whispered in her ear—which was completely unnecessary, since no one else was interested—and soon Spikey and Bambi floated off into the shadows of the room.

It was the same thing that had happened for two hours now. The women came, they sat, and when Jack didn't devote his entire attention to their loveliness, they found another stool to occupy.

He just couldn't rally the interest. Maybe he was too tired. He'd worked doubly hard to complete the training sessions for his clients so he could be finished by eight o'clock. He'd wanted the rest of his weekend free.

Now he wished he was back in the clients' conference room, standing in front of a circle of executives who were each resentful of the fact that their Saturday was being wasted by a work session. He hadn't been popular there, either, but at least he hadn't been bored.

He must be too old to meet women in bars. After all, he'd given up this sort of thing several years ago, when he realized he needed to get to know a woman to fully enjoy her. That was when he'd made a rule to date no more than three at a time. He knew his limitations.

And his approach had been successful enough before he moved out to the sticks. There had always been an ample supply of women who found it acceptable to share a part-time boyfriend, as long as he kept them feeling encouraged.

But he'd tried calling the remaining two girlfriends from his hotel room earlier. They hadn't answered their phones. It did nothing for his pride to realize that Diane and Zuzu had replaced his attentions in a month.

He'd left messages on their machines, making sure to keep any hint of desperation out of his voice. Desperation would imply something that simply wasn't true, and in spite of his many failings, he tried to be honest.

He wouldn't want to imply that he missed their company specifically—he didn't. He just wanted a woman's company. He didn't care which one called him back.

After waiting a couple of minutes in case one of them had been out picking up her mail, he'd left for the bar. He'd chosen the one that had been his favorite nighttime roost in his younger years, figuring he could make a connection with someone there.

He knew that with more than fifty women populating the bar this evening, one or two must be attractive and intelligent enough to take his mind off those damn little sand-colored freckles.

These women hadn't taken his mind off the things for a minute. He figured he must have outgrown the desperado lifestyle he used to love, so he gave up and left the bar long before the night's crowd had even begun their uprising.

He returned to his hotel room and paced around the phone.

He wanted to call Abby, but she was out with The Hulk

tonight and probably wasn't home yet. If she was, she might have company. Jack should leave her alone.

He stripped bare right there in front of the phone and headed to the shower. And stood under the hot water and imagined some muscle-bound man kissing Abby goodnight.

Jack wished it was him kissing her. He wished kissing her was all right. He fought to remember why it wasn't.

Complications.

Kissing her would cause complications.

She was too special, and wouldn't be as easy to leave as the others. That was it. Monumental complications.

Still, the thought of kissing Abby, and more, had him turning the nozzle to frigid for a long couple of minutes before he jumped out of the shower.

And then he wrapped a towel around his waist, went straight to the phone and dialed his own home phone number. If she was alone, maybe she'd answer it. His curiosity, at least, would be appeased.

But she didn't, even after ten rings. She must still be out with The Incredible Hulk.

Phenomenal.

Chapter Seven

After her mother left, Abby gave the babies their second bath of the day, simply to have something to do with her time. She didn't want to think about Jack's weekend, and she didn't want to listen for his key in the lock. She put the twins to bed, changed into her T-shirt and robe and wandered through the dark house as if she was searching for something. Or someone.

When she passed Jack's office, a twirling mass of colors caught her eye. He'd left his monitor on, and his screen saver was illuminating the otherwise dark room. Unable to resist, she tiptoed in. She looked around in respectful silence, admiring the careful clutter that signified a clever mind at work.

The telephone in his office erupted with a ring that sent her heart through the ceiling. She glanced at the handset, tempted to pick it up and silence the offensive jangling.

But instead she stared at it, barely moving, waiting for the person at the other end to give up. After ten rings, it fell silent.

Abby let the air back out of her lungs and turned toward the door, too guilty to enjoy her snooping. As she went past the telephone, a Post-it note that was sticking halfway out from under it flapped in the air current. Glancing down, she read, "Buy Abby a..."

She bit her lip, listening for sounds in the house. When she only heard the hum of the refrigerator and the rush of air circulating through the vents, she reached down to tug the note out from under the phone.

"Buy Abby a robe before you ravish her." That was all it said, in Jack's precise handwriting.

She snickered. Then frowned.

The note was solid evidence that he'd been tempted, and as tickled as that made her feel, it also added to her confusion. Despite her best efforts, he'd been tempted. And she was supposed to be upset about that.

A tiny click had her dashing from the room to evade discovery, and she bolted into the kitchen. After several breathless seconds spent wiping a spotless countertop, she realized that the noise wasn't caused by Jack coming in. The click must have been some mysterious house sound, and it was quiet now.

The house seemed too big tonight. With the twins upstairs asleep, and Jack missing, she was reminded too much of the night of her sister's death. Once again Abby was in this house, waiting for someone's return.

And again the hours seemed to stretch out endlessly.

She headed out to her greenhouse to putter around among the pots, carrying the baby monitor with her. There wasn't much out here that needed doing, but the smell of rich earth and the vigor of plant life helped calm her. She checked each variety for signs of disease, and pinched off a few straggling ends.

She told herself as she worked that she didn't really miss Jack that much. That he was just like Tim, and wasn't worth missing. He'd sure surprised her, though. Every step of the way. He wasn't at all self-serving, as

Play the

Lucky
Hea

and get...

2 FREE BO
and a **FREE MYST**

yes! **YOUR**

I have scratched off
Please send me my *2 FREE*
FREE Mystery GIFT. I unders
under no obligation to purchas
explained on the back of this ca

354 HDL DUZ4

FIRST NAME	

ADDRESS

APT.#	**CITY**

STATE/PROV.	**ZIP/POSTA**

Twenty-one gets you
2 FREE BOOKS
and a **FREE MYSTERY GIFT!**

Twenty gets
2 FREE BO

Offer limited to one per household and
subscribers. All orders subject to appro

▼ **DETACH AND MAIL CARD TODAY!** ▼

HARLEQUIN®
Live the emotion™

Visit us online at
www.eHarlequin.com

The Harlequin Reader Service® — Here's how it works:

Accepting your 2 free books and mystery gift places you under no obligation to buy anything. You may keep the books and gift and return the shipping statement marked "cancel." If you do not cancel, about a month later we'll send you 4 additional books and bill you just $3.99 each in the U.S., or $4.74 each in Canada, plus 25¢ shipping & handling per book and applicable taxes if any.* That's the complete price and — compared to cover prices of $4.75 each in the U.S. and $5.75 each in Canada — it's quite a bargain! You may cancel at any time, but if you choose to continue, every month we'll send you 4 more books, which you may either purchase at the discount price or return to us and cancel your subscription.

*Terms and prices subject to change without notice. Sales tax applicable in N.Y. Canadian residents will be charged applicable provincial taxes and GST. Credit or debit balances in a customer's account(s) may be offset by any other outstanding balance owed by or to the customer.

BUSINESS REPLY MAIL
FIRST-CLASS MAIL   PERMIT NO. 717-003   BUFFALO, NY

POSTAGE WILL BE PAID BY ADDRESSEE

HARLEQUIN READER SERVICE
3010 WALDEN AVE
PO BOX 1867
BUFFALO NY 14240-9952

NO POSTAGE
NECESSARY
IF MAILED
IN THE
UNITED STATES

she had imagined. He'd been generous with his time and money, and he was amazingly sweet with the babies. He didn't seem bored with them, or with her, or with living in the country.

Come to think of it, he wasn't much like Tim at all.

Which made carrying out her plan that much more difficult, but enjoying his company very easy. Abby felt a tenderness toward him that seemed too powerful in combination with the wallop of physical need she felt every time she looked at him.

Sighing, she picked up the monitor and returned to the kitchen, pausing at the table to trace the grain of the oak with her finger. A series of circular patterns repeated across its surface.

Every line and every flaw went all the way through to the underside. Although the top was polished to a rich beauty, and the bottom was rough, the flaws were still there.

Just as hers were. No matter how hard she tried to polish them out, she was flawed through and through. She was starting to repeat the biggest mistake of her past.

She was setting her sights on an impossible man. Again.

Jack was generous and witty, and he made her feel sexy.

He was very nearly Tim's exact opposite, except for those wandering eyes. He was thirty-one, and he'd never committed to a woman—in marriage or anything else. He'd made it clear that he didn't want that sort of life.

If Abby got involved with him, it would only be for a while. At some point he would leave, and he'd have every right to steal away the baby boy sleeping upstairs.

She couldn't let that happen. Wyatt belonged out here

on the farm. He belonged with his sister. Most of all he belonged with Abby herself.

It was late enough now that she was fairly certain Jack wouldn't return tonight, and she needed to relax. She poured herself a glass of wine, locked the back door and turned out the kitchen lights.

She'd just have to stick to her plan. Somehow, she had to keep protecting Wyatt.

She went to the living room and flopped down on the sofa. She removed her hair band and undid her braid, then crossed her feet on the coffee table. Grabbing the TV remote, she started clicking through channels. Even though she hadn't watched television in a long time, she couldn't find a thing to hold her interest.

She told herself she wasn't really waiting for him, but she was. Heaven help her, she kept wishing for the moment he'd come through that door.

But she kept dreading it, too.

JUST AFTER DAWN, and about halfway between downtown Kansas City and rural Topeka, Jack drove past a sign propped up against a farm gate. In hand-painted black letters, it read Young Ducks For Sale.

He slowed to look, but didn't stop. Most folks would still be asleep at this time of day.

But everyone knew farmers woke early, and Abby had said that her sister wanted ducks on the pond. Maybe a couple of ducks would make a nice conciliatory gesture.

He backed up to the gate and pulled off the road into the ditch. Chickens were scattered everywhere around the house, but there was no sign of a farmer.

Determined now that he had stopped, Jack got out and maneuvered his way past the hens onto the porch. The inner door was open. Someone must be up. He tapped on the screen, and a ruddy-cheeked woman appeared within seconds.

"Mornin', young man," she said. "What can I do for you?"

"Is it too early to see the ducks?"

"Not at all," she said. Whipping her head around, she hollered into the house, "Fred, there's a youngster out here asking to see the ducks."

A squarish man in overalls came to the door and peered through the screen. "You drove out here at sunrise to see some ducks? Where ya comin' from?"

"Kansas City."

The farmer took a look at Jack's baseball cap, then squinted past him at the car he'd parked out by the road. "Ya ain't plannin' to keep ducks in some bachelor apartment, are you?"

"No, they're a gift for a friend who has a pond."

The farmer stepped out the door, plowing his way through the chickens without a glance. "Must be livin' right, to get on your way so early," he said. "Or missing your friend."

Jack didn't comment, but he let the farmer's words weigh on his mind. Did he miss Abby?

Absolutely.

Even though he'd been around fresh faces all weekend, he'd missed her. That had never happened with another woman.

As he followed the farmer through the doors of a weathered gray barn, the distinct smell of animals and hay enveloped him, reminding him of the single summer he'd lived in the country as a boy. Squawks sounded from a couple of round pens on the floor of the barn. Jack stepped close to one of the pens, grinning as he watched a half-dozen gangly ducks scramble all over one another, each striving to reach the top of the pile.

As he concentrated on trying to choose the best pair, the farmer said, "Ya know, most men just take flowers to their lady friends."

"She has plenty of flowers," Jack replied. "She doesn't have a single duck. I'll take the two on top."

"Fair to middlin' choices, if ya want a coupla brothers," the farmer said. He turned to pick up a tall, thin-looking bird from the other pen. "Now this'n has a proud look about 'er. She'll make a fine layer."

"Oh. Then I'll take the two you think are best."

The farmer set Jack up with a cardboard box, a starter supply of duck food and a few minutes of instructions. Then he helped carry everything out to the car.

Before Jack drove off, he rolled down his window. "By the way," he asked, "how did you know my friend was a woman?"

The farmer leaned one hand against the hood of the car. "I've been breedin' animals mosta my life," he said. "I recognize the look of an affected male."

"What look?" Jack asked, trying not to be offended at being compared to some farm animal.

"A man has a certain look about 'im when he's shoppin' for a lady," the farmer said. "He makes a careful choice, knowing it'll matter to a female. If you'd a been shopping for a buddy, you'd've had me throw a couple of ducks in a box and been on your way."

Jack drove the rest of the way to Topeka with the radio off, listening to the ducks yammering instead, and thinking. Did it matter what Abby thought?

It did. Absolutely. He definitely cared that she approved of his gift. And as much as he told himself that it was because choosing a pet was a serious decision, he knew he'd just wanted to please her.

When he arrived at the farmhouse, he was thrilled by the empty driveway. At least there wasn't some monster truck parked there, signaling the presence of Duke, the seven-foot-tall legend who had taken Abby out last night.

Jack pulled into the garage, trying to decide what to do with the ducks. The farmer had said that they should be kept close to the house for a while, until they got used to their new home.

Jack carried the box through the back door and put it in a corner of the kitchen farthest from the rest of the house. He opened the flaps and set a bowl of water inside, dropping some pellets in a clump beside that.

Then he went back outside to get his bags, intending to unpack quietly until everyone else woke up. A sudden shriek had him tossing the gear on his bed and hurrying out to the kitchen. Maybe a duck had gotten out and was searching for its mother. That cry had sounded demanding.

But one peek made Jack realize it hadn't come from the birds. They were curled into matching gray-and-yellow fluff balls, asleep.

The cry must have come from one of the twins. Jack flew up the stairs, trying to reach them before Abby woke up. She'd done her share of the work this weekend. Since he was up anyway, he might as well handle this shift.

Wyatt was awake and bawling, sitting up in his crib and looking around for an adult rescuer. Apparently, neither baby had awoken last night, since the bottles in the warmer were still full.

Jack picked Wyatt up and began to feed him. Luckily, Rosie was still asleep. He and Wyatt could enjoy the quiet of the morning without interruption. It felt right, being back. He felt at home.

After Wyatt was fed and burped, Jack dressed him in a white T-shirt with a yellow duck on the front, and smiled at the thought of Abby's reaction to his gift. But he worried about it, too.

He sat down on the floor of the nursery and watched Wyatt play, whispering words of encouragement. Rosie should awaken soon, and Jack decided to stay up here and handle her morning feeding, too, allowing Abby to sleep in for once.

As expected, the little girl began stirring in her crib within minutes. He picked her up before she even opened her mouth to cry.

As he fed her, Wyatt started batting a ball around on the floor. Jack was surprised when the ball rolled a few feet away, and Wyatt crawled to retrieve it.

Jack was saddened by the knowledge that his brother had missed seeing his son crawl for the first time. That he'd miss all the first times. But at least Jack was here. He could treasure the twins, just as Brian would have.

After Rosie had been fed and clothed, he decided to show them the ducks. He tucked a baby under each arm and headed downstairs. When the living room came into view, however, he missed his footing and plunked clumsily down on the last step, barely managing to hang on to Rosie and Wyatt.

Abby was asleep on the couch.

She was curled up as contentedly as a feline. Her hair flowed off the sofa, sexy in its abandon. She was wearing her robe, but it had fallen open to reveal a long strip of freckled skin that nearly gave away every one of her secrets.

Jack's body exploded with a shock of desire that he didn't want to feel. Not while holding a couple of babies.

Rosie's unexpected chatter caused Abby's eyes to open and look directly into his own. Unable to move, he watched as she sat up and pulled the robe across that skin.

Abruptly, she tumbled off the couch and headed straight toward him. He jumped up and lurched out of the way, allowing her to pass by on her way up the stairs.

When she reached the landing, she said, "I'll be back down in a minute."

He realized she had left the belt to her robe on the end of the sofa, so he put the babies down to grab it. A wineglass lay on its side on the coffee table, with a few drops of wine dribbled out.

He put the belt in his pocket and hurried to the kitchen for a towel. He couldn't remember Abby drinking wine at home before, and she usually wore a T-shirt and sweatpants around the house. She'd sure switched things around last night.

And then he remembered. She'd been out with the banker. An image of her lounging around half-naked and sipping wine with some grotesque banker had Jack clenching his fists.

Apparently, her weekend had been more fruitful than his.

ABBY SCOWLED at her reflection in the mirror, perturbed that she had fallen asleep and let Jack find her sprawled out in some disgraceful state. Her mouth had probably been hanging open, and now her bangs were flipping up in an unnatural curl.

She dressed hurriedly, throwing on her standard attire—oversize T-shirt, baggy jeans and cheap white tennis shoes. Running a brush through her hair, she braided it with deft fingers and wrapped a band around the end.

Then she squared her shoulders and jogged back down, prepared to start another day with twins and chores. After all, there was no better cure for a foolish heart than a day filled with good, hard work.

The chattery sounds coming from the kitchen indicated that her housemates must have gone in there. She followed the noise, and discovered the twins in their high chairs pushing around a few slices of banana. They were also squealing at something in a box on the counter.

"What's this?" she asked, peering into the box. A couple of ducklings were hopping around in a bowl of water. Pellets and water were scattered everywhere.

Jack was rinsing dishes. "I wouldn't know," he said, sounding brusque. "I found them here in the kitchen."

She put her hands on her hips and stared at his profile.

Finally, he turned to look at her, and he was scowling. "I bought them for Wyatt and Rosie," he said.

Abby tried to lift the corners of her mouth in a smile, but that proved impossible with the rest of her face pinched in a frown.

What on earth had made him so mad?

"They're way too young to appreciate any pet," she said, "let alone a duck!"

He looked pointedly at the babies, who were chortling in merriment. "They're enjoying them now."

"I can see that. But these ducks look pretty mature. They'll need to be moved out to the pond soon."

He turned back to the sink and retrieved a wineglass from the basin. As he dried it, he said, "I got a pair. Next year you can raise a pondful of ducklings, for Rosie to enjoy when she's older."

Abby ran her index finger along the soft yellow back

of one duck. "You shouldn't have done this," she said. "You weren't supposed to bring me anything else."

"They're not for you," he reminded her. "They're for the twins and the farm. I promised to help run this farm for one year. After that, you can sell it all. I don't care."

He whipped open the cabinet and set the wineglass inside with a quick, angry movement that had Abby waiting for the sharp clink of breaking glass. But she only heard the slam of the cabinet and the stomp of Jack's feet as he exited the kitchen.

"Oh," she said, not at all pleased that they seemed to be returning to the cold war of last week.

She decided the greenhouse would be a better place to keep the ducks, and moved their box and food out to a corner shelf. They could live out here for a while, until they were mature enough to be released to the pond.

And she took care of the babies alone most of the morning. She refused to knock at Jack's office door to ask for help. She knew she could handle her greenhouse chores when the babies were napping.

He came out every once in a while and went into the kitchen or down the hall to his room. But he and Abby managed to avoid one another quite well.

By Monday morning, they had returned to their normal routines. Almost. Jack offered to help with baby and kitchen duties, but the teasing light in his eyes was gone, and he didn't seem to be enjoying himself. He was so serious-minded Abby barely recognized him.

Until late Wednesday morning, a week later, when the doorbell rang, and Abby answered it. A raven-haired woman in a leather miniskirt and a skintight turtleneck stood on the porch. Her well-endowed chest swelled out in a way that reminded Abby of the bust-enhancing ads she'd seen in the backs of magazines. When the woman saw Abby, however, her chest seemed to shrink a couple of inches.

"May I help you?" Abby asked.

"I'm here for Jack," the woman answered as she stepped through the door.

"He's in his office," Abby said, waving her hand down the hall and frowning when the woman trotted off in that direction. "Would you care to wait in the living room?" she called after her.

"Just point me to his office," the woman said.

Jack's door opened abruptly, and he stepped out and nearly collided with his visitor. His arms went around her. "Diane, what a surprise!"

Abby stood at the end of the hall, watching as the woman pressed her chest and lips against his. "Jacky boy, I was upset when I missed your call," she said when she finally let go. "I wondered how long it would take you to come to your senses. I adjusted my schedule to drive out to this godforsaken place, just so I could see you."

Jack's reply would always be a mystery to Abby, since he and the trollop went into his office and shut the door.

Great—he returns from his wild weekend and the revolving door starts spinning again, Abby thought. He must have been forgiven for moving in with her. Maybe he'd convinced his harem that Abby was nothing but a big fat zero to him.

She returned to the greenhouse, intent on finishing her pruning. She couldn't help hearing the woman's loud whoops of laughter and wincing every time.

Occasionally, Jack's vigorous chuckles joined in, and Abby finally marched all the way up the stairs to get the baby monitor. She took the receiver into the greenhouse with her and shut the door.

There. Now she'd hear the babies upstairs if they needed her, but not the babe downstairs, who most assuredly didn't.

Just as Abby had finished transplanting some calendula sprouts into larger pots, a knock caught her attention. Jack was standing at the door, grinning through the glass.

What could he possibly want from her, when Miss Sexpot herself was in his office hooting it up? Abby headed for the door, pulling off her garden gloves on the way.

"I was wondering, do any pizza joints deliver out here?" he asked as soon as she stepped into the kitchen. "Diane and I have decided to eat lunch here today."

Abby slapped her gloves down on the counter. "We're only fifteen minutes from town, Jack. Of course they deliver out here. There's a number by the phone."

"How would I know that?" he asked on his way out.

"I guess you wouldn't," she said softly. "Sorry."

He turned immediately and leaned against the doorjamb. "Do you want to join us?" he asked amicably. Miss Sexpot must've put him in a better mood.

"No."

He came back into the kitchen. "You may as well, Abby. Diane won't bite, and we don't want to eat much. We're going out to dinner later."

Abby's heart fell, and not only because she was jealous. It also meant that Diane would be here all day, leaving behind her trail of perfume and making Abby feel uneasy in her own house.

"I don't want to intrude," she said, knowing she couldn't handle watching Jack flirt.

He touched her shoulder. "Please, Abby. Let's call a truce. Join us."

"I'm not hungry." She hoped the rumbling in her tummy wasn't loud enough for him to hear. Take-out pizza actually sounded good. It was something she seldom indulged in, since she usually ate alone. But she couldn't share one with them. She'd starve before she did that.

"Suit yourself," he said, disappearing back into the hallway. A minute later, he returned, pulling Diane along behind him. "Check out Abby's greenhouse while I order," he was saying. "She has a way with plants."

Diane glared at her.

Abby wanted to tell her to relax—her boyfriend had just pointed out she had a way with plants, not with men. And certainly not with Jack.

He picked up the phone to dial the pizza parlor, and Diane chose to stand at his side and examine her long red fingernails instead of looking out at the flowers.

Nevertheless, Abby knew there was no way she'd get any work done in the greenhouse with that woman loitering on the other side of the French doors. She decided the chores would wait, and headed upstairs to check on Rosie and Wyatt.

Wyatt had rolled to a corner of his crib, and his sweat-dampened curls were crushed against the edge. She moved him back to the center, pulling his blanket away. He nestled back down in sleep, not ready to wake. Skewed across her mattress diagonally, Rosie, too, was deep in slumber.

Tiptoeing into her own room, Abby caught her reflection in the dresser mirror. Now that two of Jack's girlfriends had visited, she realized he must like excitement—fireworks for eyes, and a carnival for a mouth. Color. Splash. Verve.

He went for stargazer lilies and Oriental poppies. How could she compete with women so exotic they caught a man's attention at first glance?

And why did she keep forgetting that she wasn't supposed to compete at all? The sexpot's visit was a good thing.

Wyatt's whine sent Abby scurrying into the nursery. She'd just finished changing his diaper when Rosie followed suit with a few hiccups. Abby scooped up the baby girl, changed a second diaper and sat down in a rocker with both babies.

She was glad they were awake, thankful to have allies in the house, even if they were tiny. It made Abby feel as if she was the one who belonged here, not Jack. And certainly not Diane.

But the cuddles only worked for a short while, and when the twins began to cry in earnest, she knew she had to take them downstairs to feed them.

Hopefully, the pizza party was over and Jack and his girlfriend had left the kitchen. Maybe Miss Sexpot had gotten her press-on nails all tangled up with mozzarella cheese; maybe she'd had to leave for Kansas City to glue on new ones.

But they were still there, sitting at the table and chatting. Seeing them there hurt almost as much as watching Jack flirt. That table had a history and a character all its own, and Abby had gotten used to the idea of sharing a lifetime of meals there with the twins. No one else should sit there, unless she invited them.

Lifting her chin in the air, she marched up to the table. Wordlessly, she placed Wyatt in Jack's arms, then scooted Rosie's high chair about four feet away, to the opposite side of the table.

If she had to share the kitchen, she wanted to be far enough away that she couldn't hear them breathe.

"How cute! Are these your twins, Jacky boy?"

Abby ignored them as best she could, securing Rosie in her seat and returning for Wyatt.

"They're not mine," Jack said. "Wyatt is my ward, Rosie is Abby's. You've heard the story."

Abby practically tore Wyatt from his arms. With her foot, she shoved Wyatt's chair next to Rosie's and put the boy inside.

Finally, she pulled out a chair for herself, centering it in front of the babies.

Diane got up and walked over. Abby watched in horror as the woman pressed her lips to Wyatt's forehead. The baby was too young to recognize deceitfulness when he saw it. He kicked his feet and said, "Agagaga."

Then he grabbed a handful of short black hair and yanked.

"No, shoo can't hab my hayur, punkin," Diane crooned. "I pay too much to keep it wooking wike dis."

She patted her hair, attempting to restore it to normal, but only marginally succeeding.

Abby went to the refrigerator to grab a bowl of pureed apples, and to the buffet drawer for a couple of baby spoons. She sat down in front of the twins, still trying to ignore the woman who was invading her space. Rosie opened her mouth, and Abby popped a spoonful inside.

"How adorable! Look how she eats that food," Diane said. "May I try to feed the baby boy?"

"Suit yourself," Abby said, handing her a spoon.

Jack carried a load of lunch plates and utensils to the sink to begin cleaning up. Diane's smile, and her silly chatter, vanished with Jack's attention elsewhere.

She spooned small mounds of apples and tried to stuff them into Wyatt's mouth without getting too close, and only came back to life after Jack had finished loading the dishwasher and returned to watch. Then she scooted closer to the baby, grinning again. "Does the itty-bitty boy wike his apple-wapples?" she sang.

But Wyatt stole the show by spitting a huge mouthful of food back onto the tray and trying to make a grab for her wayward tuft of hair.

Diane jerked back, smiling stiffly. She looked up at Jack and shook her head, as if she knew the baby had been about to do that. "What a scamp," she said. "You're so lucky!"

Meanwhile, Wyatt was patting both hands in the puddle of apples. Abby considered cautioning Diane about the potential for disaster, but she bit her tongue and waited.

Miss Sexpot didn't deserve the warning.

In seconds flat, Wyatt flung most of the puddle onto Diane's face and clothes. The woman looked down in horror, and the genius baby squealed and grabbed her nose with the same apple-covered hand.

Abby sprang up to head for a roll of paper towels, grinning all the way. She stopped for a minute, trying to contain her amusement, and only returned when her face was composed again.

"Here you go," she said, handing a paper towel to Diane, who was making a keening sound through clenched teeth.

Abby listened closer, trying to distinguish it. It was…a laugh, she supposed. Jack's friend was trying to fake a laugh through wooden lips.

Diane began to blot at her face and clothing with the towel. Wyatt gurgled in pleasure at the commotion, and Rosie began to fuss at having her lunch interrupted.

"I'll take over the feeding duties," Jack said with a thoughtful look at Abby. "Help Diane clean up? Please?"

Reluctantly, Abby headed for the hallway.

Diane followed, still dabbing at her blouse. Mercifully, the strange laughter died as soon as they got to Jack's bathroom. Abby found a washcloth in the linen closet and handed it to the now scowling woman.

She watched from the doorway as Diane blotted. After a few minutes, Jack's friend handed back the cloth and said with much disgust, "I'm going to have to borrow something of yours. I can't go out to dinner tonight with this slop all over my outfit."

Diane reached back to unzip her skirt, while Abby stared at her face. The entire middle of it, around her nose, was now a mottled white. The previously white washcloth was an attractive shade of tan. Half of her color had transferred to the rag!

"Aren't you going to find me something to wear?"

Wincing, Abby flung the cloth down in the basin and headed upstairs. Jack's girlfriend was one of the most domineering women she'd ever met, and she'd give her the nicest outfit she owned if it would hasten her departure.

But Abby had simple tastes. Her closet contained only a few dressy items, unless you counted all the T-shirt and jean combinations. She debated about which of her outfits the horrible stepsister downstairs would find acceptable.

There was the somber gray dress that she'd worn to the funeral, and a delicate lavender floral that she'd worn to the twins' christening. But neither seemed suitable for Miss Sexpot. Except…the new blue business suit Abby had worn to dinner last weekend was in her dry cleaning pile. Maybe Diane wouldn't notice that it was slightly rumpled. Pulling it out, Abby smoothed its wrinkles. It didn't look too bad.

She hung the suit on a padded hanger and carried it

downstairs. She was sure she'd made the right choice, and it was magnanimous of her to offer her best outfit. Diane didn't deserve it.

Still, Abby wasn't surprised when the woman stood in her bra and panties and said, ''Is that all you could come up with? That's the most repulsive suit I've ever seen.''

Abby turned it around, looking at it again. ''It's either this, or a T-shirt and jeans,'' she said. ''You choose.''

Diane grabbed the hanger and scowled as she stepped into the elastic-waisted skirt. It fit perfectly, being only an inch or two short. Pulling the jacket from the hanger, she slipped that on, too.

It barely met at her waist; Diane had to suck in her breath to get the buttons closed. And when she worked her way up to her bust, the jacket wouldn't close at all. Abby held her own breath as Diane tried to wiggle her way inside.

''Oh, for God's sake,'' the woman finally snarled, turning her back to Abby. She unclasped her bra and removed it. Two wads of tissue fell to the floor, which she didn't bother to pick up. Then she turned, buttoning the jacket easily.

Apparently, Diane had found padded bras and tissues a cheaper alternative to those miracle magazine cures.

The suit would work, and Abby debated over whether she should tell Diane about the face problem. She was tempted to let Jack see the hilarious white-and-skin-tone bull's-eye, but she couldn't do it. ''Um, Diane? You might want to check out your face in the mirror.''

Diane whirled around to look, and nearly screamed. ''My God, this is a nightmare. I need my purse from my car.''

Abby waited.

''Please, bring me my purse?''

"Certainly," Abby said, heading for the door.

But after retrieving the handbag and depositing it near the basin in front of Diane, she left the room. Anything else that woman wanted, she could get herself.

Abby found Jack in the living room, playing with the twins. "Did you find everything she needed?" he whispered.

"Hardly," she answered, sinking onto the sofa.

"Would you mind if Diane and I left this afternoon to run some errands, and I came home after dinner tonight?"

"Please do," Abby said with a nod. The sooner Jack's friend left, the sooner she could feel like the woman of the house again.

"She's not that bad," Jack said, his eyes enigmatic.

"She's not that good, either."

Surely Jack was aware that most of the gewgaws on that woman were as fake as her personality. He must know, if he'd gotten close to her at all.

Diane came in then, looking a bit less glamorous than the temptress who had come to visit a few hours earlier. She smiled brightly at Jack as she tugged at the front of Abby's jacket. "I'm all put back together," she announced.

Jack jumped to his feet. "Diane, I insist on having your clothes cleaned," he said. "Let's head out early to take them to a cleaner, and we can browse the shops downtown before we go to dinner."

"Sounds wonderful," Diane said. "Jacky boy, I left my bag and soiled clothes in your necessary room. Be a doll and get them?"

Jack left, and Abby was quite surprised when Diane sat down beside her on the sofa. She leaned her newly painted face in close and whispered, "Don't even think about getting involved with my Jacky. He likes to play the field, but eventually I'll win him. He and I are two of a kind.''

Abby raised her eyebrows, but didn't bother to argue. She knew the truth—he might play the field, but he was nothing like Diane.

When he returned, Diane left the sofa in a swirl and followed him toward the kitchen. As he paused in the doorway to check his wallet, she turned to direct an exaggerated wave toward the twins.

Her expression could only be described as relief, but she couldn't be half as relieved as Abby was, as soon as the door had closed.

Chapter Eight

Abby took the twins into the kitchen with her, opening the refrigerator to finally scrounge some lunch. She grinned when she found the pizza box in front, with a note attached that simply said, ''Knew you wanted some. Enjoy. J.''

She warmed a slice in the oven, and let the twins gnaw on pieces of toast in their high chairs. Later, she took them on an afternoon stroll through the orchard. The last crop of peaches was on the verge of perfect ripeness, and Abby had already called in her harvest crew.

After today's escapade, she intended to spend a portion of the profits on something new to wear. Maybe a pair of overalls. Miss Sexpot could keep the suit.

While the twins were napping, Abby went to the greenhouse to tend to the plants and the ducks. It had been thoughtful of Jack to bring the birds. Despite his claim that they were for the babies, she knew he'd bought them partly because of what she'd told him about Paige.

She wondered if he was as attentive with the women he dated. Right now, for instance, exactly how much attention was he lavishing on Diane?

He'd probably tell that caricature of a woman that she looked phenomenal, despite the repulsive suit. He'd make her feel desirable, and before the night was through, he'd probably kiss her.

Just as he had kissed Abby in a couple of weak moments.

But with Diane, he wouldn't stop with a few kisses, and his caresses wouldn't be abandoned at the smallest of interruptions.

That woman would probably get the whole man, with no holds barred. And as crazy as it was, right now Abby wished she was in Diane's shoes, wearing her own new suit.

Or not.

No matter how many times she reminded herself to keep her feet on the ground and stay away from Jack, her heart craved something as unattainable as the clouds.

She wanted to be the woman Jack directed his smile toward, across some elegant restaurant table.

She wanted to be the one he flattered and kissed and touched.

She wanted to be the one he didn't resist. The *only* one.

Stupid, flawed heart.

JACK LEANED AGAINST the counter of a stuffy downtown dry cleaning shop while four tired-looking women glared at him from the other side. He couldn't really blame them for being mad. Diane had pitched a pretty disgusting fit just awhile ago, and had insisted that they all stop work and get out of her way so she could use their back room to change clothes.

They weren't happy at the rude interruption, and neither was he. But he was glad she was changing.

He hadn't liked seeing her in Abby's suit.

He could still remember the sweet agony of watching

Abby walk away from his car in that well-fitting skirt the day they'd gone to court. She'd been explosive in that skirt.

Diane seemed to fizzle out.

When a flurry of motion caught his attention, he realized the women were rushing toward their chores in the back, and Diane was strutting out in her own freshly cleaned clothes.

"Ready for our date?" she asked with a too bright smile.

"Ready."

And though he bought Diane the promised dinner a few minutes later, he hardly considered the next hour a date. It was more like the mutual consuming of food across a table. They ate, but they barely talked.

He knew Diane was probably insulted that he'd taken her out to a fast-food restaurant. She was accustomed to wine and crisp linen tablecloths, and she acted as if she didn't know what to do with a paper napkin.

It wasn't an intentional slight. The taco stand was just the only eating establishment he could find that was on the way back out to the farmhouse, and he wanted to get there as soon as possible to see Abby.

Anyway, he didn't care if Diane was mad. Today's escapade had been an eye-opener. Those long legs suddenly didn't seem stunning enough to make up for all of her rude behavior.

She'd embarrassed him in front of Abby. He'd embarrassed himself by letting his jealousy over Duke the banker affect his behavior.

Now he wanted Diane to finish nibbling at her confounded burrito so he could get back home and point her, her car and her too tight clothes back toward the city.

And then he wanted to go inside and see if Abby was still awake, so he could apologize.

ABBY PULLED OFF her bathing cap and heard the phone ring. She ignored it and stepped out of the tub to towel herself off. She'd finally gotten the twins to bed, and it was her time to relax. A hot bubble bath had worked wonders, but she still wasn't ready to deal with the world.

Diane's visit had turned a day of good, hard work into a day of hard-fought emotions. Abby needed this time alone.

The phone was still ringing.

As she pulled on her robe, she realized the belt was missing. She held the robe closed with one hand and made a mental note to get a phone line put in her room. Then she rushed downstairs. Of course, as soon as she got there she discovered that it wasn't her phone ringing at all. It was the one in Jack's office.

She started to head back upstairs, but the darn thing kept ringing. She'd counted at least twenty-three very insistent peals before she finally picked it up.

A woman with a childish sounding voice said she'd known someone would be home, and she asked for Jack.

Abby opened his desk drawer to grab a pen and paper. "He's not here now," she said. "May I take a message?"

"No, thanks," said the voice. "I'll talk to you."

Abby frowned into the phone. "Who is this?"

"Zuzu Clark."

It wasn't a name Abby recognized, but the caller seemed familiar with her. "And you said you'll talk to me?" she asked. "What about?"

"I was so sorry to have missed the two of you when you were in the city," Zuzu said. "I wanted to meet you."

"You wanted to meet me? Why?"

Abby's thoughts were completely scrambled by the madness of this phone call. Apparently, this Zuzu thought Abby had gone to Kansas City with Jack. And she'd wanted to be introduced.

"I was hoping we could be friends."

"You're kidding."

"No, I'm not," Zuzu said. "I always stay friends with my exes. I'd like to think that I'm gaining you as a girlfriend, instead of losing a boyfriend to you."

Abby smiled now. This Zuzu must be a part of Jack's harem, and she must think Abby was part of it, too. "But you haven't lost him to me," she soothed. "Jack and I aren't together."

"Really? He's still blind?"

"Uh...I don't think so," Abby said. "He's got his eyes wide open, and it isn't me he wants."

"But it is! Will you sit for a reading?"

"A reading?"

"I read tarot cards—and I'll do you free."

"No, thanks," Abby said with a chuckle. "But I'll tell Jack you called. Goodb—"

"Don't hang up," Zuzu interrupted. "I want to visit. How's the tenth of next month? I'll be in Topeka that afternoon to run a booth at the Juco Career Fair, but I could stop by beforehand. I'll have to do Mrs. Dimwitty's massage early, but then I—"

"Zuzu!" Abby interjected. "I'll tell him."

The sugary-voiced Zuzu sounded pleased. "I'll be there at ten, maybe nine-thirty," she said. "I'm so excited."

And with that, she hung up.

Abby scowled at the phone. In spite of the odd friendliness of this girlfriend, she felt as if the revolving door had whacked her again.

Here Jack was, out with Miss Sexpot, and Zuzu the Psychic was waiting in the wings. Except she wasn't very psychic, or she'd know that Jack wasn't interested in his roommate.

She'd find out the truth when she visited, and Abby wasn't going to stand around to watch her gush in gratitude. She usually had errands to run. She'd just take the twins that day, and leave early.

She climbed up the stairs and fell into bed. The bath had helped her relax, and she was too tired to stay awake long, but she did have one final waking thought.

The day of Zuzu's visit, she'd leave Rosie and Wyatt home with Jack. There was no need to allow him the run of the house with another girlfriend for a whole morning. The babies might put a perfect damper on Zuzu's enthusiasm.

If Abby was smart, she might be able to ram a wedge under Jack's spinning door.

Sabotaging his romantic involvements didn't fit in with her plan at all. She knew that.

But it might make her feel a whole lot better.

She knew that, too.

A BABY WAS CRYING.

Abby stumbled to the nursery, half-asleep. Rosie had pulled herself up to stand at the side of the crib, and was grinning at Abby in the darkness.

"Hey, you," Abby whispered. "Did you wake up to play, or do you need something?"

"Adaga," chirped the sweet girl with flippy curls.

"You think so, huh? You need to go to sleep or we'll wake your brother. It's not time to play."

"Deek."

"That's right. Sleep." Abby checked her diaper and discovered it was wet. After changing it in the dark, she laid Rosie down again.

Tiptoeing back to her own room, Abby crawled into bed a second before a huskier cry sounded. By the time she had jogged back to the nursery, Wyatt was getting up to full steam.

Rosie was sitting up in her crib and gurgling.

"You two are giving me fits tonight, aren't you?" Abby said as she rushed to Wyatt's crib to pick him up.

She'd begun to head for Rosie's crib again when Jack's voice came from the doorway.

"Do you need help in here?"

Abby looked up gratefully, and down just as quickly when she noticed Jack's eyes on her bare legs. She was back to her oversize shirt and skimpy panties. "Thanks," she mumbled. "I don't know what Rosie wants, but Wyatt is probably hungry. I recognize that howl."

"I'll feed Wyatt," he said. "You work your magic with Rosie." He pulled the baby boy from her arms, brushing his fingers against her breast in the process.

Heat flooded her body. She didn't even attempt to speak, in case her lusty thoughts had somehow altered her voice. Nodding instead, she lifted Rosie from her crib and carried the chattery girl into her own room to grab her robe from the end of the bed.

She plopped Rosie in the middle of her mattress just long enough to pull on the garment. She'd ransacked her room earlier for the belt, but hadn't found it. Tugging the sides together, she glanced in the mirror to see if she was decent.

The image she saw was that of a woman with bright eyes and a glowing face, thinking hopelessly sinful thoughts. Abby scowled at herself, picked up Rosie and padded back out to the nursery.

"That looks better on you than it was supposed to," Jack said as she entered.

"Sorry about my state of undress," she muttered. "Guess I can't get used to having an adult roommate."

"I'm not complaining," he teased. "That robe was more for your modesty than mine."

Abby wrinkled her nose at his blatant flirting, and sat across from him to offer Rosie a bottle. "Now there's some typical playboy behavior," she said. "You go out with one woman, and a few hours later you're ready to flirt with another. Aren't you ever tired of the game?"

"Was I flirting?" he asked, grinning.

"Humph," Abby snorted.

And tried to ignore him.

Jack set Wyatt's empty bottle on the floor beside him and patted the baby's back. "I know Diane was difficult today and I'm sorry," he said, whispering now. "She likes to be in charge."

"I survived."

"You didn't deserve it, but don't take it personally. She's always been sort of stiff with women."

"If you know that, why do you date her?" Abby asked, whispering now, too. The babies were both looking droopy.

"I have no idea. I suppose she's just another rotten apple, but I didn't realize that until tonight."

Abby stifled a laugh as she lifted Rosie to burp her. "Diane's not an apple at all."

"She's not?"

"She's a potato head."

Jack's burst of laughter sent Wyatt into giggles, too. "A potato head. Why?"

"Shh!" Abby said, tittering.

When he kept staring at her expectantly, she explained quietly, "In Diane's natural state, she's starchy. She softens with heat, but even then she's just a great big blob of blather. She needs things added to be truly good."

Jack seemed ready to explode with laughter.

Abby gave him a dramatic look and put a finger to her lips. Then she tiptoed to the crib with Rosie. As she laid her down, she pointed to Wyatt's crib.

Jack put the boy down, and they hurried into the hall.

As Abby shut the nursery door, she whispered, "If we get them started laughing, they'll keep us awake all night."

Jack stood three feet away, on the landing. "Don't worry. I was following your train of thought."

She couldn't help it; that train of hers chugged right through her bedroom door, with Jack attached like a caboose.

She wanted him.

"Are you following it now?" she asked.

"No. What are you thinking?"

She wished she could tell him the truth. "The last group of peaches will be ready for picking in about a week," she said with a sigh. "Be prepared to share the farm with a few extra bodies on afternoons and weekends, for a while."

Jack leaned against the wall, looking wide-awake. "Let me know if I can help."

Again Abby's alter ego thought of a few ways he could help. She felt her body react to the thought, and crossed her arms in front of her chest. "Sure," she said.

"Who will be here?"

Abby leaned against the door to her room. "We hire

a small crew,'' she explained. ''Mostly kids from neigh-boring farms who pitch in for extra spending money.''

''What about your Duke fellow? Will he be hanging around?''

''Duke?''

''The banker,'' Jack said with a frown. ''Your date?''

''Oh! You mean Dwight.''

Jack's face grew darker. ''I thought his name was Duke.''

''No.'' She shook her head, and the movement put enough pressure on the door to release the latch. The door drifted open. Abby caught her balance and looked behind her. Her bed seemed quite inviting with the covers strewn about.

It beckoned her, telling her to risk chugging that train right into the station.

''No, he's not Duke? Or, no, he won't be helping?''

When Abby turned back around, she realized Jack had moved forward a few steps. He was eyeing the bed, too. ''Dwight won't be here,'' she squeaked. ''I don't think he ever gets his hands dirty.''

Jack stepped even closer and said, ''You sound as if you don't like him.''

His words were harmless, but his voice was sort of growly. He was close enough now that she could reach out and untie the belt to his robe, if she was so inclined.

She closed her eyes and tried to remember the conver-sation. It had been something about the dweeb banker.

Oh. Did she like him?

''He's probably a genius accountant, but he can't figure out women very well,'' she said, and opened her eyes.

Jack's expression was turbulent, and he stared at her mouth and stepped close enough to kiss her.

And then he did. And she didn't stop him.

That old train blew its whistle and started chugging. Abby didn't know whether he was pushing her to the bed or she was pulling, but within seconds the back of her legs hit her mattress and she fell onto it, bringing him down with her.

Never once did their mouths break apart to breathe, or nibble, or say anything at all crazy or sensible.

Such as "Stop."

Someone slid a hand between their bodies to pull Jack's belt loose, and his robe practically fell off his shoulders.

Hers fell off, too. Of course it would, without a belt.

Her T-shirt was more secure, but that didn't keep his hands from touching her breasts with a gentleness that made her shiver.

Finally, he backed his head away for a second, allowing them both to gasp for air.

Then he bent down to lick her breast through the thin cotton fabric of her shirt. She stared down at the wet spot, and felt that crazy need spiral through her soul.

At the very instant she needed to feel his mouth against her bare flesh, her shirt flew off her head, propelled by her spellbound arms.

He paused, watching her movements, then homed back in on her mouth while bringing a thumb to each nipple. Abby met his tongue with thrusts just as heated, and she placed her hand flat against his belly and slid it downward.

He was hot and smooth, rigid and ready. She wanted to experience him in every way. First, however, she wanted to feel him against her. Using her free hand to coax him closer, she wrapped her legs around his body.

They fit together as perfectly as sun and shadow. She

sighed against his mouth, accepted his hardness against her hollows.

Still kissing.

Still caressing.

Still wanting more.

Until she remembered.

Then she brought her hands up to his chest and used every ounce of her strength to shove him off.

And got out of the bed, hurrying to the door. She could still feel his burning heat against her body when she was two steps down the stairs.

She'd had to get away. The overpowering need he provoked was stronger than anything she'd experienced before. It stunned her, in much the same way she'd been stunned the first time she was stung by a hornet.

She'd been only six years old, and helping her father in the flower shop, but she could remember wanting to concentrate on the sting for a minute, to get a handle on the feeling.

Now, the sting of her wanting was just as powerful. She knew she'd remember this ache just as clearly.

By the time Jack caught up to her, she was standing downstairs in the living room, looking out the window at the blackness of a cloud-covered night in the country.

"Man, I'm sorry," he said softly when he reached her side. He stood behind her, not touching her.

"Me, too," she answered, without looking at him.

"We really can't do that," he said, sounding uncertain.

She turned to look at him then. "I know."

Her eyes slid down a long, strong and splendid torso. The gray flannel boxers did little to conceal the desire he was still feeling. Her eyes flew back up to his face.

"Jack?" she said.

His eyes jerked up from her naked body, too.

He blew out a shaky breath, closed his eyes and shook his head. Then he reached out one long, strong hand and jerked the floor-length curtain right off the rod.

He wrapped it around her body several times, quite carefully. He even went so far as to lift her arm and work the material underneath.

She shivered again.

These feelings were too confusing.

He was so tender, and she wanted him so much. She didn't want to remind herself that she couldn't *have* him.

He took the other end of the curtain and wrapped it around his waist, tucking the end into his boxers. Then he put his arm across her shoulder and drew her toward the sofa.

She nearly tripped over the trailing length of curtain, so fashioned it into a sort of a clumsy tail behind her. It made a swishing sound as she walked across the room, and she snickered. Only Abigail Briggs would find herself walking across her own living room in a curtain that a nearly naked man had folded around her body.

He didn't laugh at all. He just sat on the sofa, staring straight ahead. After a minute, he said, "We need to get this all out in the open."

"Okay," she said.

She couldn't stifle a giggle, despite her need. He didn't seem to notice that they were both enfolded in a plum jacquard curtain.

He seemed completely serious. "I want you, but I can't sleep with you."

She smothered another giggle. "I know."

"Sleeping together would be a mistake."

Now she laughed out loud. "A huge one."

He turned to look at her, and smiled when he noticed her laughing. But his smile was wry. "Maybe now that we've admitted that, we can work out some sort of arrangement.''

She stopping laughing. ''What kind of arrangement?''

''Let's agree to be friends,'' he said, still serious. ''Surely two adults who are aware of the complications of an ongoing sexual relationship can have enough willpower to resist.''

''Surely.''

''Especially now that we're both admitting the problem.''

''You would think so, wouldn't you?''

''So, we're attracted to one another. We can't act on it.''

She shook her head. ''Uh-uh.''

''Tomorrow morning when we get up, we'll both know we're just going to be friends and nothing else.''

''Fine,'' she said.

When he didn't say anything else, she figured the matter was settled. ''I'll see you in the morning,'' she said. She gathered the curtain around her and stood.

And frowned.

Should she jerk the curtain panel off him, or just make a run for it?

The absurdity of the situation hit her with such force that she had to sit back down, she was laughing so hard.

''Why do you keep laughing?''

''Oh, no reason,'' she said, with as much dignity as she could muster. ''But there is a problem.''

''What?''

''How do we retreat to our separate quarters?''

He glared at the wad of curtain she had balled up in her fist, and then followed the end of it all the way to where the end was tucked in his underpants.

His laughter was loud and uncontrolled. And she just grinned as she watched him.

When he finally calmed down enough to talk, he shook his head and lifted an eyebrow. "Get ready," he said with a barely stifled snort. "We're going to count to three and run."

Within seconds, the curtain swished to the floor between them as they both let go and turned to run. Abby caught a glimpse of Jack's fine-looking backside as she made her way up the stairs, and she smiled at the memory.

But as she paused on the landing to catch her breath, she frowned, wondering how her gleefulness could change so rapidly to regret.

Chapter Nine

What is that diabolical racket?

Jack tried stuffing his pillow over his head to drown out the noise and nab a few more minutes of sleep. Wasn't it the middle of the night? Who would be talking? And whoever it was, why were they doing it outside his window?

Eventually, he realized it wasn't the noise that was keeping him from drifting back into oblivion.

It was the questions.

Why was there a crowd standing outside his window, and wasn't that Abby's voice raised slightly above the others? What was happening?

As soon as some lucidity flowed to his brain, he rolled across the bed to peek through the blinds. A small group was gathered at the opening in the woods that led to the orchards, and Abby was standing in front of them with a baby on each hip.

Apparently, the peaches were ready now. At the crack of dawn. He just couldn't get used to these country mornings, which always seemed to start several hours too early.

Groaning, he went to his closet to grab some clothes and throw them on. He'd told Abby he wanted to help with the harvest. From the look of things, she could use a baby-sitter about now.

Heading out the back door, he strode quickly to her side, waited until she paused between sentences, and then held out his arms for the babies. "You could have knocked on my door to get me up," he said quietly.

She looked at him from under fluttering lashes, handed over the twins and immediately began to address her tired-looking group again.

As he returned to the house, he decided it was lucky that the harvest had begun. Even though there were six extra helpers out there, handpicking the peaches would require time and care.

Both he and Abby would have to add a few responsibilities to their load, which should make his efforts to stay away from her a little easier.

He dragged the high chairs into his office, buckled a baby in each one and dropped a handful of crunchy oat cereal and a couple of toys on each tray.

Then he sat at his computer desk and stared out the window at Abby.

In fact, despite his efforts to work and take extra shifts with the twins, he spent most of the day watching her. Somehow she managed to organize the workers and tend to the greenhouse, and still had the energy to offer him an occasional hand with baby-care duties.

He'd never seen a woman work harder. She handled the group of teenagers with a gracious manner and decisive command, making them glad to be working for her. Jack knew some business managers who never accomplished that feat.

His respect for her grew with every moment. And with every second, his body let him know that he was in for a troublesome year.

The lack of desire that had plagued him in Kansas City—making him wonder if he was too old to care about sex—was completely remedied by watching her lithe little body moving around the house and yard.

But still, the reasons for resisting remained. He couldn't hurt Abby by beginning a casual romance with her, and she'd admitted herself she knew that would be a mistake.

It helped that there was a constant stream of people coming in and out of the house. The kids made frequent use of the kitchen and bathroom facilities, and amazingly, Abby was able to keep up with their demands for food and drinks—and attention.

On Monday morning, he got up a few minutes after the teenagers usually arrived, and was surprised to find Abby sitting at the kitchen table alone. "Where's your crew?"

"School," she said, as she removed a slice of bread from a bagged loaf on the table. "They'll come later this afternoon, and work until seven."

Jack had been repeating the mantra that the peach harvest was a lucky break, so it didn't make sense to feel lucky that he had Abby and the twins to himself again. But he did.

He stepped over to the coffeepot to pour himself a cup, and refilled Abby's before he sat across from her and watched her take a bite of the bread. "That's what superwoman eats for breakfast?"

"Superwoman?"

He smiled. "Able to handle infant twins, fledgling ducks, six teenagers and a greenhouse full of plants without a single break. Doesn't require a decent amount of sleep, and subsists on next to nothing."

He directed a wry look toward the bread.

She shrugged. "I didn't have the energy to make anything requiring dishes this morning. Besides, Rosie and Wyatt should wake up any minute."

He let his gaze linger on her face. She hadn't seemed to appreciate his humor at all, and her eyes looked tired. The extra work must be catching up with her.

As if on cue, an enthusiastic bawl sounded from upstairs. Abby started to spring up, but he put his hand on her shoulder to push her back down. "Eat your bread. I'll bring them down."

At lunchtime, he had a surprise waiting for her when she brought the twins into the kitchen. It was only a roast beef sandwich, but it was a vast improvement over her breakfast.

Her appreciation was apparent in her smile, and by the time they'd worked together to get the babies fed and the mess cleaned up, he'd teased her to giggles again.

That night, when he heard one of the twins crying, he listened for a minute, hoping Abby could handle it alone. But also praying that another little voice would join in so she'd need help.

After the hushing of the first wail stretched into a long span of silence, he decided to go up there, anyway. But by the time he'd donned his robe and made his way to the foot of the stairs, all noises had ceased and both upstairs doors were tightly closed.

He was relieved. And crushed.

He'd wanted to talk to her. He'd wanted more than that. His body was beginning to react to a baby's cry as if it was the most cunning of aphrodisiacs.

But he loped back to his bed, deciding to force himself to work through a program in his head. He stared at the ceiling in a quiet house, wrestling with his will.

Using every ounce of it to keep from bounding upstairs

again to beg Abby for a completely different arrangement.

He was just congratulating himself on his phenomenal self-restraint when he heard the opening of a door, followed by footsteps. Of course he had to check that out.

He started up the stairs as Abby was coming down.

She didn't seem at all surprised to see him. She stopped when they met, halfway up and halfway down, and smiled a greeting. Then she toyed with the bottom edge of her T-shirt and stared at his chest.

He couldn't find his voice. After an eternity of standing in the middle of the stairs, she seemed to wobble. He stepped closer to grab her elbow, but his hand slid instead to her waist.

It was a sensuous waist—a perfect combination of firm and curvy. It felt so good under his fingertips that he kept them there even after she'd regained her balance.

He slid his hand up her rib cage a few inches, and watched her eyes spark when his knuckle grazed against the base of a very tempting breast. Then he let it slip down along her curves again, to a very erotic hipbone, and watched her bite her lip. He stepped closer.

"Were you coming upstairs for something?" she asked.

He kept his hand resting lightly against her waist. "I heard a noise," he said.

"Oh."

"Were you coming down for something?"

The pretty pink color flowed across her freckled cheeks. "Yes, um…a glass of milk?"

"Oh." He let go of her waist and followed her down to the kitchen, leaning against the counter as she poured her milk. "Things are going well with this new arrangement," he said, just to make conversation.

''Sure they are,'' she agreed. Then she scooped her hair behind her ears, said good-night and left the room.

The full glass of milk was still sitting on the counter.

BY THURSDAY EVENING, the harvest was nearly complete, and Abby was still a whirlwind of activity. She alternated between the orchards, where she kept tabs on the crew, and the kitchen, where she stirred bubbling kettles of delicious smelling concoctions.

She was so busy that she'd broken down and sent one of the teenage girls upstairs to entertain the twins in the nursery.

Jack was in his office, attempting to work, when he heard a shout, followed by so much commotion he couldn't imagine what sort of atrocity had happened.

The sound came from the greenhouse. He ran out there with his heart pounding, wondering if some stranger had invaded the farmhouse to hurt Abby.

But she was unharmed and alone, except for the ducks. With wild arm movements, she was shooing them along a path in the greenhouse, scolding them as they flapped out of her reach.

The cause of their disgrace was evident when Jack noticed a long green stem drooping from the bill of the young female. Both ducks were squawking in disapproval at being treated so indelicately. As Jack stepped into their path to block their escape, he realized that several pots were overturned. Dirt and greenery carpeted the pathway.

''Abby, what happened?''

''What do you mean, what happened? Those ducks of yours decided to have my ornamental grasses for a snack.''

Jack surveyed the greenhouse. Except for a single low

shelf empty of pots, most of the plant life was intact. "Sorry," he offered, trying to hide a smile.

Abby put her hands on her hips and glared at him. "Well, are you just going to stand there grinning, or are you going to help?"

"What can I do?"

She pointed to the ducks, which were now hovering in a corner, squabbling over the tendril. "Start by cornering those creatures and putting them in the garage," she said. "It's time for them to make a life outside."

He snatched up the ducks and carried them out, smiling all the way. Everything Abby did, she did with spirit. Indignation added a blush to her cheeks and a fire to her eyes, making her look…red-hot.

Sighing, he found a deep box for the ducks and set up temporary holding quarters beside his car. After equipping it with food and water, he returned to the greenhouse. By that time, Abby had picked most of the pots back up off the floor and was beginning to sort through the tangle of plants.

"Need help?" he asked, and winced when a shock of sexual awareness tore through him. Somehow those two words had taken on an extra meaning when he said them to Abby.

She didn't seem to notice, though. Without looking up, she said, "Start by filling these pots three-quarters full with new soil from the bag near my workstation. I'll take it from there."

Jack carried pots to the table and filled each, leaving them for her to finish. Silently, Abby repaired most of the damage and returned the pots to their shelf.

Meanwhile, Jack found a broom and began to sweep up the debris. "Hope they didn't create too much calamity."

"Now that things are in order, I realize they didn't," she said, snickering. "When I walked in, it looked as if they'd demolished an entire season's crop." Her smile turned to a chuckle. "Wouldn't you have loved to see them having their little duck party?"

And with that, Abby bent over her workbench with her hand on her belly, laughing heartily at the thought.

Jack could only watch. The one thing more intriguing than the flash in her eyes when she was mad was the twinkle there when she was laughing.

He was still admiring it when she pulled off her gloves, strode to the French doors and peered back over her shoulder at him. "Are you planning to help?"

"Absolutely," he said, following her over to pull open the door and wait for her to go through. "Help with what?"

She rolled her eyes as she passed. "You did put the ducks in the garage, right?"

"Yes."

"Then we need to move them, unless you want the elegant charcoal finish on your hot-as-you-know-what new car to get covered."

"With...?"

"Duck muck."

Within minutes, he was walking out to the pond beside Abby, each of them carrying a duck. Abby stopped at the side nearest the shelter and nudged the female into the water. As it swam off, she said, "Welcome to your new home, Calamity Duck."

Jack smiled. "What's this one's name?"

"I don't know," Abby said, tilting her head. "What do you think?"

"Since they work as a team, what about Wild Bill?"

''Wild Bill and Calamity. That's perfect,'' she pronounced. ''See if he'll follow her.''

Jack put the male down at the edge of the water. Sure
enough, the drake swam along after his companion, seeming confident in his new surroundings.

Jack and Abby stood side by side, watching as the
ducks waddled onto their island and circled around the
shelter Paige had built. When the pair began to forage at
water's edge, Jack knew they would adapt.

The mellow afternoon sunshine provided the ducks
with a peaceful initiation to the outdoors.

Standing out here with Abby didn't seem to be a bad
way for a man to end the day, either. Jack was surprised
at how much he was enjoying his time in the country. At
some point he'd stopped thinking of the house as a mon-
strosity, and started thinking of it as home.

That thought was not only incorrect, it was dangerous.
This was Abby's home. Eventually he had to leave her,
and the house, and Rosie. But living here was anything
but dull.

He had an urge to take hold of Abby's hand—an urge
he throttled, of course. Exactly the way he had throttled
most of his impulses when he was around her.

They were far too dangerous.

ABBY SAT AT THE END of a long table in a bustling corner
of Topeka's most popular pizza place, and grinned at the
jovial camaraderie of her companions. The three teenagers—half of her harvest crew—had all grown up together
and were good friends. The two blond boys were
Sharon's sons, and the brunette girl lived on the ranch
down the road.

Eating dinner together in town was a rare treat and a
nice gesture. And hadn't been Abby's idea.

Just before they'd left the orchard this afternoon, Jack had walked out among the last baskets of peaches and offered to treat every one of the crew to dinner. And since Abby had heard the offer at the same time as everyone else, her protests had been drowned out by the enthusiasm of six hungry teenagers.

She'd put her hands on her hips and glared at him, but that had only provoked a triumphant grin. He'd known what he was doing when he mentioned it in front of those kids.

Later, as he'd helped her cart the peaches to the kitchen, he had anticipated her arguments and countered them before she had a chance to voice them. He'd said that the crew had worked hard and deserved a party. He'd pointed out that Abby's mother had been thrilled when he asked her to baby-sit the twins for the night. And he'd reminded Abby that he owned the orchard and had a right to treat everyone to dinner. She'd been left speechless.

Now he walked across the restaurant behind the rest of the crew, and slid into the chair beside her. "That hot-as-you-know-what new car of mine is already proving its practicality," he said with a wink as the other teenagers found seats around the table. "I had room for three long-legged farm hands, and I still could've squeezed in a few computers and a crate or two of formula."

"You don't get to gloat about the car, since it was my idea," Abby retorted, wrinkling her nose at his teasing.

He gave her a bright-eyed look that traveled from the top of her head all the way down to somewhere in the vicinity of her chest. And then he cleared his throat and met her eyes.

"And it was a very good idea," he said.

Then he turned to their chattering dinner guests and

bellowed, "What kind of pizza are you people planning to devour?"

The next few minutes were filled with boisterous declarations of topping preferences, a few dissenting groans, some jostling and a general air of chaos as the six teenagers tried to reach a consensus.

Abby smiled as she watched, but her thoughts were about four miles away, back at the farmhouse. Recalling the night she'd come close to succumbing to Jack. Or rather, to her own silly desires.

She'd thrown herself completely into her work over the past couple of weeks, trying to forget that night and the way she'd felt with her body wrapped around his.

She remembered it all too well.

The hard work had added a dull ache to her muscles, and had helped her pass the time, but it hadn't taken away the memory. And ever since that odd discussion on the sofa, she'd been trying to get a handle on her emotions.

Being friendly with him was a lot riskier than being contrary, but she couldn't go back to her much safer plan now. Heaven help her, she didn't want to go back.

When the pizza choices were finally made, Jack waved the waitress over to their table, and Abby pulled herself back to the present.

She listened while Jack gave the order, and was surprised by the sober efficiency of the waitress as she took it. The young woman didn't seem to notice how handsome Jack looked in his button-down shirt and khakis, and the only smile she directed toward anyone was a grinning "hello" to one of the teenagers, who claimed he went to school with her younger brother.

Jack's behavior was even more surprising. He spoke seriously to the waitress, and only smiled when he turned to Abby to ask her opinion about drinks.

After Abby suggested that they buy several pitchers of soda, the waitress hustled away to prepare their order, and the teenagers started talking about the upcoming high school football season. There was no way to break into their excited chatter about bus trips, past victories and the homecoming dance.

For all practical purposes, they had left her alone with Jack. "I hope you don't mind pizza again," he said softly.

She shrugged. "It's what they wanted, and it's their party."

"But it's yours, too," he said, grabbing her hand under the table to squeeze it. "You worked hard."

"Thanks," she said, and waited for him to remove his hand. But he left it there on her lap, and his thumb started rubbing against the flesh of her palm. Her throat went dry.

"Someday I'd like to take you to a nicer restaurant," he said, and he kept those attentive eyes right on hers for an impossibly long time.

She pulled her hand away. "That's not necessary."

He lifted an eyebrow and brought his hand up to rub his chin. "But it is, to thank you for all you do," he said, and still he kept gazing. It made her squirm.

When she noticed the waitress walking across the restaurant with a trayful of pitchers and glasses, she jumped up and snatched the tray, insisting that she wanted to pour drinks for her guests.

It bought her five minutes to get her bearings. By the time she sat back down beside Jack, Abby was determined to change the subject. "Do you miss the city?"

"Not really," he answered, surprising her. "I hit all my old party spots last time I was there, but it wasn't the same. I must be getting old."

She laughed. "Then I must have been crotchety in my senior year of college," she said. "Tim used to go to bars when we were married, but I never felt comfortable."

"Let me guess," Jack said with a grin. "You were acing your botany exams, feeding the hungry and working as a poster child for the rewards of serious study."

"Are you making fun of me?"

"Absolutely not," he said quickly. "I admire you for finishing a degree when you were a newlywed."

"It wasn't all that admirable." She rolled her eyes. "Although Tim would argue this point, I practically let my life revolve around him."

"Abigail Briggs, otherwise known as superwoman, let her life revolve around a man? I can't believe it."

She still couldn't believe it, either.

She sighed and looked down at her hands, which she'd folded in her lap. "I worked weekends, studied every day and waited for him to get home so I could fill some little pocket of my life with fun."

Jack touched her shoulder, causing her to look up again.

"You sat at home while your husband went out?"

"Sounds pathetic, doesn't it?"

"Sounds saintly," he argued. "Why did you marry him?"

Abby shook her head. "He was my first serious boyfriend. I think young girls attach all sorts of imagined sentiments to their first relationship. I thought we were in love."

"Weren't you?" Jack asked, looking disturbed.

"He said he loved me before we were married. Later, he said it had only been lust, and that wives were boring by definition. He told me to get over it."

"Maybe I'm the wrong person to say this, Abby, but your ex-husband sounds like a snake."

"You think so?" she asked, smiling. Now that she knew Jack better, she knew the comparisons between the two men were few. Tim had been a snake, and Jack was anything but.

"Absolutely," he said, and frowned into her eyes.

She could tell he wanted to say something else, but his comment was interrupted by the arrival of four large pizzas.

By the time the crew had all scuttled around the table to claim a slice or two of the kind they wanted, the conversation was lost.

As they ate and talked to their dinner companions, Abby watched Jack. He was kind and amiable as he asked about their schools and families and interests, and he listened intently when anyone else was speaking.

Several times he even pointed out something he admired about Abby. To all those teenagers and her.

He was definitely not a snake.

The friendly arrangement he had suggested on that sofa destroyed the very intent of her plan. She could hardly bore him into leaving if he was enjoying himself.

But he'd been unpredictably tenacious about sticking around, anyway. In spite of her best efforts, he would likely stay a year, as Brian had requested.

And in a small way, the new arrangement made things easier. Since she knew he was resisting, too, she didn't have to work so hard to repel him. And as long as they kept things simple, her pride would be intact when he left.

Then, she knew, she'd have to deal with the issue of Wyatt. Then she'd argue her case for keeping both twins.

And then, if she had any luck at all, Jack would leave only with some sweet, private piece of her heart.

"THAT TRUCK OF YOURS must have a race car engine under its hood," Jack said as he came through the kitchen after dropping off his carload of passengers. Abby had already changed out of the sexy flowered dress she'd worn to dinner, and was back to her customary jeans and T-shirt.

She grinned at his comment, but didn't turn from her spot near the sink. "Well, I only had two stops to make," she said. "You had three, all over the countryside."

He halted in the middle of the room when he realized what she was doing—peeling peaches. At ten o'clock at night, after a frenzied teenage pizza party and a hard day's work before that, she was peeling a humongous pile of peaches. "Don't you ever rest?" he asked.

"Not during the harvest," she said with a shake of her head. "I still have a good week's work ahead of me."

Her movement made that long braid sway against her back, sending his eyes down to its end. It didn't matter that she was wearing the jeans again, she was ravishing.

He wanted to remove her hair band and spread those locks out around her bare shoulders. He wanted to grip his hands around that firm little tush. He wanted all his *wanting* to be all right.

But it wasn't.

He'd agreed they were to be just friends.

He coughed, and walked over to lean against the counter beside her and watch. Her movements were precise and quick as she peeled each peach and tossed it into a kettle.

He frowned. He'd thought the party tonight would be

a nice reward for her, but apparently he'd only put her further behind. "What do you have left to do?" he asked.

Her hands were covered in peach juice, so she brought her arm up to swipe her bangs out of her eyes with the back of her wrist, and sighed when they fell back across her face.

"Sharon said she'd help me in the kitchen this week," Abby said. "We'll finish the preserves and prepare the baskets. I'll start delivering them by this weekend."

"I had no idea," he said, watching her try to blink the hair off her eyelashes. "I thought when the harvest was done, you just sold the fruit."

"This orchard is too small to compete with the big growers in milder climates."

She grabbed a peach from the pile, peeled it quickly, tossed it the kettle and grabbed another. Her movements were nearly hypnotic. "We profit by processing the goods and marketing them in a package," she said, with a quick glance at him.

"Hmm." He reached a thumb to her chin to pull her face toward his, and tucked an offending wisp of hair behind her ears.

When he finished, he realized she was only about three inches away. He could practically feel the hot discomfort burning on her face. He was pretty hot, too. But not from embarrassment.

He backed up immediately. "Thanks for taking time out to go to dinner with us," he said to her braid as she returned to her chore.

When she didn't respond, he left the kitchen.

He went to his office and picked up a stack of new orders. He knew he should try to work. The twins were still at Abby's parents' house, and he had nothing better to do.

But something Abby had said at dinner was still bothering him. She was so admirable. Hardworking, nurturing and as sexy as a whispered sigh.

It was hard to believe her ex-husband hadn't known what a treasure she was. Just knowing she'd suffered at the hands of that clod made Jack angry. He needed her to know that he wasn't in the same class as Tim.

Besides his mother, he'd never once told a woman he loved her. He always made sure, by the end of the first date, that his lady friends knew he wasn't a forever man.

Before Jack knew it, his feet had propelled him back to the kitchen doorway. He stood watching Abby work for a minute, and finally cleared his throat.

She whirled around with a startled expression, and chuckled when she saw him.

"There's something I need to tell you," he said.

She nodded emphatically. "Me, too. In fact, I was about to come looking for you."

He frowned. "You go first."

She rinsed her hands under the faucet, wiped them on a tea towel and relaxed against the counter. "I don't know if I remembered to thank you for dinner. The break was actually pretty welcome."

She smiled, and a single dimple danced charmingly across one cheek. It caught his attention just as fully as her braid had awhile before. Suddenly, every inch of his body was brimming with the knowledge that they were alone in the house. He lost his breath.

Abby seemed to be aware of that fact, too. She pushed away from the counter and stood a little straighter, causing her breasts to jut against the fabric of her shirt. When she put her hands on her hips, he could see the pucker of her nipples from all the way across the room.

''You're welcome,'' he whispered belatedly, and forced his eyes up.

She wasn't smiling, and a tiny frown wrinkled her brow as she waited for him to talk.

He coughed again. ''Remember when we were talking about your ex-husband at dinner?''

''Of course.''

''He had no right to treat you that way.''

She chuckled again and folded her arms in front of her. ''You don't have to convince me of that.''

Jack frowned as he struggled to make his point clear. ''He should have realized you were something special.''

''Thanks,'' she said, just before she turned her pink-and-freckly face back to her peaches.

She'd dismissed him again, but he didn't feel as if he'd said what he wanted to say. He rubbed his chin and stared at her braid again. Something felt odd about this whole situation. He was a man who was rarely at a loss for words, but he sure was now.

He loped past his office and down the hall to the bathroom to shower and shave. Abby would probably be up at dawn, working, and maybe he could help.

Besides, he knew he wouldn't get anything done tonight. He was bothered even more than before. He'd said words that were soothing, just as he had intended.

For some reason, however, he kept feeling as if he'd barely scratched the surface.

Chapter Ten

"It was generous of you to take the boys out for pizza last weekend," Sharon said from across the kitchen, where she was helping Abby with the seemingly endless chore of canning fruits while the twins napped upstairs.

Jack finished tightening a screw on the leg of Wyatt's high chair, and stood up. "Oh, that was nothing," he said. "I just thought a party was appropriate after a harvest."

Sharon turned away from the counter to offer her trademark smile. "You're right about that," she said. "That's why the community throws an annual harvest party. But your separate pizza feast for the kids was generous."

Jack moved his eyes to Abby, who seemed oblivious to the conversation as she peered into a pot on the stove.

"There's another party?" he asked. "Why don't I know about it?"

"Oh!" Sharon's eyes grew round and flew to Abby, too. She tapped Abby's shoulder, and as soon as she had her attention, shrugged and made a face. Abby shrugged back.

It seemed to be some secret language for country women.

Then Sharon looked across at him again. "It's Saturday night at seven,'' she said. ''And I guess you're invited. Okay, Abby?''

''Sure, he can go,'' Abby said, seeming unconcerned as she returned her attention to the bubbling pot.

''You sound as if you're not going,'' Sharon said.

''I'm not.''

''Why not?'' Jack interjected. He returned the screwdriver to its pantry shelf and walked over to stand near the two women, waiting for Abby's answer.

''I never go.''

''Well, you're going this year, even if we have to drag you. Right, Jack?'' This was from Sharon again.

''I'm not going,'' Abby repeated.

Now Sharon started using that strange sign language on him. She looked directly at him, smiled that huge smile and winked.

And the stranger thing was, he got it. They would wait a while, develop a stronger argument and try again.

He nodded.

Since the twins were still asleep, he knew he should use the time to work. He also knew it was highly unlikely that he'd get anything done, so he looked at Abby's profile and asked if there was anything else he could do to help.

That got both the women's attention. Sharon did her megawatt smile thing, and Abby turned completely around to tilt her head at him.

He smiled, too, and waited. Surely, with all that was left to do, there was something more that needed a man's touch.

Abby joined in the smiling party and pointed to the kitchen table. It was set up with a pile of wicker baskets, a tangle of navy-blue ribbons bedecked with sunflowers, and stacks and stacks of chubby mason jars. Apple Man's Acres, read the label on each one.

"You can help assemble baskets," Abby said, sliding into a chair and patting the one beside her. "Sit."

He scowled at the table. "What?"

"That's right…we're decorating baskets. I make peach jelly, apple butter, strawberry preserves and candied pears. We arrange the jars in these baskets and sell them."

"You want me to put jars in baskets and tie ribbons?"

"Absolutely. If I had to do this alone, I'd never get done," she explained. "Paige and I used to have a great time with this phase of the process."

Jack shrugged as he sat down. "I'll help," he said. "But only if I get to taste it before I devote time to packaging it. I won't promote shoddy products."

Abby's jaw dropped. "These are superb, but you can judge for yourself." She started to get up, but Sharon was already charging across the room, so she sat back down.

As discreetly as the most professional of waitresses, Sharon came to the table bearing a tray loaded with four open jars and a pile of toast and crackers.

"I saw that one coming," she said, and then slipped back over to man the stove.

Jack bit into a toast point slathered with peaches. Its fresh, sweet taste was superb, exactly as promised. As he chewed, he watched Abby take a basket from the pile and fill it with blue and yellow corrugated confetti. Then, taking a jar from each of the stacks surrounding the table, she plunked them inside. Finally, she tied a ribbon around the whole thing and set it in a box on the floor.

"You get that?" she asked, and giggled when Jack rolled his eyes.

He began to follow her lead, frowning in concentration as he tried to tie his ribbon into a bow as perfect as hers. "This whole operation has been amazing," he said. "And this is an ingenious marketing tool."

"I figured a big-city boy would find all this a bit too rustic," Abby said as she finished her second basket and placed it in the box.

Jack was still fumbling with the first ribbon, and he shook his head. "When I was a kid, we lived in the country for an entire year while my mom was involved with a farm hand. I'd forgotten how much I loved it."

"I always wanted to live out here," Abby said as she started another basket. "When we were kids, Paige and I would gather our stuffed animals around us and pretend we were running a farm."

"I seem to remember pretending I had a dog," Jack said as he continued to battle the ornery ribbon. "We moved around so much I never had a pet, but I begged for a puppy twice every year—just before Christmas— and just before my birthday."

Abby pulled his basket away and tied a perfect bow before sliding it back to him. "Don't you dare go out and buy a dog, Jack Kimball."

"No. I won't do that," Jack said, disappointed that she'd squelched his idea. Then he brightened. "We could all go to the pound together and adopt one." He pulled another basket from the pile and threw a handful of filler inside.

"And how would we divvy up this pup when you leave?" she asked in a sober voice that was sweetly familiar.

He didn't answer, and he stopped working for a minute to look at her face.

He didn't want to leave.

Frowning, he watched her freckled hands move nimbly from task to task. Just barely, he shook his head.

The bar hopping and woman juggling that had been getting old for a while now held no lingering allure, and neither did the prime downtown apartment he had once coveted.

He wanted to stay here on the farm with Abby. He wanted to try a real relationship.

That was what had been bugging him.

He reached across the table for a jar of peaches and nestled it carefully in the basket. He wanted to help her fill these baskets again next fall, and probably the year after that.

He could even imagine the two of them sitting across this same table in five years, chatting about the twins' school days and sampling the year's harvest.

He glanced at Abby's face again. A tiny crease marred her brow as she concentrated, but she seemed unaware of the changes occurring across the table from her.

Of course she'd be unaware.

He separated three more jars from their stacks and slid them sluggishly across the oak surface as he struggled to process a bombardment of feelings. He winced at the grating of glass against wood, then started at a clanging of metal from across the room.

Sharon had lifted a pot lid and returned it clumsily. He'd forgotten they had company.

He arranged the remaining jars in the basket and rubbed his chin as he stared at them. He'd have to wait until he was alone with Abby, but then he'd admit his own proposed arrangement was a flop.

Just the possibility of sharing her bed at night sent a cannonball of anticipation rocketing through his body.

He sneaked another peek at her, wondering how to

approach the subject. Would she feel threatened by his news?

Probably, and he didn't want that.

He had to find the right words. He had to explain.

She was still working, so he tugged a single ribbon from the tangled mass and tried to tie a bow as perfect as hers.

His was crooked. He blinked a few times and bent closer to the ribbon, struggling again to make it neat. After three failed attempts, he slid the whole thing across to Abby with a pleading expression.

Chuckling softly, she tied the ribbon and put the finished basket in the box. Without planning it, they developed an assembly line of sorts.

Abby filled a basket with confetti, Jack put the bottles inside and she tied the bows. The work went faster, and the lack of conversation in the kitchen made the thoughts screaming through his head more bearable.

After the pile of baskets had eroded to a foothill, Jack said, "Since I'm part owner of this farm, I should have been told about this party."

"Well, you were," Abby said, glancing across to Sharon.

He looked at Sharon, too, who gave a slight nod as a go-ahead. This secret language was a piece of cake. "No, I mean by you," he said. "I think we should go together, in a show of cooperation between the owners of Apple Man's Acres."

Abby laughed. "But I'm not going, and you're not really an owner, anyway. You're more of a squatter."

"I'm no squatter, and I have papers to prove it," he said. "I want to attend this party. What do I have to do to get a date?"

"A date?"

He stopped working and crossed his arms in front of his chest. "I'd hate to invite one of *them*," he said. "I don't seem to care for apples or potatoes anymore."

She snickered, but kept working. A stack of partially finished baskets began to accumulate in front of him.

He touched her hand. "I'd rather escort a real person."

Abby's mouth smiled, but her eyes looked confused.

"You," he said.

She blinked a few times and said, "I can't go."

"Why not?"

He could practically see the gears turning in her head. Finally, she said, "I don't have anything to wear."

That was when Sharon leaped in. "You'll come shopping with me," she said. "I need a dress, too."

Abby shook her head. "I can't shop, I have to deliver these baskets."

"I'll help you," Jack and Sharon said, both at the same time.

BAMBOOZLEMENT! That's what it was.

Abby scowled as she made her way down the concrete steps of the cellar. For the past twenty minutes, Jack and Sharon had ganged up on her and practically forced her to say she'd go to that silly party.

And with Jack, to boot.

She was still scowling as she pulled the chain to light the damp, dark space. She hadn't been down here since this spring, but she knew Paige had stored some extra jars of preserves down here.

When the strawberry supply had run low upstairs, she had immediately offered to come down and get more, just to escape all that persuading. Very soon, she was going to have a chat with Sharon about loyalty between friends.

Metal shelves lined one long wall in the back, and

Abby went to rummage through the boxes stacked there. She was surprised when she encountered a couple of cartons of personal things.

After Paige died, Abby and her parents had sorted through her belongings. They'd donated much of it to charity, but they must have missed the boxes down here.

She pulled one of them down and opened the lid to look inside. Brilliant red and green Christmas balls and bright tinsel lay in a jumble inside. She smiled and returned the box to the shelf. She would always try to make holidays special, for Rosie and Wyatt. A few extra decorations would come in handy.

She pulled another box down and opened the lid. As soon as she saw what was inside, she sank to the floor.

Soft, sweet newborn clothes filled most of the box. She sat cross-legged and sifted through the contents with trembling fingers. On one side, there was a plastic bag containing several tiny silk headbands and a miniature bow tie, in cornflower blue. On the other side was a smaller bag containing the twins' hospital bands.

Paige had probably been smiling when she put this box on the shelf. She'd probably been thinking of that day in the future when she'd show her children the things they'd worn when they were just born. She must have already thought of some of the anecdotes she would tell, about what they were like as babies.

She must have been so happy, thinking about it all.

And now she was gone.

Abby sat on that cold, hard cellar floor and started quaking. When the tears appeared from nowhere, she didn't bother to wipe them away.

"Abby, do you need help carrying the boxes up?" Jack said from the top of the steps.

She knew he would come down here if she didn't answer, but she couldn't talk just yet. She closed her eyes, drew her arms around her middle and rocked. And let herself cry, really hard.

And let herself miss her sister, and all that was lost.

Within seconds, she felt Jack's fingers against her hair. He didn't speak, either, but sat down beside her, wrapped his arms around her and rocked with her for a long time. After a while, her tears started subsiding. Only then, did he whisper consoling words against her hair.

She turned, just slightly, to look at him, and realized his eyes were wet. That cosmopolitan man was crying, too—and she knew he'd just claimed another big chunk of her heart. She drew closer to kiss him for his kindness, and he kissed her back, very softly. His lips tasted salty.

They felt warm and vital and alive.

She couldn't pull away. She opened her mouth and kissed him the way she'd wanted to for a long time. She let the built-up longing take over, and swayed in pleasure at his eager response.

She felt his hands roam down her back, and let hers sculpt the firmness of his chest. When he dipped his tongue into her mouth, she met it eagerly.

He tugged her next to his heat.

She tugged him down to the floor.

The hard, cold concrete was strangely arousing against her back. His hard, hot body was definitely arousing against her front.

Their kisses grew bolder, and so did their hands. Before long, both of their T-shirts were gone.

Jack stopped kissing her and started running his palms over the peaks of her breasts. With soft touches, he teased her nipples until she squirmed, and he smiled at her moans.

She loved his tenderness, but she needed something

more elemental. She grabbed his hands and pressed them against her breasts, then inhaled a hissing breath when he moved her bra out of the way and swirled his tongue against her skin.

As his body settled on top of hers, the coldness of the floor seeped painfully into her muscles, but she didn't care. It suited her mood. She wanted more of his heat.

''I need you,'' she whispered, sliding a hand between them to grasp his arousal, leaving no doubt about what she wanted now.

He groaned and pulled her hand up to kiss it, then moved away to slide off the rest of his clothes. She trembled as she watched, wanting him to hurry back and warm her again with his vibrancy.

In the time he was gone, she hurried to undress, too, and was ready when he knelt beside her. As he covered her body with his, he kissed her once, hard, then backed up slightly to search her eyes. ''Are you sure, Abby?''

She nodded. She wouldn't run away this time.

Swiftly and completely, he filled her. She gasped and felt tears dampen her eyes again.

The intimacy was stronger than she remembered. The satisfaction was immediate and intense.

She closed her eyes, sending a few straggling tears down her cheeks as she began to rock with him, welcoming more of his comfort. Soothing more of his sorrow.

This was what she'd needed. To feel this deeply alive.

She moved her hips to his rhythm, clutching his back to keep him close, and never allowing him to slow. His roving kisses warmed her neck and lips, his hot puffs of breath batting against her skin with each growl of approval.

As if they were one, she quickened her pace with his through the sharpening sensations, until she couldn't see or hear or feel anything except the high, lingering comfort of release.

Then they lay hand in hand on the cellar floor, listening to their breathing slow and staring at the bare white light-bulb above them.

''Jack? Abby? You guys okay down there?''

''We're fine!'' Jack hollered, squeezing Abby's hand.

They bounded up together. Jack threw her shirt into her hands and pulled his over his head in practically the same movement. When she had her shirt on, he winked at her.

''I wouldn't bother you,'' Sharon hollered again, ''but the twins woke up a minute ago, and I couldn't handle both of them and the stove.''

''Be up in a minute,'' Abby shouted, responding to Jack with a roll of her eyes and an embarrassed grimace.

He chuckled and kissed her again, softly and sweetly this time. ''Did you find the extra jars?''

She pointed to a separate stack of boxes on the shelf, with bold black marker clearly detailing the contents.

He scooped up the rest of their clothes, handing hers to her before pulling his on, and went to grab a box.

''Take your time,'' he said on his way to the steps. ''I'll make up a story about us ransacking the cellar in search of these strawberries.''

Abby waited to dress until Jack was gone. She needed a few minutes to pull her emotions together. Things had gone further than she had intended, but she felt no regret.

She felt glad.

She stopped in the middle of buttoning her jeans, and sank down on the cellar bench. How was it possible that she could be glad? She'd let herself surrender to a de-sire she'd resisted from the moment she met Jack four years ago.

No, that was wrong.

She hadn't surrendered this afternoon, she had led the march into battle. And the total rush to oblivion she'd felt down here could be nothing but a victory. She'd never experienced it before.

She'd always thought her ex-husband was right when he told her she was too controlled to enjoy sex. She'd enjoyed it just now, though.

It was hard to imagine never allowing herself this feeling again. It was hard to imagine even looking at Jack without blushing as pink as a tea rose and wanting to repeat the whole thing over and over.

Now, all her dogged resistance just seemed silly. What had happened was a natural part of life. They were adults.

She tugged the band off her braid and worked her fingers through to the ends of her hair. She didn't have a mirror to check, and she didn't want Sharon to notice anything amiss.

She wanted this development between her and Jack to remain private. It was nobody else's business.

As she rebraided her hair, she tried to sort out her feelings. She already felt affection for Jack, but the experience they'd shared down here was powerful. She knew it had brought them closer, and her emotions were teetering between joy and confusion.

Her feelings for him were deepening, but a physical relationship could complicate her ability to fight for Wyatt later. Eventually, Jack would return to his other women and his other life.

In the meantime, keeping her feelings secret seemed to provide her with one last vestige of safety.

She wrapped the band around the end of her braid, which she tossed over her shoulder, then checked her clothes one last time.

Before she left the cellar, she looked down into the box of infant clothes still on the floor. Tenderly, she tucked the soft pink sleeve of a sleeper back inside. She folded the lid across the top and returned the box to the shelf.

Someday she'd come back down here and look through it again. She would study each item and try to remember everything she could about the twins' birth and their first few months of life.

She'd think of some anecdotes she could tell, about what they were like as infants.

And as soon as they could understand, she would begin to tell them a lifetime of very special stories about her sister, and their mother.

MORNING WAS FINALLY HERE. Even before Jack opened his eyes, he felt an energy stirring him to action. Today he would talk to Abby. Today their future could begin.

He sprang out of bed, grabbed his robe and darted down the hall to shower. The house was oddly quiet. The twins weren't babbling in the kitchen, and Abby wasn't bustling around doing a hundred different things at once. He must have gotten up before them.

It was truly a rare day.

Even though he was anxious to get everything out in the open, he took his time with grooming. He shaved with hot lather and a razor, and used his best cologne. Then he spent ten minutes trying to tame his hair with a comb and styling gel while he rehearsed his speech in the mirror.

He'd tell Abby that she'd blown him away, down in that cellar, and that he was excited about the changes. He was ready for something more.

Returning to his room, he dressed with care, too. Just

jeans, he decided, since he'd want to help her deliver baskets today. But he chose nice ones that he knew fit well. And he picked out a tan shirt that the salesgirl had said brought out the light in his eyes.

After he finished, he roamed around the house, trying to be patient and listen for sounds coming from upstairs. The rehung curtains were still tightly drawn across the window, and the two upstairs doors were latched shut. There were no sounds of his family waking.

His family—that sounded good. And right. And except for Abby, it had always been the truth. He'd simply never thought of them that way before.

Since they nearly always started their day in the kitchen, he went there to wait. The sunny room, usually brimming with activity, was calm and tidy this morning.

Every basket, ribbon and jar from yesterday had been assembled, tied and boxed. By late last night, it had all been loaded into Abby's truck.

No wonder she was sleeping late. She'd been working hard, and it was time for a break. He'd make sure she had a phenomenal time at the party Saturday night.

He'd make sure she had a phenomenal time every night—if she'd let him.

Since he was up first, he decided to make coffee and breakfast for the two of them. He pulled eggs and cheese from the refrigerator, hoping she liked omelettes.

As he opened a cabinet to pull out a skillet, he grinned at Abby's big kettle, already scrubbed to a shine and replaced on the shelf.

Neglecting his work yesterday afternoon had resulted in a time of great discovery for him. The only thing that hadn't truly surprised him was Abby's scorching response.

He'd suspected she'd be a passionate lover, and she

hadn't let him down. She made love with the same vigor she brought to everything else. She was incredible.

But she'd seemed quieter than usual after they returned to the kitchen, and she'd asked him to take care of the twins so she and Sharon could keep working. Later, he'd put the babies to bed while Sharon helped Abby work out her delivery schedule and invoice receipts.

It was only then that they'd pulled the truck around to the side of the house to load it under the post light in the driveway, then returned to the kitchen to clean up.

Abby had been so exhausted she'd gone up to bed immediately after Sharon left at midnight. Jack wouldn't allow himself to follow her upstairs and pound on her door, no matter how much he wanted to, so he hadn't been alone with her since the cellar.

Today, before anything else happened, they would talk.

When he finally heard noises upstairs, he started across the house to help her with the twins. But she'd carried them halfway down the stairs by the time he got there.

And she still looked exhausted.

"Hello," he said brightly, taking Wyatt.

"'Lo," she mumbled.

He followed her back to the kitchen, frowning at her silence. Usually, she talked to the babies almost constantly.

After the twins were in their high chairs and eating, he set a cup of coffee on the table in front of her and said, "I'm making omelettes. You interested?"

"Omelettes?" she asked, wincing as she sipped the coffee.

"Omelettes," he repeated. "I must still owe you a meal."

She shrugged, set the coffee down and continued feeding the twins.

Jack stood over the stove, starting to cook. Since she was quiet, he decided to begin the conversation he'd had a hundred times in his head. "We never talked about what happened yesterday in the cellar."

He glanced back at Abby, but she just kept spooning food into the babies' mouths. He returned his attention to the eggs. "I know we had an agreement, but—"

"Shh," she interrupted. "There's no need for an apology. I was the one who broke the agreement."

An apology?

He scowled down at the eggs. He'd thought what had happened in the cellar was one of the most amazing moments in his life, and he wasn't planning to apologize. He started to tell her that, but Wyatt squealed and bounced in his seat, and of course Abby had to devote her attention to the babies.

As soon as Wyatt was calm, Jack said, "We need to talk about what happened down there."

"I guess we do," she said, just as the doorbell rang.

He turned off the burner and scowled across the room at Abby, wishing whoever it was would just go away.

It rang again, and this time the tones sounded loud and long, as if the person outside was leaning against the buzzer.

As Jack strode through the hall to the foyer, he grumbled at the audacity of anyone showing up on a person's doorstep at this hour. Apparently, a man couldn't even get privacy if he moved out to the sticks these days.

"What time is it, anyway?" he hollered back at Abby as he yanked the door open.

"Nine-thirty," yelled Abby, from the kitchen.

"Nine-thirty," said Zuzu, from the front porch.

He stared at his eccentric ex-girlfriend, who appeared to be wearing a rhinestone-studded sheet.

''Hello, Jack,'' she said. ''How are you?''

He frowned and shook his head. Zuzu's timing was usually much better. ''Zuzu,'' he sighed. ''I know I left a message on your machine awhile back, but this is a horrendous time to pay a visit.''

She patted his cheek as she stepped through the door. ''You are definitely a Leo, aren't you?'' she said. ''Still so busy you can't keep track of your social calendar?''

''Huh?'' He held an arm out to block her path. There was no need for Abby to meet another of his ex-girlfriends, ever.

But especially not now.

''Oh, my gosh,'' said Abby from behind him in the hall. ''I forgot about Zuzu's visit.''

He dropped his arm and turned around. Abby had been listening. And she seemed to know Zuzu. Or at least she knew about this visit. And she was clearly agitated.

''I need to deliver baskets,'' she said in a shaky voice. ''I'll be gone most of the day.''

She sprinted up the stairs before he could stop her.

''Do you and Abby know each other?'' he asked Zuzu as she fluttered past him into the house.

''Only in the sense of a shared sisterhood.''

Jack raised an eyebrow. Zuzu knew he hated her cryptic comments.

''We met over the phone,'' Zuzu explained. ''Did you make me breakfast?'' She dropped her gaze and lifted the corners of her mouth.

That was when Jack realized he'd brought along the omelette pan. He snorted, already heading for the kitchen.

And when he got there, he realized Abby had left Wyatt and Rosie in their high chairs.

They didn't seem very happy about it, either.

He tossed the still-hot pan of eggs in the sink, used a

handful of paper towels to wipe most of the food off the twins' fingers and mouths, and carried them both back out to find Abby and explain.

By the time he reached the main hallway, Abby was standing near the front door, and Zuzu was comfortable on the sofa.

"I was planning to help you deliver those baskets," he said on his way across to Abby.

"Don't worry about it," she said. "And anyway, who'd baby-sit if you came with me? You'll have fun."

Suddenly she sounded awake and cheerful.

She grabbed her clipboard from a side table and reached up to peck all three of them on the cheek. Including him.

It was an unthinking gesture, as if they'd said years of goodbyes—except he would never let her get away with such an innocuous kiss. He would always want their goodbyes to be every bit as passionate as their hellos.

He considered putting the babies down to show her that, but instead simply stared into her face, trying to send one of those secret messages. *Don't leave me now. I need to tell you something.*

She backed out the door and all the way to the edge of the porch before whirling around and vanishing around the corner of the house.

After she'd gone, he turned and glared at Zuzu. She was standing in the doorway to the living room.

"She's adorable, Jack," she said solemnly.

Sighing, he strode back into the house and put Wyatt on the floor near the sofa.

"She is, isn't she?" he said. He sat down on the sofa with Rosie on his lap, smiling at the little girl as he bounced her on his knees.

Zuzu picked up the wandering Wyatt and reclaimed

her spot at the other end of the couch. ''When did you realize you were in love with her?''

Jack looked across at Zuzu, startled.

She must have been talking about Abby, not Rosie.

And was he in love?

Probably.

He scowled. ''Yesterday, I guess.''

''Why doesn't she know?''

''I haven't had the chance to tell her,'' he said. ''We've had too many dam—*dang* interruptions.''

Zuzu swung Wyatt in the air above her head, imitating the drone of an airplane. ''Don't tell her over a pan of eggs,'' she advised. ''Wait for a romantic moment to woo her. I'd hate to see you warp your destiny with bad karma.''

Jack turned his attention back to Rosie, but Zuzu had surprised him again. He'd always considered her a harmless kook, but she was making perfect sense now.

Abby was seeming more and more like his destiny.

Chapter Eleven

Abby had nearly driven past the entrance to Sharon's sprawling ranch house before she remembered she was supposed to pick her up on the way into town.

Even then she considered speeding on by.

She'd love to forget her load of baskets and travel down some country road until she was lost, just to give herself time to sort out her feelings.

Yesterday's mixture of sensuality and tenderness had been confusing enough, but seeing another of Jack's girl-friends had hurt. The revolving door hadn't just whacked her this time, it had scraped right across her bones.

As if Jack had ripped the wheel out of her hands to make the turn, she swerved into Sharon's drive at the last minute. Abby still had to deliver the baskets, and Sharon didn't deserve to be ignored.

Maybe a busy day away from the farm would help Abby put things into perspective. She'd work so hard she couldn't think about what he was doing with Zuzu.

"I thought Jack was coming along to help," Sharon said as soon as she slid into the passenger seat.

Abby reached for the ignition. "He's baby-sitting."

Sharon put her hand on Abby's, stopping her from

turning the key. "Oh, but surely your mother would watch the babies, if Jack wants to come along."

Abby stared at a pot of mums beside Sharon's front door. "He has a visitor," she said quietly.

"A woman?"

Abby could feel herself being scrutinized, so she nodded.

When her friend didn't comment, she started the truck. She tuned the radio to soft rock, turned up the volume and drove straight to town, determined to forget about Jack.

But as she and Sharon delivered baskets, Abby felt his touch everywhere. Each time she lifted a box her clothes chafed her tender breasts, and each step she took brought a sweet, fluid ache to her thighs.

By the third delivery into a very heavy schedule, Abby realized work wasn't helping her escape this time. She felt languid and off-kilter, and she couldn't stop thinking about what had happened down in that cellar.

She had just parked in front of a gourmet food store and picked up her clipboard, intent on finishing her chores anyway, when Sharon's hand slammed down on top of hers.

Abby frowned across the seat, and realized Sharon was nodding toward the storefronts.

There was an exclusive ladies' apparel store next to the food shop, and a banner in the window announced a gigantic pre-holiday clearance sale.

"Let's take a break and shop for our dresses," Sharon said as she got out. "We'll finish delivering later."

Abby stared at the mannequins in the window display. She had said she would go to the party with Jack, but surely things had changed. Even if Zuzu's visit hadn't altered his plans, the incident in the cellar had certainly changed things for her.

It was too risky. If she walked into that party on Jack's arm, some members of her community might start pairing them up. The farm would become "Jack and Abby's place." Invitations would be issued to the two of them.

Expectations would grow.

And the worst thing was, Abby would wish the gossip were true.

Sharon was already pulling open the shop door and beckoning with a broad sweep of her hand. "Come on," she called. "It'll be fun."

Abby sighed. Sharon's acceptance of her frantic pace and brooding mood today had been big-hearted. She'd been a trouper, and Abby had promised she would help her shop for a dress. She dropped the clipboard and got out.

As she entered the shop, she looked around curiously.

She'd never let herself venture into this sort of place, figuring her style ran more to discount stores and department store clearance racks, at best.

These clothes were gorgeous. As she and Sharon browsed toward the back, they passed rows and rows of exquisite and trendy styles. Before long, Sharon disappeared behind a pair of swinging doors with an armful of dresses, and Abby waited near a floor-length mirror so she could offer a yea or nay when Sharon came out to model each one.

A silver-haired saleslady handed Abby a hanger holding a strappy bit of material in ripe-tomato-red. Abby shook her head and handed it back. "This isn't her size," she said. "But thanks, anyway. It's wonderful."

The woman forced it back into her hands. "No, it's for

you," she said. "Your friend said you needed something special, for a party."

"I doubt that I'm even going," Abby said, but she held the dress out to admire it, and couldn't help smiling a little as she imagined Jack's reaction to her wearing it.

The woman smiled back. "This dress is classically designed. It would work for any festive event."

"Oh! No, thanks." Abby hung the dress on a rack and stepped away. She couldn't let herself think about going to the party.

It was a horrible idea.

Sharon came out wearing a sparkling sea-green sheath that left her ample bosom spilling out the top. "Try on that dress," she said with her usual grin as she splayed a hand over her exposed chest and looked in the mirror. "For fun."

"Oh, do! Just for fun," urged the clerk, clapping her hands almost gleefully.

Abby crossed her arms and stared at Sharon. Once again her friend seemed to be cheering for the wrong team.

"Wise decision, Abby," Sharon said on her way back to the dressing room. "That dress would probably get your handsome roommate too worked up, anyway. Leave it alone."

Five minutes later, Abby stared in the mirror at a sultry version of herself she'd never known existed. The gown fit her curves so perfectly it was as if someone had made it for her. "If I was going, I'd want to wear this," she whispered, turning her hips to make the skirt swing around her thighs.

The door opened, and the clerk peeped in. "Your friend was right," she stated. "That's your dress."

Sharon crowded in behind the clerk, and her smile turned gargantuan.

"It's too expensive," Abby said, to both of them. She might have let herself fall for Sharon's obvious psychological ploy, but the price tag made resisting easier.

"I'll give you a thirty percent discount on this dress and any other item in the store," the clerk announced.

Abby squinted at her.

"Fifty percent, for you and your friend," the woman said. "Two items apiece, at fifty percent off."

Abby looked past the clerk's shoulder at Sharon, who was nodding forcefully and pointing to the pretty ocean-blue dress she was wearing.

Abby sighed. "Do you carry overalls?"

SHE FOUND JACK on the kitchen floor several hours later. He was lying flat on his back next to the high chairs, with his knees bent into twin arches and his hands cradled underneath his head. His eyes were closed.

She tiptoed up and put her shopping bag on the counter next to where he lay. "I'm home," she said quietly, in case he was asleep.

"Mmm-hmm."

She stood over him, looking for signs of trouble. Although his eyes were still shut, he was breathing evenly, and it didn't look as if he'd fallen.

A quick scan of the room didn't reveal too much amiss, either, unless you counted the fact that his elbow was resting next to a bucket of gray water with a yellow sponge floating in it.

"Jack? Are you okay?" she asked, a little louder.

"Um-hmm."

"Where are Rosie and Wyatt?"

At last he opened his mouth, so she knew he was

awake. But it took a few seconds for the sound to come out. "Naps," he said, and breathed a couple of times. "Finally."

"It's almost five o'clock! Did they start late?"

"Oh, yeah."

She surveyed the room again, starting to smile, and tittered when she saw the array of baby food jars stacked next to the sink. "I hadn't introduced them to baby food meats yet," she said, hunkering down. "Did they like it?"

"Not a bit." Finally, he opened his eyes. And stared at her hair.

"Where's your company?" she asked.

"Company?"

"Zuzu."

"Oh. Well, Zuzu left right after you did, about a hundred years ago. She said she only came to meet you."

"You're kidding." Abby bit her lip to keep from chuckling, but a sigh escaped when she felt her entire body relax and a hundred taut nerves and muscles untangle themselves.

"I'm not kidding at all," Jack answered, springing to his feet.

She followed him up, and he stood before her, whistling under his breath at her new hairstyle.

She ignored the whistle.

She'd tried desperately to pull her hair back into a braid after Sharon's daredevil stylist had finished snipping. The scores of layers kept falling out of the band to curl softly around her face. She'd had to leave it down.

"Why would she want to meet me?" Abby asked, just noticing *his* hair. It was actually wilder than usual, with bits of pinkish food strewn among the curls. She bit down on her lip again.

"Zuzu has her own way of doing things," Jack explained, circling her slowly and with intense interest.

"I noticed that."

As he came back around in front of her, she noticed his shirt, too. She would have thought the pretty chestnut shade would camouflage most flavors of baby goop, but the evidence of his ill fortune was visible in the crusty smears.

She thought he'd never looked sexier.

"Did you have a good day?" she asked sweetly. She tried to keep a straight face, but wound up bursting into a fit of giggles.

He stuck his hands in his pockets and rocked on his heels, smiling at her enjoyment. "Oh, the twins did," he said. Then he added, "Your new hairstyle is phenomenal."

She ignored the comment. "What did they do?"

He rubbed his chin. "Let's see. They crawled around the living room and had a diaper change. They played in their room and had a diaper change. A late lunch, a bath and an eternity of play. And that brings them around to their nap."

"Sounds like a long day."

"Did I mention the word *eternity?*" His smile was huge.

She grabbed her shopping bag from the counter behind him. "You look wiped out," she said. "I'll repay the favor when I can, but I still have a few deliveries to make in the morning."

His comment was interrupted by a faint, husky cry.

One of the babies was awake. Abby headed up, and only realized Jack was following when she was nearing the landing.

"You didn't get finished?" he asked from two steps down.

"No." Abby glanced back at him and ran a finger across her shortened bangs. "Sharon was in a makeover mood."

"You look as sexy as you-know-what," he said, lowering his voice as they entered the nursery. "I can't wait to show up at that party with you on my arm."

Abby picked up Wyatt, who was sidestepping along the rail of his crib. "I'll probably feel like staying home to rest tomorrow night," she whispered. "You go have fun."

At first Jack seemed dismayed by this news, but he recovered quickly. "You agreed to go to the party *with* me," he whispered back.

"I seem to remember being bullied into it."

Jack stepped in close and put his lips near her ear to murmur, "Agreed—bullied or dragged along by the elbow—the results are the same. I'm collecting my favor."

THIS YEAR'S HARVEST PARTY was being held at the stately home of Art and Nancy Klein, who had propped up a scarecrow between the sculpted shrubs of their front lawn and pointed one of his grassy fingers toward their back terrace. The simulated usher was dressed to the nines, with a crisp white shirt and a black bow tie. His only concession to scarecrow tradition was the tattered straw hat that threatened to fly off in the wind.

Abby grinned at the Kleins' flair for whimsy as she pulled Rosie from her car seat and paused on the lawn to let the baby girl chatter at the scarecrow's inked-in face.

"We just got here, and already you're eyeing some other man," Jack said as he walked up with Wyatt. "Have you no discretion?"

"I was only thinking about swiping his hat," Abby said as they started together down a pumpkin lined path to the back. "Do you think anyone would notice?"

A movement in the front window caught their attention, and they both waved at several party guests who were watching their arrival.

Jack didn't respond to her question until they reached a secluded spot beside the house. Then he swooped his free arm around her shoulders, turning her to face him. "You'd manage to make that raggedy old hat look sexy," he said, and pressed a firm kiss against her lips. "Before we join the party, I want to thank you for giving in."

"Giving in?"

"Agreeing to be my date."

"Well, there's still time to escape," she teased, looking back toward his car.

He chuckled, but his grip tightened as he piloted her on along the walkway. "We've already been spotted," he argued. "And your mother's probably waiting to show off the babies."

"All right," Abby said with a sigh. "But only if you agree that we're attending as platonic roommates. No repeats of that kiss in front of the others."

He stopped again. "No repeats?" He slipped a palm under a strap of her dress to turn her around again.

She started to protest but he was ready with a kiss that, despite its brevity, managed to melt her defenses. The heat of it reminded her of his middle-of-the-night visit to her bed last night. It had begun soon after Wyatt had cried and been calmed, and hadn't ended until hours later when both babies woke for their breakfast.

"I suppose that one will have to tide me over," Jack said gruffly, just before he winked and let go of her.

Abby shifted Rosie higher on her hip as they rounded

the corner to the terrace, and waited for her stomach muscles to clench when she saw the crowd. She'd always felt out of place at parties.

But the terrace was vacant. Although it had been adorned with arrangements of hay bale seats and pumpkin votives, the unseasonably hot and windy weather made it less inviting. The tall sepia candles were unlit, and beyond the terrace a glistening pool seemed to dare the bravest souls to shed their clothes and swim under the harvest moon.

The back door stood open, and the lighted rooms within beckoned guests to enter.

As soon as Jack pulled the screen door open, they were greeted by Abby's mother. She offered both adults a kiss on the cheek before claiming the twins and hurrying off into the house. Jack and Abby followed the lure of jazz guitar music into a large den, where much of the crowd had congregated.

Abby loved the solicitous feel of his hand on her back as she introduced him around to her friends. Featherlight against her skin, his touch was warm and arousing.

Somehow, with a rub of his thumb and a squeeze of his fingers, he communicated volumes. He said he wanted to be there, by her side. Touching her. And that he wanted to keep touching her when they were alone.

The promise of that hand was every bit as sensual as the new red dress she wore.

It had started with that spark in his eye in the farmhouse kitchen, no more than a half hour ago, when she'd come in wearing her dress. The naked desire in his expression had sent an intense jolt of need throbbing through her body. And another piece of her heart had shifted, just a little.

Just enough.

It could simply be the fact that she hadn't been to a party since her sister's wedding reception. Or maybe it had something to do with her dress and hair. She supposed it could be the strange tidal forces of that big orange moon hanging in the sky.

Whatever the reason, she felt different tonight.

She felt a few hormones sexier and a few impulses wilder. And she was very glad she didn't have to resist something that her heart and body craved, when everyone around her kept telling her to relax and enjoy life.

Tonight she'd respond to Jack out of pure, hedonistic pleasure. She'd allow him his clandestine touches and whispered flirtation.

And later on at home, when they were alone, she'd respond to him again, in all the ways she wanted to.

"Did I tell you how amazing you look in that dress?" Jack murmured next to her ear as his fingers traced the straps in back.

Abby smiled brazenly, grabbing hold of his taupe silk tie to straighten it and then using it to pull him a step closer. "You look good, too," she whispered.

A pair of teenage girls giggled from their spot on the sofa, so Jack led her toward a quieter corner. "I've been waiting for a good time to tell you something," he said.

Abby twirled a long strand of her newly liberated hair, and wondered at his seriousness.

"What happened in the cellar the other day was a real eye-opener for me," he said. And paused when their host passed by, intent on some social errand.

Abby felt her cheeks color. "For me, too."

Jack pulled her closer and whispered, "I'll never intentionally hurt you, Abby."

She wasn't at all sure what he meant, but she said, "I don't want to hurt you, either."

Although his hand still rested boldly against the small of her back, his forehead furrowed and his lips parted. He seemed surprised.

"You in here, Abby?" called her mother from the doorway.

Abby offered Jack a shrug and a smile before plunging back through the crowd. "I'm here, Mom."

"I told Nancy I'd help set up the buffet," her mother said as she handed Rosie to her. "And this darling girl needs a diaper change. Thanks, dear. Your dad has Wyatt."

Abby found a vacant bedroom to change Rosie, and by the time she came out, Jack was huddled with a group of men, talking.

She had only taken a step in his direction before she was stopped by Sharon, who was enchanted by Rosie's party dress. Soon Sharon was whisking the baby away to show her husband, and Abby's attention was claimed by another group of acquaintances.

Though she and Jack spent the next half hour mingling in different circles, she was always aware of his presence in the room. She was listening to a group of farmers discuss the prospects of this year's winter wheat when she felt a tingle run up her spine and knew he was watching her. She grinned when his laughter sounded out above the music and chatter.

That's when she realized she was smiling constantly, at everything and nothing. She was having a great time, and that dreaded old feeling of being lost in the crowd was absent.

She felt connected to Jack, even when he wasn't at her side. Heaven help her, but it felt good.

By the time the buffet line started forming, Abby had Rosie on her hip again.

"Come on," Jack said, on his way to the kitchen. "If we share a plate, juggling a baby and eating shouldn't be too complicated."

With his hand on her back once more, he escorted her to the dining room. "Much better," he said next to her ear, as soon as they'd found a place at the back of the line.

At her questioning glance, he said, "This," and rubbed his hand back and forth across her skin. "Touching you again."

"Shh!" Abby hissed, but she couldn't manage a frown.

When their turn came, Jack filled a plate with a sampling from every serving dish, then led her to a spot near the window.

"What do you want to try first?" he asked, surveying the overfilled plate. "Some sort of veggie bruschetta, or coconut shrimp?"

"The bruschetta," Abby said, stretching her free hand toward the plate. But he was already lifting a round to her mouth, and when she opened it to protest, he slipped the crusty morsel in.

Abby blushed hotly and bit into it, glaring at him as she chewed.

His teeth flashed whitely as he popped the rest into his own mouth, seemingly unconcerned by her distress. He offered a bit of bread to Rosie, and was ready with a plump shrimp as soon as Abby swallowed.

Abby opened her mouth to take the shrimp, but leaned forward at the last second to nip his finger, too. She'd meant it as a reprimand, but she knew her teasing had backfired when he stared at her lips and neglected to pull his finger away.

The next few minutes had Abby trying to smother her laughter, to escape attention. Every time she tried to grab the plate with her free hand, he held it up over her head; every time she finished a bite, he was ready with another.

When her dad appeared through the crowd, she clamped her mouth shut on a bite of stuffed zucchini and backed away, telling herself she was relieved by the interruption.

"The ladies are feeding Wyatt pumpkin custard in the kitchen," her dad said with his arms outstretched. "Your mother asked me to bring Rosie."

"I'll come help," Abby said, even as she handed Rosie across.

Her dad chuckled. "Wyatt already has four women feeding him, and there's hardly room for another body in there. Get yourself a drink and relax."

When her dad left, Abby glanced at Jack, who immediately plucked the last remaining shrimp from the plate and dangled it in front of her face.

She laughed softly and shook her head. "I couldn't eat another bite," she said. "Let's follow Dad's advice."

They found the bar and made their drink selections, and were soon immersed in conversation with Sharon and several others. An old school chum of Abby's broke into the circle, and stared so pointedly at Jack that eventually the entire discussion halted.

"Your friend is so familiar," she said to Abby. "But I can't quite place him."

Jack extended his hand. "I'm Jack Kimball," he said. "My brother, Brian, was married to Abby's sister."

"My word, that's right!" the woman exclaimed, and sobered dramatically. "How awful for both of you. Are you okay?"

"We're handling it," Abby said, and glanced over in time to catch Jack's nod. "Paige and Brian would have wanted us to get on with our lives."

"I couldn't believe how it happened," the woman continued. "They were so young, and the crash was so violent. I get upset just thinking about it."

When several other members of the group joined in a lengthy retelling of the details of that night, Sharon caught Abby's eye and backed out of the circle.

Abby took Jack's hand to pull him away, too. "It's time for my escape," she said softly.

He led her outside beyond the patio, to the pool deck. They stood together, sipping their drinks and staring at the shimmer of moonlight on the crystal-blue water. "Our being here together would bring it all to mind, wouldn't it?" she said, without bothering to elaborate further. He knew what she was saying.

"I guess it would," he agreed, taking her hand to squeeze it. "I miss them, too, but it defeats the spirit of the party if people spend time dwelling on it. This is supposed to be a celebration."

"I'm ready to go home, anyway," she said. "I'll tell the Kleins we're leaving. Will you get Rosie and Wyatt?"

"Wait…listen," Jack said, tilting his head to the faint sound of the stereo. "I think that's a waltz. How about a dance before we go?"

"No one's dancing, Jack."

His gaze swept down her body, causing a thrill everywhere it touched. "Now that would be a perfect waste of that dress.'' He took both their glasses and set them near the edge of the pool.

Abby looked up into those brilliant eyes and knew that, at least for this moment, she was the woman for Jack.

And she was grateful.

Why not dance? After all, there was a full moon to explain her crazy behavior. Why not make the night magical?

It was true, no one was dancing. The air was too hot, and the Kansas wind tugged at her skirt and ruffled her hair into artless abandon. Several people inside had just looked at her and been reminded of the sister she had buried nearly two months ago. The situation was altogether inappropriate.

The song wasn't even a waltz, as Jack had claimed. But she heard its rightness, as clearly as he did. And she knew everything was perfect.

She closed her eyes even before they began to dance. He whispered about how perfectly she fit in his arms, and she sighed, knowing exactly what he meant.

The first time she'd danced with him, years ago at Paige's wedding, she'd felt perfect in his arms.

Without thinking, she reached up to kiss him gratefully, but he didn't let her get away with a simple peck. He slanted his gin-and-olive-scented mouth across hers and demanded heat. Hands that had rested against the straps at her back now pulled her as close as skin. As flesh.

Abby tangled her fingers in his hair, making sure the kiss didn't end anytime soon. She forgot where she was, and that her feet should be moving in time to the music. She forgot everything except her private moment of joy.

When they stopped to breathe, Abby glanced over Jack's shoulder toward the house and saw a windowful of people watching them. Gasping in surprise, she began to dance again, but faster.

Jack's expression was so surprised, she giggled. ''We forgot about our audience.''

He pulled her back into his arms, smiling in a way that told her he didn't care who saw them. And after another kiss, she didn't care, either.

The moon would rule tonight.

When they finally ventured back inside, Abby ignored the way the crowd stilled as they walked through in search of the twins. Abby's mother was sitting on a love seat playing with Rosie, and her dad was on his way across the room, carrying Wyatt.

Abby reached her mother just as her dad spoke. ''Jack, let's step outside,'' he said quietly as he handed Wyatt to Abby.

Abby's dad always spoke quietly, and people always listened. He was only medium in height, and soft-spoken in manner, but he was a giant in the hearts of many.

He'd bought his quaint little flower shop soon after his marriage to Faye thirty years ago, and he'd been sharing his flowers and wit with the community ever since. Abby and her sister couldn't have asked for a more benevolent father.

But he had definite opinions, and one of them was that couples shouldn't live together before marriage. Abby had grown up hearing him say that she was too special to settle for anything less than a man who would cherish her for a lifetime.

Who knew what he would say to Jack now?

Abby turned to watch Jack follow her dad through the crowd. She wanted to protest, but the crowd was too big and the eyes too curious. She'd have to let them go.

She sank down onto the love seat beside her mother and listened to Rosie babbling at Wyatt.

"It looks as if you have your hands full with more than the twins these days," Faye said.

"Mother!" Abby whispered, wondering if anyone had missed the spectacle outside the window.

"It's all right, dear," her mother soothed. "Just enjoy."

Chapter Twelve

When Jack wound his way back through the crowd, Abby was already standing with Wyatt on one arm and the diaper bag on the other. He grinned as he took Rosie from Abby's mother. Abby was always on time and ready to go. Right now, so was he.

He hadn't managed to make his intentions clear to her at the party, or even out by the pool, but his kisses had been reciprocated for three days in a row, and they weren't followed by confused looks or vows to cool things off.

She was in the right frame of mind. The drive home should provide ample time for talk.

If everything went as well as their kisses, he had every reason to believe she'd be receptive to his revelations, and now he had the added power of her own father's opinion to back him up.

After they'd been on the road a minute or two, she brought up the subject herself. "I guess my dad didn't humiliate me too badly, since you're still smiling."

Jack put a hand on her knee. "Your father said that in a community of this size, we should consider how things look."

"Dad has old-fashioned ideas."

"He's right, Abby. Many of your friends saw you kissing your male roommate in a very unplatonic way. You'll be the talk of every pool hall and church kitchen in the county."

She was quiet.

He didn't need to see her to know that she was biting her lip, and he loved the idea of knowing her that well. "It was worth every bit of gossip," he said with a chuckle.

"Was that all he had to say?"

"He said I should marry you tomorrow, or move out and court you properly."

"He didn't!"

Jack didn't answer. He reached over to pull her closer, and she came willingly. She rested pliantly against his side, and he drove in silence for a moment, enjoying the privacy that traveling at night afforded them.

"Seems to me that you'd make an entire community happy just by marrying me," he said.

Even as he said it, he knew the words he'd chosen were all wrong. That truth was verified when he felt her muscles turn rigid against his side.

"I'd make the *community* happy by marrying you?" she said in a squeaky voice. "Surely you're kidding!"

She skidded back across the seat and practically wedged herself against the passenger door.

Jack stared out at the glowing arc thrown by the headlights, wondering how to rephrase things. Wondering if every man had such a hard time professing his feelings for the first time.

I'm falling in love with you. The words were simple enough to think, but saying them seemed to be another thing entirely. And not just because he'd never said them before.

It was because he knew she'd already heard them from someone else, and suffered through a venomous retraction of them later.

The words, the timing, the mood—it all had to be right.

But now he was nearing the farmhouse, and since they were on a rural road he couldn't exactly drive around the block a few times to keep talking. He couldn't hold her captive in the car, either.

The damned romantic moment had escaped him again.

He parked in the garage and slid out. "Wait here," he said. Seconds later, he opened her door and took her hand to help her out. He led her to the back entry and unlocked the door, but kept one hand wrapped around hers.

When she tried to pull away, he didn't let go. They would sit down and talk all night, if necessary.

She tugged again, and finally wrenched her hand away.

"Relax, Abby," he said in the doorway. "I didn't mean that marriage comment the way it sounded."

"Good," she said with a wry smile. "I need to get the twins from the car, at any rate."

"Oh. Right."

He followed her back to the car, and watched as she unbuckled the sleeping twins and carted them both inside. Jack didn't offer to help, because she seemed to have gone into superwoman mode. She might punch him in the stomach if he did.

Her mood had definitely changed, and it was his fault. He'd tried to use the protectiveness of her father and the curiosity of her community to broach the subject of marriage. He hadn't even realized he was receptive to the idea, but it obviously didn't scare him as much as it scared her.

Within minutes, she was carrying the babies through

the nursery door, and he was standing at the bottom of the stairs, thinking.

He'd hoped to follow her straight to her bedroom just as soon as the twins were in their cribs, but now he wasn't at all certain he'd be welcome.

Still, if he was lucky, one of the twins would wake up later. It had been an exciting day, and routines had been broken. With Rosie and Wyatt, daytime commotion often led to nighttime wakefulness. Jack was counting on it tonight.

It took three hours, but he was patient. He sat in the darkened living room and listened to the tick of Abby's antique wall clock. At a little before midnight, he heard a baby whimper.

He sprinted up the stairs, rushing through the nursery door just as Abby picked up Rosie. She'd forgotten the robe again, and the familiar T-shirt caressed her breasts as lovingly as he would, given half a chance. She pulled a bottle from the warmer and fell into the rocking chair.

Jack sat down across from her, studying the cascade of hair around a face that was freckled and lovely, and calm again.

He let his expression say everything.

He started at her face, then let his attention slide down her body and back up. Then again. Her agitation had lessened enough for her to look at him, too, and her tiny smile gave him hope.

When Rosie finished her bottle, and Wyatt seemed as if he'd sleep on through, Abby put the baby in her crib and met Jack out on the landing. "You rascal," she said. "You were waiting downstairs, weren't you?"

He stepped closer, forcing her to back up against her bedroom door. "Absolutely," he said.

"Well, you're still in the doghouse, but I guess I can

toss you a bone,'' she said. She flattened herself against the door and frowned when he kept advancing.

When he got close enough, he reached out and turned the doorknob, so the door popped open behind her. With the help of the strong and willing arm he slipped around her waist, she kept her balance.

Both of them looked inside, at her big, inviting bed.

''The only thing I want tossed my way right now is you,'' he said. She still seemed tentative, so he pressed her hand against his arousal to let her feel the truth.

She kept her hand there for achingly long seconds, then sighed and removed it. He held his breath. He had to let her decide what to do next.

When she swayed forward and raised her lips, his relief was profound. Although it was whisper soft and sweet, her kiss electrified his veins. He allowed her to lead for a minute, accepting her nibbles gratefully.

Until she took a step forward, and he felt the supple curves underneath her clothes, and was driven to demand rather than accept. He grabbed a handful of that gorgeous hair and tugged her head back, allowing his mouth better access to hers. Diving his tongue inside, he searched for feeling, for forgiveness, for satisfaction that would never be enough.

When he slid his hands under her shirt, he discovered that she was totally nude beneath it. He gave a quick bark of laughter, nearly going over the edge with one simple touch.

Unable to resist, he tangled a finger in the hair at the juncture of her thighs, feeling the exquisite textures and groaning in approval. She broke away then, pulling his arms behind her back and drawing a shaky breath. ''Jack…slow down,'' she whispered.

Slow. She'd said slow.

Not go away. Not stop.

It *was* an exciting day.

He took his time pushing her into her bedroom, removing his shirt and socks on the way. But he kept her occupied with kisses and caresses, and when they stopped beside her bed, he ran his hands over the sweet nipples outlined by the fabric of her shirt.

Using only his thumbs, he tortured himself awhile longer. Then he pulled the shirt over her head and nuzzled his lips against a dusky nipple. Even if her hand wasn't gripping the back of his head to pull him closer, her moan would have let him know he was on the right track.

When she slid to her knees beside her bed, he followed, not wanting to give up his treasure. A persistent hand returned to her silky oasis of curls, and he slid a finger inside.

The snug feel of her already dripping heat drove him to near madness, and he pumped one and two fingers inside her, frantic in his excitement.

Abby clutched his hand in hers. ''Slow,'' she reminded him.

But he couldn't go slow. Not now, anyway. He unzipped his pants, took her small, gentle hand and pressed it against him. He wanted her to hold him. To let him know this was all right.

She stroked him softly, seeming to enjoy the feel of his body as much as he did hers. When her grip firmed, he gritted his teeth, inadvertently biting her nipple and provoking a yelp that had him apologizing with his lips and tongue.

She sighed encouragingly as he worked harder to please her, with little nibbles, some suckling and a soft nip here and there. But her hand kept touching him, and he felt his body pulsate threateningly. He pulled her hand away then, pivoting her around so she was facing the bed. Letting his pants slide down, he nestled his hungry body behind hers as he nuzzled her neck.

It was nearly too much. His brimming shaft rested against that delectable tush, and his hands had free rein on those perfectly soft and pebbled breasts. He couldn't hold out much longer.

Abby's moans grew wilder. She rammed her elbows against the edge of the mattress and shoved back against him. ''Now,'' she said hotly, ''I'm ready now.''

That was all he needed. He sought her wet and swollen center and pushed inside in a single driving thrust.

She pressed her face in the mattress to muffle a scream, and then lifted it again to whisper approval as he pumped himself inside her.

He opened his eyes, wanting to see. Wanting to watch in sweet hot agony as his body found joy inside hers. Her skin gleamed in the light of a single bedside lamp, and she moved against him in perfect synchrony.

Reaching around her, he found her firm female nub and stroked it. Again she buried her face against the bed, stifling her cries. When he was sure she'd found complete pleasure, he let himself go, coming quick and hard and completely.

After a few seconds of breathless bliss, a glowing Abby climbed onto her bed and patted the spot beside her.

Jack followed, smiling the smile of a contented man. He waited while she turned off the lamp, then pulled her into his arms as they caught their breath. When he thought he could speak again, he finally got the words out.

''I'm falling in love with you.''

ABBY CHUCKLED. Jack Kimball was the last man she'd expect to be sentimental in bed. "What did you say?" she asked.

"I love you," he whispered.

She shoved against his chest. If he was teasing, it was cruel. "Don't say that."

"Why not?"

She turned the lamp on again so she could see his face. As tired as she was, this was a conversation that needed the reality of light. "This little interlude is for now," she said. "Not a lifetime."

"Abby, you're going to have to put up with me for more than some little interlude." His eyes twinkled as he grabbed her waist to pull her close.

She pushed his hand away and blinked a couple of times, trying to settle her emotions. "No," she said fiercely. "I'm just like your other girlfriends."

"Not really," Jack said.

When she frowned questioningly, he explained, "You're sexier than Diane, more fun than Zuzu, and you make Paula's polish seem gaudy."

Abby shook her head. "No, I meant I'm temporary, like them."

He leaned closer and lowered his voice. "At the party tonight, when you said you didn't want to hurt me, I realized you could devastate me. No one else ever could."

"Don't say that," Abby said, and realized she wasn't breathing. She raked a hand through her hair and let out her breath in a long, slow release.

"Why?" he asked, frowning as he reclined against her pillow.

"Can't you just take my word for it?"

Jack's face cleared as he pulled her down beside him. "I'm not your ex-husband, Abby."

"I know," she said, and immediately sat back up. She pulled the sheet over her chest and held the edge in a tight grip.

He followed her up and rubbed her bare back. "You need more time?" he asked.

She knew he was watching her, waiting until she met his eyes. After another breathless moment, she did.

"Well, yes."

He smiled. "I can be patient."

ABBY TENDED HER CHORES the next morning with trembling hands and a skitterish heart. She kept reminding herself that last night was just a fluke. Jack's words could only mean he was infatuated.

Exactly as Tim had been, years ago, in the beginning.

She couldn't let a few nights of madness turn into a relationship she couldn't trust.

She couldn't.

His words had been momentous, though, and his actions powerful. She didn't know how she could dismiss either one.

As usual with Abby, inner turmoil sent her into overdrive. She tried to calm her thoughts by quickening her work pace. She finished tending her plants within an hour, and moved right on to housecleaning.

When Jack came down the stairs, she was dusting the mantelpiece while the babies played on the floor of the living room. He said good morning, and asked if she needed help with the twins.

She answered that she had everything under control, and he said he'd be in his office, working.

And he left.

She was greatly relieved by a conversation that had taken less than a minute from start to finish. If they could really go back to some semblance of normalcy, maybe she would be all right.

If they could be cordial and polite and the perfect roommates by day—and down to earth about their nights—perhaps she could allow herself a little more time.

And it worked that way, for a while.

In the next couple of weeks, Abby devoted her days to the babies and the greenhouse. She started several rows of cut flowers for the holiday season, and watched the twins learn to stand alone and take their first supported steps.

Jack spent long hours in his office, but was always willing to lend a hand with babies and cleanup duties. And he kept a comfortable distance, most of the time. Although he joined Abby upstairs on many nights, he didn't ask for promises, and he didn't make any.

Sometimes she felt as if she had solved some sort of cosmic riddle—she had a roommate to ease her daytime burdens and a lover to add passion to her nights.

At other times, she was sure she was crazy.

One Friday morning in late October, Abby watched through the greenhouse window as Jack played with the twins in the side yard. He'd bundled them up in coats and hats, and sat them down under the big cottonwood tree.

Over and over again, he tossed leaves in the air above the twins' heads. The leaves drifted down, the babies cackled and Jack grinned at their pleasure before snatching another handful and flinging it upward.

Their circle of fun was tempting, but Abby forced herself to return to her chores, reminding herself of all the reasons it was necessary to stay away.

She was still working an hour later when Jack's arms

wrapped around her waist from behind. Unwittingly, she sank back against him, and smiled when he moved her hair aside to kiss her neck. "Where are Rosie and Wyatt?" she asked.

"Sleeping. The fresh air must have worn them out."

Abby didn't respond—she was too intent on the heady sensations he was rousing with his lips and hands.

"I just got a phone call from a client with an emergency," he said. "I'll have to head to Kansas City late tomorrow morning and stay a couple of days. Come with me?"

Abby studied the mottled green foliage of a cyclamen, wishing she could say yes. Kansas City was where he lived that other life...the one he would return to in less than a year.

She didn't want him to go, now or ever, but she couldn't go with him, either. She had a farm to tend and deliveries to make. Most importantly, she had a pair of twins to raise, and a lot of convincing to do in order to be allowed that privilege. She had to remember.

"I can't," she said.

"I'll hurry back."

"Just do your job. Don't hurry."

She turned in his embrace, unable to resist testing herself, and him, and the emotions she was more and more sure she recognized as true.

She didn't resist, either, when his hands finagled their way underneath her shirt to her very responsive breasts.

Within minutes, she was running through the house with him, to his room and his bed.

As he shut the door, he made some comment about stealing her T-shirt and underwear to pack in his suitcase, so he could at least smell her scent in his hotel room.

She felt her thighs turn to rubber, but she laughed anyway. Even without his touching her, she felt that delicious oblivion again.

She led him across the room, shedding her clothes on the way. She threw herself on his bed with a bounce, and watched as he stripped in front of her.

When he joined her, she lay beneath him, face-to-face, and kissed him so deeply she felt him shudder. Then, still keeping her eyes open, she accepted him inside her.

The intimacy was still potent. Her eyes filled with tears, and she had to close them when she saw the matching wetness of his.

She wrapped her legs around his torso and felt him sink more deeply inside. He lingered there for a while, without moving, and she was happy to allow the respite.

Movement would start them toward the end. It would bring him closer to packing and leaving. She wasn't ready for that.

She'd never be ready for it. She knew that now.

After a while she felt his body pulsate, and she clamped her muscles tighter around him. He groaned and began to move, but she led this time, with whispered commands. She told him how fast to go, and when to pause, and how forcefully to continue.

He listened well and followed every instruction.

And between the two of them, their cadence led them to a shattering end that she knew would be unforgettable.

FOR NEARLY AN HOUR, Abby loitered in her parents' flower shop. She chatted with her dad and the customers, helped her mother arrange flowers, and kept her ears attuned for the twins, who had fallen asleep in their stroller and were still napping in the back room.

The naps were her excuse. She'd told everyone she wanted to let the babies enjoy a nice long snooze before she headed home. She hadn't frittered the time away in this manner for several years. She always had plenty to do.

But she'd finished her errands, and she wasn't ready to go home. She'd left the house before Jack was done packing for his business trip, and she wanted him to be long gone when she returned.

Even though he'd been respectful and quiet after yesterday afternoon, she knew she couldn't handle watching him leave. Her feelings were too conflicted to handle anything more than a simple goodbye.

She was glad he'd be gone a few days. Apparently, she needed time and space to figure things out.

She'd spent the morning finishing every chore she could generate away from the house. She delivered her flowers and cared for the twins and filled in the time.

But her thoughts had stalled on Jack.

After three hours of avoiding home, she thought it would be safe to return. She said goodbye to her parents and left the flower shop with the waking twins, congratulating herself all the way out to her truck for avoiding the subject of roommates with her dad.

But as she buckled the babies into their car seats, she realized the air felt eerily still, and it was noticeably colder than it had been an hour before.

She glanced at the sky and her heart quickened. Ominous black clouds were stacking up on the horizon, and the atmosphere felt charged. A storm was blowing in.

As soon as she started the truck, she turned on the radio and listened to the weather report. The meteorologist warned of possible tornadoes, with high winds and hail inevitable. For the first time that day, she could only think of getting home with the twins.

She headed straight for the farm, but rain started falling

before she'd gone halfway, and came down so heavily she could scarcely see the road five feet in front of the car. She drove as fast as she dared, wincing when a clap of thunder sounded seconds after a huge streak of lightning.

The storm was nearly on top of them.

When she pulled into the drive she discovered the garage door opener wouldn't work. The power was out. She'd have to carry the twins through the downpour.

Quickly, she unfastened them, picked them up and sprinted onto the porch without bothering to close the doors to the truck.

The house was dark without the benefit of lights, even in the afternoon. Still carrying the babies, she fumbled her way upstairs to resupply the diaper bag, then looped it over her shoulder and crept back down. In the kitchen she set the twins on the floor while she grabbed a couple of bottles from the refrigerator and a fluorescent lantern from the pantry. Then she hoisted them again and headed out to the storm cellar. Raindrops hammered her skin as she walked three yards from the back door to the cellar door, and then she realized she'd have to put the twins down again to pull open the heavy panel.

Gently she sat them on the wet grass, yanking the door open and scooping them back up within seconds. She practically slid down the concrete steps, put the babies on the floor and switched on the lantern. Then she scurried up to shut the door behind her.

That was when she let herself get scared.

She stared at the door, near to tears. She'd never been frightened of storms, but being out here alone with the babies was terrifying.

She returned to pick them up, snuggling them close as she sat on the cellar's single concrete bench. Wyatt squirmed on her knee, fretful at being confined. She wished she'd brought along a couple of toys. At least Rosie seemed content to blow bubbles into the air and jabber in curiosity at the dim little room they inhabited.

It would be best for the babies if she acted as if this were just a strange new playroom, Abby decided. If she could just relax... She let loose a harsh, lonely chuckle when she realized she'd finally accomplished this afternoon's goal—she hadn't thought about Jack again, until just now.

A trickle ran down her chin. She ran her tongue over her lips, thinking it was rainwater. But it was salty. Warm. She must have gnawed a gash in her bottom lip.

Just then the cellar door crashed open and Abby screamed in alarm, causing both babies to whimper.

Chapter Thirteen

"Abby, thank God you're down here," Jack yelled above the storm. "Is everyone all right?"

"We're fine," she hollered. And she felt fine, now. *Dammit.*

"Anything you need?" he called down.

Glistening streaks of rain fell around him, and before she'd had a chance to answer, a clap of thunder boomed through the open door. "Just get down here and shut that door!"

His form disappeared from the doorway, leaving a gaping view of the dark sky and allowing rain to invade their refuge. Then, just as quickly, he appeared again, clattering down the steps with a soggy computer box.

Abby frowned, wondering if he'd taken the time to pack up his system. As he set it on the cellar floor, however, the cries from inside divulged its contents.

He'd rescued the ducks.

Opening the top, he allowed them to flap out and voice their complaints. Nearly full grown now, they had learned to quack, and were doing so loudly.

Abby couldn't help grinning as Jack climbed the steps to pull the cellar door closed again. When he came back, he was smiling, too.

"I figured you wouldn't have taken the time to grab them," he said as he sat beside her on the bench and took Wyatt from her arms.

She didn't feel the need to say a thing for a while. Everyone was together—drenched, but safe.

Jack pulled her against his side.

"You couldn't be finished already," she said.

"No, the radio weatherman was talking about some potentially dangerous weather coming up through south-west Kansas, so I turned around. I made it back in thirty-two minutes, watching the storm all the way."

She leaned away to peer into his eyes. "We're fine."

"I know. But I needed to be here." His eyes clung to hers, saying everything he didn't.

"Jack…" she began, shaking her head.

Wyatt's giggle interrupted.

The agitated ducks were waddling in circles around the perimeter of the cellar, still quacking.

Rosie joined in with a belly laugh, and with all of the pandemonium inside the cellar, the outside noise was obliterated.

Jack's arrival had taken them from cold, dark fright to loud, clamorous fun.

Abby and Jack laughed, too, unable to resist as the babies continued to chortle and the ducks continued their waddling symphony.

From some small corner, a cricket even added its chirp, sounding out above all else as if it had a microphone. Abby thought it odd that a cricket could be heard above the din, and then realized that the thunder had lessened.

The storm must have blown past.

Jack handed her Wyatt and went to look out. When he returned, he merely nodded. It was safe to go up.

And they were lucky, this time. The storm had involved gale force winds and driving rain, but no tornadoes.

She and Jack each carried a baby on a walk around the house, searching for damage. A major limb had been ripped from the cottonwood tree, and the ducks were cooing approval as they rested under the fallen branches.

Abby frowned into Jack's eyes, and he nodded. He seemed to understand that she'd want to check the orchard.

They jogged out there, with the twins laughing in innocent glee at the bumpy ride. As they neared the first group of apples, they slowed. Abby's heart was heavy as she surveyed the jumble of limbs, leaves and fruit littering the ground.

The last crop of apples was wrecked, and some of the trees might not survive. Suddenly, the storm and its aftermath seemed appropriate.

For in that instant, she knew without a doubt what she had to do about Jack.

She'd let it all go too far, and there would be no use trying to return to a platonic relationship. Now that she'd experienced the all-encompassing power of their passion, she'd never be able to backpedal fast enough.

She knew that.

She also knew that he fancied himself in love with her. But she'd heard the same words, or similar ones, from the only other man she'd ever slept with. She couldn't risk her heart, or the welfare of an innocent little boy.

So it all had to end.

She wouldn't tell Jack now, as they stood outside among the ruinous tumult of the storm. That memory would be too surreal. She'd wait until later, when she and her world were more settled.

For now, she'd take care of this other, less daunting

mess. Wordlessly, she continued along beside Jack to check the rest of the orchard. Many of the younger trees seemed undamaged, but a few older ones had major wounds.

"I need to make repairs," she said in a trembling voice that had little to do with the storm's aftermath. "Can you watch the twins?"

"Absolutely." Jack took Rosie from her arms. "You take as long as you need. I'm here."

She started to walk toward a garden shed at the corner of the orchard, where she kept a stock of arborist's supplies that had been there since the days of Mr. Epelstein. But something compelled her to turn and wait until Jack had disappeared down the wooded path to the house.

It seemed important, his walk down that path. Everything would change as soon as she finished here, and followed that same path home.

At dusk, she came in to find that the power had been restored. Jack had bathed the twins and put them to bed.

He was waiting in the kitchen, but when he saw her damp hair and glum expression, he insisted that she head straight to the shower.

She didn't argue. She dreaded the things she had to say to him tonight, and she was so chilled she was trembling. She might as well allow herself the comfort of warm, dry clothes.

When she came back down, she was fully dressed and dry, but still shaking. Jack pulled her to the kitchen table and helped her to sit. Then he filled a couple of bowls from a soup pot and came back to join her.

The fact that all he'd done was open a can of clam chowder and heat it on the stove was irrelevant to Abby. The gesture itself broke her heart. He'd made dinner. He'd waited to share it with her.

They ate for a few minutes, and she answered his questions about orchard damage with stilted words and a quavering voice. She couldn't meet his eyes.

When the soup and the refuge of the moment had had time to calm her tremors, he lifted her chin with gentle fingers and waited until she did look at him.

He took his turn speaking then, in a strong and sure voice. He told her he realized he hadn't been clear enough about things. He said he loved her, and the twins, more than anything in his life.

He pulled a red velvet jeweler's box from his pocket and set it beside her soup bowl. He chuckled when he said he'd stopped on the way out of town this morning, just to buy her this ring. He said the past few weeks had been incredible—that they had given him the courage to try.

She started shaking again. "No," she whispered, forcing the box back into his hands without opening it. "I can't accept this, and you'll have to pack up and leave as soon as you can."

He seemed disbelieving. "What? Abby, why?"

"This isn't working," she said, shaking so hard that she knew he must be able to see her tremors. "I can't live with you anymore."

He didn't say anything, but she could imagine his questions. She knew he deserved answers.

"I should never have gotten involved with another playboy."

He smiled at that, and flipped open the box to look inside. "I'm not a playboy anymore. I've only wanted you since the day I moved in."

She pretended interest in her soup and refused to look at him or the ring. "You're only intrigued because I'm a challenge," she said. "Just like Tim."

"I never met that damned ex-husband of yours, but he couldn't have loved you or he wouldn't have hurt you that way," Jack said. "I won't do that."

She heard the jeweler's box snap shut, and realized Jack had returned it to the table between them. "I can't risk it—I have the twins to consider," she murmured.

"I want us all to be a family."

"You think you do, but marriage would turn me into a wife, and wives are boring," she said, looking up now. "After a few more months, or a year, or two years, you'd want to leave."

He shook his head emphatically, but she ignored him. "It's better that you go now," she insisted. "As soon as possible."

"Even after all that's happened?" he asked, his eyes blazing as hot as blue fire. "In our bedrooms? That afternoon in the cellar? Even at the car dealership, I know you felt the same connection I did. Can't you trust it?"

"No."

He picked up the box. "You're turning down my proposal?"

"Yes."

He laughed, but the sound was hollow. "I'm sure you won't believe this, but I've never told any other woman I loved her. Never, Abby. And I've never neglected to use a condom before, either."

She clamped her teeth so hard against her bottom lip that she tasted blood again. Then she shrugged. She'd known she was taking a risk; she would handle the responsibility, if necessary.

He studied her face and shook his head.

Then he stood and shoved the box into his jeans pocket.

"I'll need to call a mover," he said. "But I'll find a

way to get Wyatt and me out of here tomorrow…if that's what you want.''

''No.'' She stood, too, and put a hand on his arm to stop him from leaving.

Wordlessly, he stared across at her.

''I want Wyatt,'' she whispered.

He raised his eyebrows. ''What, Abby?''

''Wyatt needs to stay here,'' she said as she withdrew her hand. ''Brian asked you to take custody because he thought you two had missed a father figure growing up.''

''That's right.''

''But the real problem was a lack of stability, not the lack of a father. Your mom's lifestyle wasn't very stable, was it?''

''Probably not,'' he admitted.

''Wyatt's childhood would be just as miserable with all of those inappropriate women circulating in and out of his life.''

''Inappropriate women?''

Abby smiled sadly. ''Don't you realize? Every woman you date has some strange personality flaw that allows you to keep your distance.''

He scowled. ''Everyone has flaws, Abby, and I didn't keep my distance from you.''

She ignored him. ''I can provide a stable life for both twins. Please, leave Wyatt here.''

''I wish it were that easy,'' he said. ''But I love both of those babies, too. And, for whatever reason, my brother asked me to raise Wyatt.''

''Wouldn't it be better for everyone if you just visited often, like a favorite uncle?''

Jack's narrowed eyes pierced hers as he shook his head, just once, from left to right. ''I can't become my dad.'' He let his gaze fall down to some spot on the table and said, "All things considered, Wyatt will be fine with me. At least I have a healthy attitude toward the opposite sex."

A healthy attitude? She frowned.

"If you never learn to trust a man, you'll wind up becoming the hermit you seem to think you are now," he said. "Would that be a healthy thing for a boy to experience?"

She recognized the truth, and couldn't answer.

Jack ran a palm along his jawline. "I'll start packing tonight. Will you gather Wyatt's things?"

She nodded.

He left to head down the hall toward his rooms, and she remained in the kitchen trying to think, but not able to think at all.

She felt as if she'd passed beyond heartache to numbness—just as she had on the night of her sister's death.

Except this time her wounds were self-inflicted.

Abby took the soup bowls to the sink and ran water over them. As she opened a cabinet to gather half of the baby bottles and set them out on the countertop, she was very aware that her composure was superficial—as if she were a puppet on a string. She knew she'd remember every detail about tonight.

After she'd boxed up every downstairs toy and blanket, every spoon and dish and hat that she thought Wyatt might need, she stacked them in the front foyer and tiptoed past Jack's closed bedroom door on her way back to the kitchen.

She stared out at the greenhouse plants, running through a mental list of all the places in the house where Wyatt's things were stored.

There was just the nursery left, but she'd have to pack those things in the morning, after the twins were awake.

When she remembered the box of infant clothes in the cellar, she knew it was right that Jack should take those, too. He'd be the one to guide Wyatt into adulthood. He'd be the one to tell stories about babyhood's sweet memories.

She also knew she could trust him to handle that gently and well. During the past few months she'd seen Jack deal with enough people to know that he was full of integrity and kindness, as well as charm.

The boy would grow up strong, sturdy and caring under Jack's tutelage. He'd miss growing up in the same house as his sister, but he'd benefit from his bond with a good man.

Before Jack left, she would talk to him about keeping the twins in close contact. Perhaps they could grow up like cousins, or the children of amicably divorced parents. They needed every opportunity to be close to one another.

She knew Jack would agree.

She dragged the box up the cellar steps and set it in the middle of the living room floor. As the clock ticked toward midnight, she knelt beside the carton and meticulously separated blue from pink, and his from hers. She made separate stacks of neatly folded clothes all around her on the floor.

When the box was empty, she began to put Wyatt's things back inside, and noticed the edge of a pink envelope sticking out from under the bottom flap.

Frowning, she tugged at it. The scent of roses drifted up and caught her by surprise. Paige must have put the envelope in here.

Abby cried out when she turned it over. In her sister's round lettering, the envelope was addressed to the lawyer's office. There was a stamp, carefully placed, but no cancellation marks. The letter must have gotten lost in this box. Paige probably never knew she hadn't sent it.

With trembling hands, Abby turned it back over and slid an index finger under the flap. Gingerly, she pulled out the familiar stationery, unfolded it and read:

Dear Abby,

A few days ago, Brian and I came to an agreement about how to handle our will, and the intent of this letter is to explain my decisions. You are a wonderful aunt. You've been around from the minute the twins were born, and I know you'll be a constant source of love in their lives. I also know that if I die, you'll be as good a mother as I would have been. We're asking you to raise Rosie.

But here's the hard part—Brian wants Wyatt to go to his brother. Jack will do a good job. He's always been an attentive brother to Brian. I know you so well. You gave up on some dreams, after your divorce. If we leave everything to you, you'll put all your energy into the twins and the farm. That's admirable, but I hate thinking about you missing out on loving a good man. It's a joyful part of life—and I know you still want it. We asked Jack to take responsibility for the farm for a year, in hopes that you two would develop a friendship, and realize Rosie and Wyatt need to grow up knowing one another. I hope that happens. Most of all, love Rosie. Give her everything you think she needs. But take time for you, too. For my sake.

I love you—

Paige

Abby wiped away a few tears, then slowly got up and crossed the room with the letter. She sank down on the sofa and read it again. After the fifth or sixth reading, she tucked the letter back into its envelope and leaned forward to slide it between two magazines on the coffee table.

She smiled as she rested against the sofa cushions and stared at the pink tip of the envelope jutting out. Her sister had been four years younger, but she'd always had a way of helping Abby put things in perspective.

Even now.

The faint sound of a drawer sliding shut caught Abby's attention, and she listened intently. Jack must still be packing. She chuckled out loud and put a hand to her chest when she felt her heart pounding, heavy and fast.

She felt okay about sending Wyatt with Jack, because she knew Jack would take the utmost care in raising him. Despite the lifestyle he'd led, Jack was an honorable man.

He was a man who wouldn't have been insincere when he said he loved her. He would have meant it.

And her childhood dream of the country home, teeming with kids and animals, would never be complete without the smiling man who now had Jack's face. Her dream had evolved.

As she started for the hallway, she glanced down at the edge of her sister's letter. She'd remember to put that away for safekeeping, later.

Right now, she had something more important to do.

JACK CLOSED THE LID on another box and set it near the bedroom door. He'd stared at the doorknob every time he was within reach of it, but he always returned to his packing.

His excuses for going out and finding Abby hadn't been good enough, until now.

Now that he'd had a chance to think about things, he realized he'd been wrong to tell her she couldn't keep that baby boy.

She would put her entire heart into the task of raising him. Although it tore Jack apart to give up any of the three people he considered his family, he could live with some sort of visitation agreement.

But Rosie needed her brother and Abby needed her babies.

He picked up the tie to Abby's robe, which he'd meant to return weeks ago, and finally turned the knob.

She was standing in the hallway. "May I come in?" she asked politely.

Jack pulled the door open wider, and frowned as she stepped around boxes and suitcases to perch on the edge of his bed. When she patted the spot next to her, he sat down and handed her her belt.

Then she handed him the porcelain rosebud he'd given her months ago, in the beginning. "Do you remember what you said when you gave me this?"

He smiled as he accepted it, and felt the first glimmer of hope. He couldn't remember his exact words, but he knew they'd had something to do with honoring the occasion of their moving in together.

He shook his head. He needed her to tell him.

"You said it commemorated a new beginning," she reminded him, with eyes so full of feeling they'd turned to burnished gold. "I'm giving it back to you, to share."

He nodded, and felt the hope grow.

"Let's start over," she said. "I love you, Jack."

He didn't answer, but only because she didn't give him a chance. She tackled him with a kiss that sent them both sprawling across the bed, and nearly made him forget he had something to ask.

As soon as he could, he reached over to put the rosebud on his pillow, then stood to remove the velvet box from his jeans pocket. Although he'd felt its uncomfortable bulk all evening, he hadn't taken it out.

Now he knew why.

He knelt beside the bed, pulling the ring from the box and holding it on his open palm. "Will you take this?"

She did.

"I chose this ring for a reason," he said. "The marquis diamond in the center signifies permanence, and also the perfection of a decision that's right."

She touched the stones. "And the others?"

He looked at the two satellite diamonds next to the marquis. "The twins," he said. "Because I want all of us to be together. I love you, too, Abby. All of you. Will you marry me?"

She slid down to the floor, answering on the way. "Yes," she said, with no hesitation.

She felt good in his arms, and even better on his lips. He'd managed to kick a couple of boxes out of the way before Abby absorbed his full attention.

"We may have to have the ring adjusted, though," she murmured.

"It doesn't fit?" He sat up, and realized she was still holding it. He took it back long enough to slip it on her finger.

"Oh, it fits," she said with a brilliant smile. "But we may have to add a stone or two, later."

He raised an eyebrow and let his gaze drift down to her belly.

She laughed. "No, not this soon. Probably not, anyway. But would you mind another baby?"

He pulled her close again and answered against her ear, "I was counting on it."

Epilogue

Fifteen months later

Abby carried Rosie's cake across to the table and set it down next to Wyatt's, and smiled at the mixture of voices drifting in from the living room. The last time she'd checked, her dad was on the sofa talking with Zuzu about herbal cold remedies, her mom was trading chili recipes with Earl Hauser, and Sharon was on the floor beside Jack's mother, playing with the twins and their train set.

The company filled the living room, and Abby's heart. She knew each of today's visitors would want to celebrate many of her family's milestones through the years. As soon as Jack got home, this year's first party could begin.

She scanned the decorations one last time, making sure every balloon and streamer was in place, and then sank four candles into the frosting. Two red ones for Wyatt and two purple ones for Rosie.

She and Jack had agreed that they would always acknowledge each twin's individuality, but so far, Rosie and Wyatt wanted everything to match their clothes, their toys, even today's birthday cakes.

Abby had managed to sneak in a hint of variety with

the candles and cake flavors, but the outsides were fashioned into twin dog faces. Puppies had become a common topic around the farmhouse lately.

The sound of the back door opening sent Abby scooting across the room, and she met Jack at the door to peer into the crate. "Oh, she's adorable," she whispered, reaching in to pull out a frisky black-and-white puppy and cradle it atop her rounded belly. "They'll love her."

"I thought of the perfect name on my way home," Jack said as he put the crate on the floor.

Abby grinned. "For the baby or the dog?"

"You still don't want to take Zuzu up on her bid to name the baby after her?" Jack asked, pulling both Abby and the puppy into a hug.

When he let go, Abby stepped back and waited while he took off his coat and hung it near the door, and then she grinned broadly.

"When Zuzu offered her feng shui expertise to bring good fortune to our home and marriage, and said it was her wedding gift to the two of us, I didn't have the heart to tell her 'no,'" Abby said in a low voice. "Through the months of decorating she became a friend, but she's still a mystery. A few minutes ago, I heard her tell Sharon that Zuzu was just a name she made up to sound exotic."

"It is?" Jack glanced toward the entry to the living room and lowered his voice. "What's her real name?"

Abby laughed. "She wouldn't say."

"Hmm. Well, we still have a month or two to negotiate baby names," he said. "I was talking about the dog, anyway, what do you think of Diamond Lil?"

Abby studied the puppy. "It's perfect," she pronounced.

"It goes along with Calamity and Wild Bill."

He took the puppy from her arms and returned it to the crate. "There's another reason for the name."

"Why am I not surprised?" Abby chuckled as he swept her into a stronger embrace. "What's the other reason?"

"A diamond is something that can't be easily divided."

Abby answered with a kiss meant to be short and sweet. Every adult in the other room had been asked to keep the twins occupied and out of the kitchen, but they all must have heard Jack's voice by now.

At any moment, one of the twins could break away and make a beeline toward the kitchen, with a trail of adults behind. Abby and Jack needed to go out and start the party.

But his lips lingered and deepened, and lingered a little more. Finally, Abby laughed and pulled away, whispering, "Jack! My parents are in there."

"So's my mom," he answered. "But it's all right, they all watched us dance at our wedding."

He bent down to pick up the crate, and then offered an elbow. "Are you ready, Mrs. Kimball?"

She reached out to straighten the bow on the side of the crate, and looped her hand through the arm of the man she loved. "I'm ready." Enough time had passed to ease the first wondrous days of their marriage into responsibilities and routines, but Abby still felt thrilled at Jack's touch.

Gently, she pressed her fingers into his muscles, silently acknowledging her feelings one more time. She'd always feel lucky to enter a room beside him.

As they rounded the corner into the living room, Wyatt spotted the crate and started running toward it, and Rosie stared from her spot on the floor. "Puppy home?" she asked in her sweet, high voice.

The dog's answering yip made everyone laugh.

And Abby knew it was an entire family, who'd found a home.

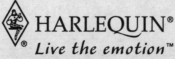

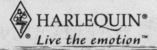

eHARLEQUIN.com

Sit back, relax and enhance your romance with our great magazine reading!

- **Sex and Romance!** Like your romance *hot?* Then you'll *love* the sensual reading in this area.

- **Quizzes!** Curious about your lovestyle? His commitment to you? Get the answers here!

- **Romantic Guides and Features!** Unravel the mysteries of love with informative articles and advice!

- **Fun Games!** Play to your heart's content....

Plus...romantic recipes, top ten lists, Lovescopes...and more!

Enjoy our online magazine today— visit www.eHarlequin.com!

INTMAG

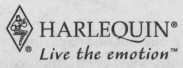

If you enjoyed what you just read,
then we've got an offer you can't resist!

Take 2 bestselling love stories FREE!

Plus get a FREE surprise gift!

Clip this page and mail it to Harlequin Reader Service®

IN U.S.A.	IN CANADA
3010 Walden Ave.	P.O. Box 609
P.O. Box 1867	Fort Erie, Ontario
Buffalo, N.Y. 14240-1867	L2A 5X3

YES! Please send me 2 free Harlequin American Romance® novels and my free surprise gift. After receiving them, if I don't wish to receive anymore, I can return the shipping statement marked cancel. If I don't cancel, I will receive 4 brand-new novels every month, before they're available in stores! In the U.S.A., bill me at the bargain price of $3.99 plus 25¢ shipping & handling per book and applicable sales tax, if any*. In Canada, bill me at the bargain price of $4.74 plus 25¢ shipping & handling per book and applicable taxes**. That's the complete price and a savings of at least 10% off the cover prices—what a great deal! I understand that accepting the 2 free books and gift places me under no obligation ever to buy any books. I can always return a shipment and cancel at any time. Even if I never buy another book from Harlequin, the 2 free books and gift are mine to keep forever.

154 HDN DNT7
354 HDN DNT9

Name	(PLEASE PRINT)	
Address	Apt.#	
City	State/Prov.	Zip/Postal Code

* Terms and prices subject to change without notice. Sales tax applicable in N.Y.
** Canadian residents will be charged applicable provincial taxes and GST.
All orders subject to approval. Offer limited to one per household and not valid to current Harlequin American Romance® subscribers.
® are registered trademarks of Harlequin Enterprises Limited.

AMER02   ©2001 Harlequin Enterprises Limited

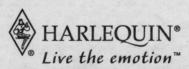